Sherlock Holmes
Consulting Detective

Airship 27 Productions

Sherlock Holmes: Consulting Detective Volume 3

An Airship 27 Production
www.airship27.com
www.airship27hangar.com

"The Lucky Leprechaun" © 2011 I. A. Watson
"The Adventure of the Mummy's Rib" © 2011 by Aaron Smith
"The Singular Affair of the Sultan's Tiger" © 2011 by Joshua Reynolds
"The Adventure of the Injured Inspector" © 2011 by Aaron Smith
"The Adventure of the Towne Manor Haunting" © 2011 by Andrew Salmon

Editor: Ron Fortier
Associate Editor: Charles Saunders
Production and design: Rob Davis
Illustrations ©2011 Rob Davis
Cover © 2011 Brian McCulloch

ISBN-13: 978-0692259979 (Airship 27)
ISBN-10: 069225997X

All rights reserved under International and Pan-American Copyright Conventions. No part of this book may be reproduced in any manner without permission in writing from the copyright holder, except by a reviewer, who may quote brief passages in a review.

Second Edition

Printed in the United States of America

10 9 8 7 6 5 4 3 2 1

Sherlock Holmes
Consulting Detective
Volume Three

The Lucky Leprechaun..4
By I. A. Watson
Are a rich man and his children being duped by fairies?

The Adventure of the Mummy's Rib.................................50
By Aaron Smith
An Egyptian mummy has been stolen from a museum and replaced by another.

The Singular Affair of the Sultan's Tiger........................75
By Joshua Reynolds
A wild beast in on the loose in London–its prey an old soldier.

The Adventure of the Injured Inspector.........................114
By Aaron Smith
When Inspector Lestrade is shot, Holmes and Watson investigate.

The Adventure of the Towne Manor Haunting..............131
By Andrew Salmon
Is a thieving poltergeist at work in the old manor house? Or is there a more sinister plot afoot?

Afterword...176
By Ron Fortier

Sherlock Holmes
Consulting Detective

"The Lucky Leprechaun"

by
I. A. Watson

I was accustomed to urgent telegrams from Holmes and a hasty departure to join him on some intriguing case. None was more rushed than my hurried cab ride to King's Cross station and my chase up the platform to catch the 11:21 on that bright summer day in 1890.

"Well done, Watson!" Holmes called as I hurled my bags into the compartment, just as the guard's whistle sounded and the engine filled the platform with thick steam. "I was beginning to fear that you would have to take a later train and miss out on this fascinating little problem!"

From my old friend's demeanour, from the animation of his movements and the jocularity of his voice, I concluded that some new mystery had piqued the great detective's interest. Rather belatedly I realised that there was a third person in the carriage with us.

"My apologies," I said to the legal gentleman sitting beside the window with his back to the engine. Holmes' methods were ingrained into me by now so I took in the stranger's neat attire, the wire-rimmed half-spectacles, the brief-case laid beside him on the seat and concluded that he must be a solicitor.

"Dr Watson, may I present Mr Adley?" Holmes introduced us. "Mr Adley is from Adley and Shennister's law firm of Gainsborough, Lincolnshire. It is to him we owe our debt of gratitude for drawing our attention to this fascinating case."

Adley made the usual responses to an introduction but I could see that he was agitated. He shared none of Holmes' professional enthusiasm for whatever matter had brought him to our Baker Street consulting room.

"Adley represents Mr Leonard Manchard," Holmes went on, "of Manchard's Temperance Tonics. Mr Manchard has gone missing."

Adley nodded urgently. His fingers sought the reassuring feel of his brief-case handle. "Missing these two days now, Dr Watson," the solicitor warned me. "The family is frantic. Mrs Manchard is distraught. And Mr Manchard's young nieces…"

Holmes could not restrain himself any longer. "Mr Manchard's young nieces," he interrupted, "claim that their uncle has been stolen away by the fairies."

❄ ❄ ❄

On the journey north I learned the details of the case set before Holmes. Leonard Manchard was a self-made Lincolnshire businessman who had made his fortune in the bottling and sale of health-improving non-alcoholic beverages. He lived an abstemious life befitting a strict Methodist temperancer, maintaining a small household that usually consisted only of his wife and he, attended by butler, footman, and maid. This summer that number was swelled by the addition of Arabella and Abigail Bolton, daughters of Mrs Manchard's sister. The eleven and nine year olds were being put up over summer since their parents had business in Hong Kong. Two lively children of a less-than-strict upbringing had been something of a trial for the Manchards.

Yesterday morning Mr Manchard had not appeared for breakfast. When he was sought it became apparent that his bed had not been used. A subsequent search discovered his walking stick in a clearing in the woods behind his house but there was no other sign of the missing man. Disturbingly, Manchard had previously ordered his man of business Adley to withdraw a large amount of money from his savings with no explanation.

"Had Manchard ever withdrawn substantial sums from his accounts before?" I wondered.

"Mr Manchard was a man of very simple habits," the solicitor replied. "He made regular donations to his chapel and to certain charities but otherwise made no substantial payments. It is unprecedented for him to liquidate his investments and withdraw four thousand pounds in cash."

"And where is this money now?" Holmes asked.

"Gone, sir," replied Adley. "Vanished with Mr Manchard."

The absence of such a huge wad of banknotes was not the most extraordinary aspect of this case, though. "The fairies," I prompted. "Where do they come into this?"

"The young Misses Bolton claim to have encountered mythical creatures in the woods," Adley explained, "at the very spot where Mr Manchard's cane was found yesterday morning. Indeed that site was searched at their insistence."

"A leprechaun, I believe you said," Holmes repeated with satisfaction. "A diminutive spirit in green speaking with an Irish brogue."

"Quite so," Adley admitted. "The girls insist that they met this creature – and other fairies – on a number of occasions in the woods. They claim that he led them to fairy gold and…" The solicitor stopped short.

"And what?" Holmes prompted him. "Any detail could be of importance."

"And it is true that these last three weeks Mr Manchard banked sums of money that I cannot trace to incomes from his usual business."

"What kind of sums?" I wondered.

"Seven guineas, then fifty-five, then four hundred."

I raised my brows. "That's quite a deal of fairy gold, Mr Adley."

"I make no claim as to where the money originated, Dr Watson. It was paid into my client's account in notes and coin in the usual way."

"What do the children say of these windfalls?" wondered Holmes.

"The children will not speak of it," the solicitor replied. "They say that Mr Manchard has been kidnapped because he upset the fairies, and that if they speak of it to anyone then he will not be returned for a hundred years."

❋ ❋ ❋

The small Lincolnshire town of Gainsborough was quite charming, an old-fashioned place basking on the River Trent; but Holmes allowed me little time to enjoy the sights of England's most inland port, a place that was once the capital of our nation for six weeks under the ancient tyranny of Sweyn Forkbeard. Instead he and Adley whisked me into Manchard's coach-and-four and we vanished out into the lush meadowland beyond the town.

Through Scampton, Bole, and West Burton Mr Adley tried to make conversation, indicating points of local interest. By the time we passed through Sturton le Steeple into the light woods fringing the Manchard estate he had realised that his commentary was unwelcome to Holmes and had fallen silent.

Holmes' mood had changed from his King's Cross ebullience. How well I recognised that intense concentration, so tight as to preclude even courtesy. My old friend was now focussing the whole of his immense intellect on the disappearance of Leonard Manchard. Nothing else could intrude.

"Stop the carriage, Mr Adley!" Holmes called suddenly. "This is, I believe, the woodland wherein Mr Manchard's cane was discovered the evening before yesterday?"

"It is, sir," agreed the solicitor. "A little over that way, away from the road and down the slope."

"Then that is where I shall begin my investigations."

"But Mrs Manchard will be awaiting us, sir."

"Then Mrs Manchard must have patience. I wish to see the primary evidence without prejudice of other's interpolation."

"Holmes has his methods," I soothed Adley. "They have proven efficacious in many a complex situation."

Adley reluctantly bade the driver stop. The solicitor accompanied us into the undergrowth, Holmes striding forward to clear the way with his cane. Adley picked his path carefully and unhappily through the dry foliage between the oaks and ashes. Holmes and I had adopted comfortable country tweeds; Adley still wore his best town attire.

"Did Manchard walk these woods regularly?" Holmes asked suddenly. He dropped to his knees with no regard for the condition of his trousers and inspected some clod of soil that seemed significant to him.

"He came here very rarely in recent years," Adley replied. "When he was younger he owned a spaniel which he would walk twice daily. Mr Manchard is now past fifty and enjoys good health for a man of advancing years but does not take regular exercise."

"Others enjoy these woods," Holmes noted.

"They are private land but there is no fence on this side of the estate between these woods and the bridle path to the common."

"There are many traces of passage – including the unmistakable tramp of police boots, Mr Adley."

"When Mr Manchard was found to be missing yesterday morning the police were summoned, of course." The solicitor paused to unhook his jacket from some ambitious briar then continued. "A search of the grounds was organised and it was his nieces' suggestion to investigate this place. And so Mr Manchard's walking stick was found."

"The fairy glade," Holmes mused. "That would be the clearing we are now entering? I perceive that the forces of the law have been quite diligent in their hunt for the little people."

We dropped down into a natural hollow five yards across. The indentation was ringed with gnarled oaks that leaned over to make a green canopy. The long grass around the edges had been trampled down by many searchers. A pile of old stones had been dismantled and cast aside.

Holmes indicated the squashed remains of a mushroom ring. "That was where the walking stick was discovered?"

"It was," agreed Mr Adley. "We found no other trace of the missing man. The police brought in dogs but the animals seemed unhappy in the area, unwilling to cast about for a scent."

"You're certain the cane was Manchard's?" I checked. After all, one stick can look much like another.

"It was an old companion of his," Adley replied. "Mrs Manchard identified it by the carving on the handle and by ancient teeth-marks from the dog I mentioned."

Holmes was casting around the area in frustration. "Half of Gainsborough has danced over this spot!" he growled. "This site should have been sealed off. Trained constables should have examined each blade of grass carefully for vital evidence!"

"Nobody knew that you would be inspecting the scene, Holmes," I mollified my friend.

"That might account for the heavy-booted prints marring the site, Watson. The newly-dug holes around the glade must be attributed to the activities of enthusiastic and hopeful treasure hunters."

"When Mr Manchard was found to be missing yesterday morning the first thought was that he might have met with some kind of accident," Adley explained. "When he did not appear for breakfast Mrs Manchard sent the footman to knock upon his door. Since there was no answer the butler entered his room and found the bed unslept in. The house was searched to no avail. At the suggestion of Misses Arabella and Abigail the grounds were also examined. Some of the common searchers took the opportunity to seek the buried horde to which the girls had alluded."

"Who found the cane?" demanded Holmes.

"Help was recruited from the neighbouring estate. It was one of the stable lads from there who happened upon the stick." Adley pointed down to the sad remains of the crushed mushroom ring. "It was laid in the centre of that circle."

"In a fairy ring," I mused.

Holmes stood up suddenly. "There is nothing more to be seen here for now," he announced. "To the house."

* * *

Manchard's manor was hardly what I would have expected for a man of such immense wealth. What revealed itself to us as we broke from the treeline onto a semicircular driveway was a modest winged home of two stories, constructed of stone in a simple old-fashioned manner and covered with trailing ivy.

Holmes jumped down from the carriage before it had even halted and strode away from the front door where butler and maid awaited us. He focussed his attention on the French windows to the east of the property and then to a particular flowerbed around the corner.

The young servant who had driven the coach-and-four looked back to Mr Adley to check if he could stable the horses. "Yes. I'll return to town in the gig, Stanley," the solicitor confirmed. To me Adley said, "Mrs Manchard will be waiting in the house."

I called Holmes and reminded him that a lady was waiting.

Holmes showed no evidence of having heard my promptings. "See these imprints, Watson! The French windows have not been opened for many months but someone has been making use of this clinging ivy as hand and footholds to climb up and down to the window yonder."

I looked up at the window he indicated. On this hot summer afternoon the sash was raised and the curtain fluttered slightly.

"The children's room," Adley told us. "So Arabella and Abigail were speaking the truth when they confessed to sneaking out at night." He seemed alarmed that their testimony was accurate even as he seemed relieved by this minor demonstration of Holmes' powers.

My friend swivelled suddenly and stalked back towards the front door. "Inside," he called.

We followed him inside.

※ ※ ※

Mrs. Manchard was a thin, stern woman in her early fifties. I was surprised at first to see her in mourning garb, swathed from head to foot in black bombazine. Later I discovered that this was customary dress for the lady of the house who had strict religious convictions.

Holmes swept aside her tart welcome (which centred more on how late we were than on any actual greeting) and insisted on examining the missing man's bedroom. That at least was relatively untouched.

"The bed has not been made since?" he checked with Carrow, the butler.

"Indeed not, sir," the old man replied. He'd been in service with the Manchards for over twenty years, since the house had been built. "This is exactly as I found it when I entered the room at seven fifty a.m. yesterday."

Holmes circled the room, examining everything. "Your master's nightgown was still untouched, wrapped around this warming-pan?"

"Yes sir."

"And Mr Manchard had exchanged these indoor shoes I see discarded here for some outdoor footwear?"

"Yes sir. His regular boots are missing, sir. And his outdoor coat."

"His cane we found," noted Adley.

Mrs Manchard had trailed behind us into her husband's chamber. Her own bedroom was across the hall. "There was no reason for Leonard to leave the house the night before last," she insisted. "No reason at all."

Holmes ignored her. He paused to examine the contents of Manchard's writing desk.

"Leonard was a man of regular habits," Mrs Manchard persisted. "I see no reason why he should break the routine of a lifetime and depart the house after dark without so much as a word." She glanced coldly at Mr Adley. "I can conceive of no reason for him to withdraw as large a sum as could be quickly liquidated either."

The solicitor stiffened at the implied accusation. "I knew nothing of that, Mrs Manchard, until I checked Mr Manchard's accounts yesterday afternoon at the request of the constabulary."

"Perhaps we could clarify a few details," I suggested, seeking to divert the household so Holmes could continue without interruption. "Who was last to see Mr Manchard before his disappearance?"

"Leonard was at dinner," replied Mrs Manchard severely. "He dined with myself and our two nieces. They were allowed to join us for the meal although their behaviour had been far from exemplary. My sister has very lax ideas on how to bring up two impressionable young girls."

I was eager to avoid a catalogue of Abigail and Arabella's faults from their dour guardian just now. "The meal ended when?" I asked,

The lady of the house glanced at Callow. "A little after eight, sir," supplied the butler. "Sarah came in to clear the plates just after the big clock had chimed. I served the hot milk and normally the family would then retire after prayer but..." His voice trailed off uncertainly and he glanced at his mistress.

"But my milk was served in a dish that I would not describe as clean," noted Mrs Manchard critically. "I have never seen such laxity. There was a great greasy fingerprint on the interior of my bowl. I called Callow in to explain himself – except of course there is no explanation save for appalling sloppiness and lazy housekeeping."

The butler winced again as his fault was described.

Mrs Manchard continued mercilessly. "I went into the kitchen to remonstrate with the girl, Sarah. There I found even more evidence of a degenerate and slovenly household."

Callow moved his lips as if to protest but his discipline held. Holmes looked up from the contents of the desk drawer and watched with sudden interest.

"I found, Dr Watson, I found the direst of pagan practices being perpetrated in my home – my own home!" proclaimed the lady of the house.

"Pray describe it, madam," Holmes urged her.

"A saucer of milk had been placed on a window-ledge," Mrs Manchard recounted. "Good fresh milk, mind, in a bowl like the ones we had just been served! I called Sarah to task and asked what she meant by it. Mr Manchard and I cannot abide cats and would not allow a stray to make itself at home in our kitchens. But the girl blurted out something much worse. Much, much worse."

"She had left the milk out as an offering for the fairies," Holmes supposed.

"The little people, she called them!" snorted Mrs Manchard. "Pandering to evil spirits and worshipping the devil in our own house! Superstitious heathen tripe under this very roof!"

"You disciplined the maid?" I asked.

"I have given her two weeks notice, Dr Watson, and she will be fortunate indeed to receive any reference from me. Callow has been placed under warning also, and not even his long service will save him if any such diabolic practices ever happen again." Mrs Manchard screwed her face up to an even tighter expression of disapproval. "Mr Manchard followed me to see what the noise was about and, being of a soft disposition, attempted to dissuade me from removing that sinful idolater from our home. He was unsuccessful."

"And then?" I wondered how this strange domestic incident might inform the disappearance of the master of the house.

"And then we went to prayer and so retired. We sought special forgiveness for allowing such shameful behaviour to go on under our roof all unnoticed. Then Stanley lighted us to our bedrooms and we said goodnight."

"How did your husband seem upon retiring?" Holmes enquired. After all, the missing man had already at that time withdrawn a large sum of money for some unspecified reason.

"He was... perturbed," owned Mrs Manchard. "He was not entirely comfortable with my dismissal of Sarah and he objected to me breaking the bowl which had held the milk. I own that it was a wasteful abuse of good china. He regretted the whole incident and we lifted it to the Lord in prayer."

Holmes returned to the desk drawer. He pulled out a piece of legal notepaper and showed it to us. "This is in Mr Manchard's hand, I note. Do the figures have significance to you, Mrs Manchard, or to you, Adley?"

I regarded the numbers scrawled thus:

$11-1 \quad 7-1 \quad 11-2 \quad 8-1 \quad 14-1$

"A safe combination, perhaps?" I ventured.

"We keep no such thing in the house," replied Mrs Manchard.

"Perhaps at Manchard's Temperance Tonics?" I ventured.

Holmes passed on, drawing three coins from the writing desk's velvet-lined interior and spreading them in his palm to show to Mrs Manchard, Callow, and Adley. "Have either of you seen these before?" he wondered.

Mrs Manchard's eyebrows drew together in an expression of puzzlement. The others' faces were blank. "I have no idea about them," the lady of the house admitted.

I took a careful look at the coins. They were obviously of great antiquity and they were undoubtedly of gold. The obverse side depicted a king in a laurel wreath. The reverse showed four crowned cruciform shields bearing the arms of England, Scotland, Ireland and France, separated by four sceptres.

"Gold sovereigns of Charles II," revealed Holmes. "The diagonal edge milling places them somewhere after 1670."

"Are they valuable?" I wondered.

"They are of considerable interest to collectors," Holmes judged, "being the first guinea coins minted, from one pound of Troy gold. You had no idea that your husband might collect such things, Mrs Manchard? Nor know why one of these coins is soiled with mud such as I observed at the clearing in your woods?"

"Buried treasure?" Adley speculated. Doubtless he was thinking of the sudden deposits in Manchard's bank account.

"We shall see," Holmes told him neutrally. "Let us not theorise ahead of the facts." He placed the coins back into the desk and stood up. "I shall need to interview the maid Sarah, the footman Stanley, the butler Callow, and of course have more conversation with you, Mrs Manchard. However at this point in the investigation it would be instructive to interview the children Arabella and Abigail." He ignored Mrs Manchard's disapproving expression and added, "I wish them to direct me to the fairies."

❋ ❋ ❋

Mrs Manchard was even more reluctant to allow Holmes to question her nieces without her being present. "Those children have been upset quite enough," she insisted. "It is bad enough that their parents should fill their heads with superstition and nonsense then run off to Hong Kong and leave their daughters to come to us for the summer break from school. Now they've learned they can grab attention by making up fantastic stories that divert from urgent matters at hand."

"You wish me to locate your missing husband, Mrs Manchard?" Holmes enquired. "Then kindly allow me to conduct my investigation."

"The girls have been out of control ever since they arrived," Mrs Manchard declared. "Not content to be grateful for a roof over their heads they have persisted in playing the most abominable tricks on us; hiding hairbrushes and items of clothing, sneaking keys from doors, muddying their shoes without leaving the house. I have remonstrated with them time and again but they persist in being wilful and wayward. They wished to visit the town, to ramble like gypsies in the woods, to attend that vulgar carnival on the common. I had no truck with behaviour of that kind, I assure you."

"Come, Mrs Manchard," I offered, trying to calm things down. "Holmes must know what your nieces are saying. It's all routine. Meanwhile I'd advise you to take a little rest. As a medical man I'm concerned for your health. I'd prescribe a quiet lie down on the couch for a while and possibly a toddy of... warm milk." I remembered in time that the Manchards were such strict temperancers that they had built a fortune on selling non-alcoholic beverages.

The lady of the house finally consented to retire and allow her nieces to be interviewed providing Mr Adley remained present. She retreated to the drawing room and a pair of young girls were ushered into our presence.

Arabella and Abigail Bolton were dressed alike in sober white smocks, with ribboned hair. They did not seem abashed by their latest visitors. Perhaps by now they'd become accustomed to the attention their extraordinary claims had garnered. They sat with us in the conservatory where the summer light played through the trees and cast its own enchantment on the dour Manchard manor.

"Children, Mr Holmes and Doctor Watson wish to hear your story," Adley told them. "Perhaps you could…"

Holmes interrupted, waving the solicitor to silence. "When did you first encounter these fairies?"

Arabella and Abigail exchanged glances. "When we first came for the holidays," Abigail answered diffidently. "That would be four weeks ago."

"How and where?"

The children's account had the practised rhythm of a tale told often and recently. "We went to explore. One afternoon, before auntie told us we couldn't. We found the old clearing in the woods, where the stones are. We heard music."

"Bells," amplified Abigail. "Pretty bells."

"We heard bells," agreed Abigail. "We followed the sound and that's how we found the stones."

"And then the leprechaun talked to us," added Abigail.

"The leprechaun?" I couldn't resist interjecting. "What did it look like?"

"We didn't see it that time," Abigail answered precisely. "He told us to come back, after dark. He told us to come secretly."

"He spoke but you didn't see him?" Holmes checked.

"He was under the rocks," Abigail explained. "His voice was coming from under the rocks." I recalled the disturbed pile of old cairn-stones in the clearing's centre.

Holmes sought more detail. The children were consistent in their tale: they had heard fairy bells and had spoken with a leprechaun that hid beneath the clearing's stones in the daylight hours. They had been instructed to return that night once darkness had fallen.

"We told him we wouldn't be allowed," Abigail confessed, "but he told us how we could open the catch on our bedroom window and climb down if we were careful."

"The leprechaun knew the details of your room?" Holmes observed. "Interesting. And you kept this midnight appointment?"

"Of course. We used the ivy to climb from our bedroom and made our way back to the clearing. The moon was out and we could see quite well. We entered the grove and..." Arabella paused.

"It was strange," Abigail supplied. "Like being in a dream. Like sleepwalking."

Abigail nodded agreement. "There were sounds, beautiful sounds, and lovely smells of blooming flowers. Then later there were lights dancing between the trees, fairies swarming round in bright rings."

"You saw these fairies?" I asked curiously. "What did they look like?"

"Shining lights," Abigail told us, "like stars or candles flying through the air. But we saw the leprechaun in the flesh. And once we saw the Fairy Queen!"

I glanced at Holmes to see how he was reacting to such fabulous tales. My friend's demeanour was neutral, betraying no reaction to the children's testimony but a polite interest.

"Children, you cannot expect us to believe these wild stories of fairies," Mr Adley chided Arabella and Abigail. "This is a very serious business. Your uncle has disappeared – and a great sum of money with him. If there is information that you can offer to assist in this affair you must tell us plainly and clearly without wild nonsense about…"

"I would prefer to conduct my investigation without interference," Holmes cut short the solicitor. "I shall judge for myself the credibility of the children's' story. I should say for now that I am encouraged by the evidence to have confidence in their honesty." He turned back to the girls. "Pray continue with your account of the leprechaun."

Arabella picked up the story again. "He came to us as the fairies danced. He was small and blue-skinned, and he wore an old green tunic and smoked an old briar pipe."

"Did he?" asked Holmes eagerly, as if this was of major importance.

"He knew our names," Abigail reported, "and he was sorry for us since our mother was such a long way from us. He promised to look after us."

"And he asked for a favour," Arabella remembered. "He asked for a dish of milk. He asked us to come back the next night with a dish of milk."

"And did you?" I wondered, caught up by this strange narrative; but Holmes also stopped me. He enquired in more detail about that first encounter. He established that the leprechaun was smaller than Abigail, around three feet high, but with side-whiskers and a great bulbous nose. He wore a green coat and a brown waistcoat and a wide floppy hat. His shoes had silver buckles. He spoke like an Irishman. He introduced himself as Lucky. He appeared beside the tumble of stones in the clearing's heart. He'd pointed to the whirling lights and named the dancers. He'd shown knowledge of the children's circumstances and of their life with the Manchards which a stranger could not know. At the last he'd directed the children home to their beds. It was not until they awoke in the morning and exchanged notes that the girls could really believe it hadn't been a dream.

"But we went back the next night," confessed Abigail, "with the milk."

Again Holmes required specifics. The milk had been taken from the pantry with help from Sarah the maid, who had thought Mrs Manchard's handling of her charges too harsh. The milk-dish had been left behind when the children went home that second night but was returned emptied

"You investigated the hole in the ground?" Holmes prompted.

to the kitchen table by morning. The fairies showed their thanks for the feast by offering a gift.

"Lucky told us to place our hands into a hollow under the fairy-stones," Arabella explained. "It was the gateway to a rath, he said, a fairy palace."

"We were frightened because there might have been spiders in the hole," Abigail shuddered, "but 'Bella was brave and did it."

"It still felt like a dream," the older girl admitted. "Noise and colours and everything just made me laugh. I wasn't afraid."

"You investigated the hole in the ground?" Holmes prompted.

Arabella nodded. "It went right under the pile of stones. I had to push my arm in as far as it would go. Then my fingers touched something hard and metal and I pulled out that gold piece."

"Uncle Leonard said it was a guinea," Abigail confirmed. "He said we'd been very lucky to find it. We didn't tell him how the leprechaun had given it to us."

"Uncle Leonard kept it safe for us," Arabella said. "We gave him the other two that Lucky showed us later as well."

Mr Adley couldn't resist interrupting. "The antique coins in Mr Manchard's keeping were from a fairy hoard?" he asked sceptically. He was probably wondering what those eager searchers who had dismantled the cairn and dug up the glade might have discovered and spirited away.

Holmes gestured irritably for him to keep his counsel and encouraged the Misses Bolton to continue their remarkable account. The sum of their testimony was that each successive night they crept abroad to dance with the fairies; that they experienced first the music then the lights; that most nights the blue leprechaun appeared to talk with them at the last; that on three occasions he rewarded their gifts of milk with coins from beneath the stones.

"How often did you sneak out to the woods at night?" I wondered.

"Whenever we could," Abigail admitted. "Whenever it wasn't raining. The fairies didn't come when the woods were wet."

Mr Adley snorted. "I very much doubt the fairies came when it was dry either! This is arrant nonsense, Mr Holmes. Mrs Manchard is right that far too much attention is being given to these children's wild imaginings."

I saw Arabella and Abigail pale at the solicitor's accusations and concluded that this was not the first time their innocent candour had been criticised.

"These children's account may be key to unravelling the problem,"

Holmes replied harshly. "I have had occasion to request your forbearance during this interview on several occasions, Mr Adley. If you require my assistance in locating your employer then I insist you refrain from these unhelpful interruptions. I shall interview you again presently and will then be most interested in your opinions and observations. Until that time I must ask you to restrain yourself or withdraw."

Adley bristled but fell silent. His discomfiture was not lost upon the Bolton girls.

As I was accustomed to do, I eased the interview forward with another question. "You mentioned meeting the fairy queen?"

Adley opened his mouth as if to protest my question but he caught Holmes' glare and subsided.

"Yes, we saw her" agreed Abigail. "But we can't talk about that. She wouldn't like it." The children seemed to withdraw from us into a private little world.

Holmes intervened. "But you saw the fairies in the woods on clear nights. When did the fairies begin to visit the house?"

"We took the milk every time we visited Lucky. The dish was always in the kitchen in the morning," Arabella testified.

"Although the house doors were locked and bolted?" I checked.

"Fairies don't need doors," Abigail told me scornfully, as if I knew nothing.

"But we told Lucky that we'd be getting into trouble," Arabella explained. "Already Aunt Leah had chastised us for the state of our shoes in the mornings. We couldn't keep on sneaking milk out like that, even if the dishes were always returned to the kitchen washed clean."

"So Lucky said we could just put out a saucer in the kitchen for him," Abigail added. "He told us that if we explained to Sarah she'd understand and let us do it. Sarah believes in fairies."

"That was the saucer of milk that Mrs Manchard eventually found and broke," I surmised.

The girls looked worried. "Yes," agreed Arabella at once. "That was what made the fairies angry. That's why they stole Uncle away."

"Even Uncle knew they'd be annoyed," Abigail joined in. "That's why he was so upset about what Auntie had done."

"Hold on," I challenged. "Are you saying that Mr Manchard knew about your fairies?"

Arabella and Abigail exchanged the guilty looks of two girls that had said too much. "We can't tell you about that," Abigail said at last, "or else uncle may never come home."

※ ※ ※

"We shall return to the children presently," Holmes instructed Adley. "It will require a little more careful coaxing to convince them to impart the rest of their story."

"You cannot give credence to such undisciplined fantasies, sir," the solicitor argued. He was still stung by Holmes' earlier rebuke.

"The children are speaking the truth as they believe it," my friend replied. "It is for us to winnow the facts they present and understand the greater truth."

We'd retired back to Manchard's study, where Holmes checked through the missing man's ledgers and business diaries under Adley's watchful eye. I decided it might be best to occupy the solicitor while Holmes went about his business.

"Can you think of any reason for Mr Manchard's disappearance, Mr Adley?" I wondered. "Business difficulties? Personal entanglements? An enemy who might wish him ill?"

"Mr Manchard lives a quiet and exemplary life," the solicitor replied. "He worked for what he has, for his schooling and for his fortune. His business affairs are all in perfect order, and save for that one withdrawal of an unwarranted sum without recourse to me there is nothing of concern in his books. If by personal entanglements you insinuate some unfortunate or immoral encounter then I assure you that Mr Manchard is of unimpeachable character."

I reflected that in any case Manchard was unlikely to be let out of sight of his formidable wife long enough to stray.

Adley went on with his defence of his employer. "As for enemies, well any man of business has rivals and competitors. Mr Manchard is shrewd and determined. He has carved a name and a niche for his product and himself. I'm sure there are some who would be pleased at his disappearance; but none capable of spiriting him out of his own house by night and making him completely vanish."

"The police will doubtless make their enquiries," Holmes opined. "Does any particular name come forward as you think of rivals and competitors?"

Adley thought but then demurred. "It is a decade and more since Manchard's Temperance Tonics achieved their prominence in the marketplace. At that time, yes, there were men who blamed my client for their losses. There were lawsuits and patent disputes – Mr Manchard was strict in enforcing his rights on those who would copy his success and his formula. An American named Henshawe, for instance, claimed to have been ruined when he was forced to withdraw his own brand of tonic, but Mr Manchard proved that the composition was identical to his own. Others were angered when it was demonstrated that their temperance tonics were neither wholly teetotal nor of medicinal virtue."

"Mr Manchard was responsible for establishing that?" I asked.

"Some years ago it was Mr Manchard's crusade. As I say he is a man of strong religious sensibilities and his sect forbids the partaking of alcohol. However all of this was long ago."

"Any detail may be relevant," Holmes noted, "and a long-nursed grudge can be the worst kind of all. Watson, would you be so kind as to browse the appropriate correspondence for me when you have a moment? Mr Adley, be so kind as to direct my companion's attention to the relevant documents."

Holmes settled back in Manchard's chair, carefully stuffed a pipe and lit it. Then to Adley's dismay he did not return to his examination of the ledgers before him but closed his eyes and appeared to go to sleep.

❈ ❈ ❈

High tea that evening was a hasty cold compilation served by the red-eyed Sarah and the flustered Callow. Mrs Manchard extended a reluctant invitation for Holmes and I to spend the night. Adley made his excuses before dinner was served and had the footman Stanley drive him back to town in the smaller one-horse gig; doubtless he had reports to make to his partner Shennister on the disappearance of their most valuable client.

I had so far found Leah Manchard to be cold and critical. It was only at table as she led us in prayer before our meal that I caught the catch in her voice as she pleaded with the Lord for her husband's safe return. She did not eat much thereafter and made her departure as soon as she decently could, abandoning her nieces to finish their simple meal at table without her.

"Have you decided yet that you can fully discuss your experiences with me?" Holmes asked the girls. "Your accounts would be of significant value to my investigation."

"You don't believe us," Arabella accused him. "Nobody does. They think we're just silly children. They think we're being wicked. We know what we saw – what we experienced."

"I am willing to listen to whatever account you wish to submit," my friend assured them. "I have heard many strange stories in my time and your narrative would not be the strangest."

"But if we tell then uncle might never be let home!" Abigail almost wailed. "Auntie should never have broken that dish and said those wicked things about the fairies!"

"If you do not speak then Holmes may never get to the bottom of things and be able to help your uncle," I warned them. "It is clear that you've seen remarkable things; but now your silence is making matters worse not better."

Arabella and Abigail looked uncomfortable, but no relative was present to excuse them from table.

"It is my role to find and return your uncle," Holmes told the children. "Whatever secrets you believe you should keep must be sacrificed if I am to get at the truth and see him safe home."

The girls shook their heads and looked unhappy.

I rose from my place and squatted down beside the Bolton sisters. "Now see here," I told them, offering a smile, "You may not know it but Mr Sherlock Holmes is the cleverest detective in England. In the world. He's managed amazing feats of deduction. He's famous. When other detectives are baffled, when Scotland Yard doesn't have a lead, when the leaders of our nation are in a quandary, they turn to Holmes for his aid. So you can be sure that when he sets his mind to seeing your uncle safe and home he will accomplish what he sets out to do – so long as you will trust him with what you know."

"Thank you, Watson," Holmes told me, chuckling at my effusive endorsement, "but perhaps these young ladies would be more impressed by being shown rather than told what I can do? Perhaps if I was to describe the night-time disturbances that led to them regularly setting out their saucer for the little people?"

The girls glanced at each other again, but this time in surprise.

"There were occasions," Holmes told them, "in the first days of your arrangement for leaving a saucer in the kitchen when you neglected to do so, sent to bed early by your guardians or for some other reason. On those nights the house was plagued by mischief: objects hidden and keys turned in locks and items rearranged; as if the fairies were displaced and played their tricks."

"That's right!" blurted Abigail. "But how did you know!"

I recalled Mrs Manchard's angry complaint in Holmes' hearing but said nothing.

"There was one night where Sarah and Stanley decided to stay up and watch for the fairies," Arabella reported. "They hid in the kitchen to watch the saucer of milk they had set. Lucky did not come but there was a terrible mess in the kitchen and pantry the next day. The coal scuttle was all over the floor."

"And the doors locked fast and bolted from within," I interjected. I'd gathered that the police had been interested in these night-time disturbances but had not associated them with fey visitors.

Holmes seemed satisfied with the confirmation of his supposition. "You see I can formulate accurate theories," he assured the Bolton girls. "Now you must trust me with the knowledge of how your Uncle came to know of your association with your leprechaun."

Arabella answered reluctantly. "He made us tell him where we'd found the coins," she answered at last. "He questioned us about the fairies but didn't believe us. He went to search the glade but found nothing."

"But then we met the fairy queen," Abigail added with satisfaction.

"You mentioned a fairy queen," Holmes noted. "You saw this lady?"

Arabella and Abigail's faces lit up. "Oh yes!" Abigail cried. "She was the most beautiful thing you ever saw!"

Holmes slowly coaxed an account from the girls. After the third coin had been gifted to them, after the offerings of fresh milk were well established in the kitchen, after Manchard had expressed his scepticism and searched in vain, but before their uncle had discovered his nieces' regular midnight forays, one night the children had been told by Lucky that they were granted an audience with the queen of the fey.

"He said we'd become friends of the fairies and that the queen wanted to bless us," Arabella said. "I was worried at first, because they say that sometimes fairies take children away and keep them for their own, but we were having so much fun. When you're with the fairies – it's like flying, like being out of your own body and whirling through the skies. You can't help but laugh and sing. So we met the queen."

"We brought presents for her," Abigail cut in. "'Bella gave her that green scarf that daddy brought her back from India and I took my ribbon. You have to give presents to a queen."

I found myself being dragged along by the children's enthusiasm. "What did she look like?" I heard myself asking.

"She was beautiful," said Arabella. "All dressed in gold and silver, with a tiara in her long blonde hair. Her skin sparkled too, sparkled in the moonlight."

"The other fairies just flew around her, danced overhead," Abigail supplied.

"Even Lucky was quiet when she was there," commented Arabella. "Lucky is never quiet."

"How closely did you observe this lady?" Holmes enquired. "How near did you get to her?"

"Not close," Abigail admitted. "Mortals can't get close to the fairy queen. Not if they ever want to go home again."

Her older sister explained further. "We waited at the cairn. We were safe as long as we stayed by the old stones, Lucky said. But we saw the queen coming through the trees and she stood in the clearing. And she spoke to us."

"What did she say?" I wondered.

"She said she knew we were sad. She knew how much we missed our parents. She knew how strict Aunt Leah was with us."

"She knew auntie wouldn't let us sing and wouldn't let us go to the carnival," Abigail contributed.

"She said that she'd give our household a blessing anyhow," Arabella explained, "That she could see the future. That she wanted us to pass on a message to our uncle about what was to come."

Holmes leaned forward. "What message?"

"That first message made sense," Abigail said, as if implying that others did not. "She bade us tell Uncle come, secretly and alone."

"We told him so, and then he went back at night," Abigail continued. "When he came back after that he believed."

Holmes' careful questioning ascertained that this midnight expedition must have happened eighteen days ago, shortly after the night time saucer of milk began to be placed on the kitchen sill. Manchard had confined the children to their room and taken his stout stick into the woods. When he saw the children again the next morning he had spoken little of what he encountered. He never again sought the company of the fairies.

"But he told us we could go," Arabella added. "He told us to be cautious, but to make careful note of what we were instructed and to make a full account to him."

This was new information to us. "That makes no sense at all," I worried. "Manchard shared his wife's strict views and has hardly been depicted to us as a man to chase after stardust."

"But the timing is intriguing," Holmes retorted. "Manchard's visit to the leprechaun took place two days before the first deposit of funds into his bank."

Abigail shook her head. "Uncle never saw the leprechaun or the queen. He heard Lucky and saw the others dancing but that's all. Uncle was too grown up to see clearly, Lucky said."

Holmes continued to coax the story from the children. He determined the time that Manchard had gone to visit the grove and his demeanour upon his return – he'd seemed to the children watching anxiously from their window like a man dazzled by a dream, giggling like an infant, touched by the fairies.

"And what messages did the fairies give you to deliver to your uncle?" Holmes enquired.

"Proof," answered Arabella promptly. "Uncle sought proof that the fairies could see the future. Lucky gave us it."

"In what form?" I asked.

The girls' faces clouded with puzzlement. "We do not know, sir," Arabella admitted at last. "Five messages in all, given us to deliver to uncle, the last on the very day before Uncle vanished, but they made no sense to us. Uncle was very satisfied though."

Abigail agreed. "He said we were brave, sensible children and our fortunes were assured."

"But that was before Auntie upset the fairies," concluded Arabella bitterly. "Now everything is spoiled."

"The content of these messages?" Holmes demanded.

I wrote down the leprechaun's communications in my notebook but they made no sense at all: Edinburgh, Seraph's Queen, Rumbucket, Harper of India, Effervescent."

❄ ❄ ❄

The long summer day was over and the shadows were drawing long. Holmes seemed possessed of a sense of growing urgency. His interviews with the staff were brief to the point of brusqueness but possessed of his usual insightful technique.

From the unfortunate Sarah we heard the sad story of her dismissal, starting with her indulgent assistance in the fantasy games of two harshly-disciplined children, continuing with her growing amazement at the impossible removal of the milk from the kitchen sill, of her sole attempt to spy upon the leprechaun and its destructive consequences, and finally of Mrs Manchard's angry discovery of "pagan practices" and how the fairies had cursed the house.

Holmes asked a few questions of clarification. The kitchen was locked at night and the outer door also bolted. Only Callow and Mr Manchard possessed the keys. The disturbances and disappearances had all occurred after dark once the house was secured. Some of the items moved had appeared inside locked rooms. Some door keys to bedrooms and box-rooms had vanished and never been recovered.

"Mrs Manchard has given you two weeks' notice, I understand," Holmes mentioned to the unfortunate domestic.

"Yes," Sarah answered miserably. "For nothing." She looked for a moment as if she was about to add some tart comment about her employer but her better nature prevailed. "I don't know what I'm going to do. My mum'll be that mad."

"You were only trying to be kind to the children," I said, trying to calm her.

She looked up at me with tearful blue eyes. "Oh no, sir. I was doing my duty by the fairies."

"You saw the fairies?" Holmes asked, his own hawk-like eyes doubtless seeing far more in the girl's gaze and expression and demeanour than I could.

Sarah shook her head. "No sir. But I could tell they'd been, for things were moved in the kitchen, and betimes they played tricks when there wasn't milk left for them."

"That was when you determined to look for them and hid yourself one night to watch for their coming."

"Yes sir. Me and Tom Stanley. I wouldn't have dared on my own. But we saw nothing, and in the morning the big scuttle was spilled all over the floor and I had to spend two hours polishing away the coal dust."

"Who has keys for the kitchen?"

"Only Mr Callow and Mr Manchard himself sir. But of course the fair folk don't pay no heed to locks and bars."

"Have you any idea where Mr Manchard is now?"

Sarah looked frightened. "Why yes, sir. He's beneath the cairn, lost in fairyland. He's taken and he'll stay there till that Mrs Manchard makes her apologies to the fairies and makes good what she's done."

❋ ❋ ❋

The footman Stanley described the security of the house at night. The external doors were all locked and bolted; except that after the night when Manchard had vanished the front door was found locked without a bolt. Only Manchard and Callow had keys for the external doors and the one that sealed off the kitchen from the rest of the house. Stanley had conveyed his master to the bank on four occasions in the last three weeks and that was unusual. The final occasion had been on the morning before Manchard's disappearance. There had been a night two or three weeks back when the master's boots had been inexplicably muddy. Stanley had stood watch one night with Sarah hunting fairies because "she's a pretty little piece and I wanted to please 'er."

Stanley had more to say on the subject of Sarah's dismissal. "That was unfair and uncalled for," he argued. "She's a sweet girl, that Sarah, and she'd do no harm to a flea. She's country, she is, and they still believe in that old stuff in those parts. No harm if she sets out a sip of milk and some stray takes it – old Manchard can afford it!"

"You do not believe in fairies then?" Holmes challenged the footman.

Stanley snorted. "Catch me with that superstitious bunkum! But there was no call for Mrs Manchard to carry on like that and call Sarah all those things then give 'er notice. That'll be hard on the girl." Seeing that I was not unsympathetic to his criticisms of the lady of the house he leaned forward to me confidingly. "I was that upset by it that I've given my own notice, sir. This has always been a miserable 'ouse but that was the last straw. When Sarah goes I'll go too, and good riddance to this dark old place."

"You have no inkling of your present master's whereabouts?" Holmes asked the footman.

"He was a right stay-at-home," Stanley answered. "Part of my duties is to go into town each morning and fetch him 'is paper. The Times, that is, and the Methodist Recorder on Thursdays. I post 'is letters too, on the mornings he doesn't go to 'is office."

"Did you observe any unusual correspondence he asked you to post?" I wondered; but the footman shook his head.

"Nothin' that caught my eye, no. But if you want to know where 'e's gone, it's my belief that 'e's crept off and done a runner on his missus. I'll lay good money on it. They're saying he drew four thousand pounds before he crept away. I'd give two to one that 'e's boarding a boat for France and some jolly little mam-zelle right about now."

When reminded of Mr Manchard's strict religion Stanley expressed his view that in his experience it was always the quiet sober ones that fell the hardest.

❋ ❋ ❋

The butler Callow confessed that he'd known of Sarah's superstitious practice with the milk-dish but had not challenged it. He was aware of the strange disturbances in the household but could offer no explanation. He dismissed the idea that the children might be responsible since they had no access to some areas where things had happened. He'd known about Sarah's vigil from Stanley, who had been invited by the maid to keep her company as she stalked the leprechaun that the children had told her of. He could not account for his master's alleged conversation with the fairies. Mr Manchard was a man of strong religious belief, opposed to alcohol, gambling, wantonness, and superstition.

By careful questioning Holmes was able to piece together a timeline of night-time disturbances and pranks. It did indeed seem that events occurred in the small hours of the morning after evenings when no saucer of milk had been rendered for the little people.

At Holmes' request Callow produced the walking stick that had been found in the mushroom ring at the glade. The old ash stick had a worn ferrule and smoothed handle from much use, indentations where it had once been carried in the mouth of a small terrier, and something else.

"This stain here," Holmes said, flaking a few grains from the wood onto a twist of paper. "I'd say that this was dried blood." He pocketed the sample for later analysis. It was a worrying find.

"Everywhere was searched," fretted Callow, much disturbed by Holmes' discovery. "We searched attics and cellars and all the outbuildings. We called in helpers from the adjoining estates. We combed every inch of the woods. We sent runners to the local stations in case Mr Manchard had taken a train for some reason. Where can he be? Mr Holmes – where can he be?"

❋ ❋ ❋

"I'm at a loss," I told Holmes when we'd finished with the interviews. I'd noted the dates and times of the mysterious events within Manchard Lodge and correlated them with the alibis of the household. There was no single person who was unaccounted for on every occasion that a door had been locked, an object moved or taken, a jug or scuttle overturned. "It seems as though someone or something was indeed doing mischief at night inside the locked house, and yet no-one had the chance to do all of them, not even the girls working together. And no-one from outside could enter without someone inside unbolting a door."

Holmes snorted. "My dear Watson, you are over-estimating the security of the house. Are you forgetting that almost every night two children were able to leave their bedroom via their ladder of ivy and go dancing with the fairies? And that they returned to their beds the same way later? If they gained access to the house thus then why not others in the time they were away in the woods?"

"You suspect criminal intent, then? But nothing of value was stolen, only senseless things." I checked my notes. "A warming pan, a hairbrush, a mirror, a broken clock."

"And four thousand pounds," Holmes reminded me. He pointed to the front door. "To the post office. And then the woods again, Watson, before darkness falls."

※ ※ ※

Holmes insisted on driving the Manchard's two-man gig into Gainsborough himself. I accompanied him but knew better than to pester him for the solution that was clearly formulating in his mind. I followed him to the post office and helped him badger a clerk into sending telegrams back to London although the local office had closed for the day. Mention of a communication to Scotland Yard soon convinced the man to do his duty.

We left word for the local inspector of police to pick up any replies to Holmes' enquiries and to meet us at Manchard Lodge in the morning.

"Can you reveal to me whether you have a solution for Manchard's disappearance?" I ventured as we neared the gates of the estate.

"There are a few telling points, Watson. The hidden golden hoard, the digits on the note in the bedroom desk, the significance of the dirty thumbprint on Mrs Manchard's bowl."

"Do you know where Manchard is now?"

"I have suspicions," Holmes replied, "but no proof enough to commission a search-warrant. Not until I receive replies to my communications, and those will not reach us till morning."

"You have some theory though, as to how a grown man as well as his young nieces could meet with a leprechaun."

"That at least seems elementary. But all is supposition only until I have the final evidence," Holmes concluded. "And that awaits us in the fairy grove."

※ ※ ※

The sun was down but the twilight was yet bright enough for us to see by. The dying day gave the woods a melancholy air. The stillness and silence were profound. No birds sang as we passed under the growing shadows of the trees.

I was not surprised when Holmes trailed to the fairy glade by a roundabout route. His path took in the perimeter of the property where the woodland was bordered by a public track. Holmes examined the bridle path with his usual attention to detail.

I enjoyed the scenery. From here the Lincolnshire plains rolled away across the common down to the Trent valley. In the distance I could see the church tops of Gainsborough.

When Holmes was satisfied we pressed through game tracks back into the woods and presently made our way to the clearing. The coming night made the copse seem smaller and more oppressive. Holmes rooted in the ruins of an old campfire left a hundred yards or so from the clearing by some tramp or traveller and pressed a burned stick to my nose. "Smell," he prompted.

"Bleach?" I frowned, jerking my head back from the unexpected odour.

"Ammonia," replied my friend. "No wonder the dogs didn't wish to sniff around this place." He entered the clearing and winkled some tiny flakes of ash from the muddy footprint of a well-meaning searcher. "And this, Watson. Our pipe-smoking visitor has left traces of his habit."

"You believe the children to have actually met someone here?" I asked. "But the dancing fairies can only have been hallucination."

Holmes was looking up into the canopy of trees. "I cannot be so certain," he told me. "Not with the traces still remaining of disturbed leaves and broken twigs on those branches above."

I could see no pattern to the places Holmes indicated, nor any meaning to the pock-holed areas of bark that so excited him on the trees around the grove's edge.

"This at least then should catch your attention," Holmes told me. He parted the thick grass at the rear of the dismantled cairn and showed me a thin straight trench of recently-dug soil, no more than an inch wide but

"It means, Watson, that Lionel Manchard has indeed been taken by the fairies and that he is in mortal danger."

running all the way to the circle of trees.

"What can it mean?" I asked as I watched Holmes investigate. The digging was only a couple of inches deep.

"It means that Lionel Manchard has indeed been taken by the fairies," the great detective answered gravely, "and that he is in mortal danger."

❋ ❋ ❋

It was dark when we returned to the lodge. Mrs Manchard had not stayed up for us. The children were long since in bed, their window now firmly sealed shut to prevent further midnight wanderings. Callow remained vigilant to admit us and Stanley waited to stable our horse and trap.

"Will you take a late supper, sirs?" the butler asked us as we handed off our coats. "There is some cold rabbit remaining and I can easily warm some soup."

Holmes declined for both of us. "We yet have a little more work to do before bed, Callow. We shall be in Mr Manchard's study. There are papers there which we still have to review."

Callow had evidently been instructed to co-operate. He lit the lamps and left us in peace amongst Lionel Manchard's ledgers.

"What are we looking for, Holmes?" I wondered.

"For motive, Watson. I can now hazard a theory as to where these fairies came from and why Manchard was so enthralled. I can surmise for what purpose he withdrew his funds and why he was so distressed when his wife broke the milk dish. What remains murky is who would wish to engage Manchard in such a strange adventure. His business dealings are the most likely place for us to gain that understanding."

I began with the huge stack of yellowed legal papers from the missing man's decade-past lawsuit with Fabian Henshawe. It was clear from the correspondence that Manchard had been offended by "Professor" Henshawe's re-labelling of the Manchard tonic. Manchard had not only brought suit to end Henshawe's misuse of patent but had also taken considerable trouble to expose other Henshawe products as being "bilge and bunkum"- as he'd said in written instructions to his solicitors.

That gave me my first insight into Manchard's previous character. He'd been a sterner, harder man when he'd been making his fortune, quick to defend his rights and quicker to hold a grudge; quite different as he clawed his way to comfort from the staid charitable man of fixed and quiet habits that had been described to us by his household.

The dichotomy was striking; but more it struck me as very funny. Holmes cast me a puzzled stare as I began to chortle at the papers in front of me.

"You have apprehended something amusing?"

"My dear Holmes," I guffawed, "this whole case is amusing. Fairies! Leprechauns! Can you imagine the reaction of my readers if I write up a case wherein the great detective chases small blue men?"

Holmes' lip curled into an involuntary smile. "It would indeed cause a reaction. I wonder whether your readers would take it as mere invention or consider that we had fallen into the traps of superstition and spiritualism?"

"We shall simply have to find the leprechaun," I snorted. "Once caged and on display in Hyde Park Zoo there would be no question of credibility."

Holmes chuckled. "And I suppose we introduce the fairy queen at court and present her to Her Majesty? Perhaps as a suitable consort for Prince Edward?" The absurdity of the idea tickled him and he fell to laughing.

"It is another service you could do your country, Holmes!" I guffawed.

Holmes thought this hilarious. He laughed uproariously, almost falling from his chair as he tried to contain his mirth. For my part I had a stitch in my side with laughing and could hardly catch my breath.

"There is..." Holmes began, but his giggling overtook him. Everything seemed funny. The room seemed hot and it began to spin.

Holmes staggered to his feet and picked up Manchard's heavy document case. He staggered with it and found that immensely funny. Despite my blurred vision I convulsed with laughter at his efforts.

Holmes hurled the document case through the window. Glass and lead shattered, sending Manchard's papers billowing across the lawn.

"Come, Watson," he insisted, hauling me up by the collar and dragging me to the broken casement. "Outside! Outside if you value your life." His voice sounded giddy and ridiculous.

We both guffawed convulsively like men in delirium. Holmes hauled me to the window. Even tearing my hand on the jagged shards around the frame seemed a great joke. My friend heaved me bodily through the aperture, tumbling me out onto the flowerbed outside.

The cool night air washed over me, rousing me from the sleep that had been conquering me. My head swam and my stomach revolted. I rolled over trying to retch even as my body still convulsed with laughter.

Then another thought occurred to me: Holmes was not with me.

I staggered to my feet. The lawn seemed to sway beneath me like the deck of a ship. I cast about looking for my friend but could not find him. Like a man in a dream I realised that Holmes had been taken from me.

"Holmes! Holmes!"

My brain seemed dull and slow, reluctant to think or plan; yet some part of me remembered that I had been in Manchard's study and that Holmes had cast me from there. Holmes had never followed me through the window.

Instinct as much as intellect cautioned me to take a deep breath of the pure night breeze before I plunged back into the house. I climbed unsteadily through the shattered window and tumbled over the supine form of my friend. As I fell I took a deep lungful of the air of the room and once again I felt myself falling to delirium.

One thought sustained me, that if I fell here then Holmes fell too. I sensed a danger in sleeping here on Manchard's floor, a mortal peril that transcended the helpless giggling, the detached dreaminess, the sense of watching myself from far off undertaking trivial and pointless tasks. I was an observer who merely witnessed me dragging Holmes as he had first dragged me, pushing his lanky form through the broken frame into the clean night air; and yet eject Holmes I did.

My head swum again but I heard my friend calling to me. "Watson, you must follow. Come here."

I made for the shattered window heedless of blood on my hands from the ragged frame. My limbs weighed me down but I struggled to follow the voice.

Then I slept.

※ ※ ※

"Watson. Watson! John!"

I woke from some fantastic dream to see Holmes' pale anxious face. It took me a few moments to understand where I was, laid on my back on the lawn of Manchard Grange under the peaceful starry sky.

"Sit up slowly," Holmes advised me. "Fast movement will make you sick."

I lifted my hands to my head and found my palms bloody.

"We have had an adventure," Holmes told me. "I underestimated the determination of our adversaries and we almost died for it."

My lips felt dry and cracked. "What?" I asked. "What happened?"

Holmes heaved himself to his feet and me after him. "We were attacked, Watson. We shall now discover how."

"What attack?" I wondered. "I recall behaving strangely. Were we drugged?"

"In a sense," Holmes replied. "You will recall the euphoria which the girls reported in the presence of the fairies? And the light-hearted merriment of their usually-staid uncle after his encounter in the woods?"

"I do. Are you attributing their actions to the same cause as our recent affliction?"

"We have been subjected to a far more serious dose, Watson. Perhaps your medical experience can suggest the nature of the contaminant?"

My head was aching abominably but I racked it so as not to let Holmes down. "Nitrous oxide," I ventured. "It is now commonly used in Harley Street surgeries as an anaesthetic. It is sometimes called laughing gas because minor airborne doses of it induce euphoria and a dream-like sense of carefree disconnectedness with the world."

"Nitrous oxide," Holmes agreed. "I'll warrant though that had we fallen asleep in that study we would never have woken again."

"Someone attempted to murder us."

"We have been attacked by the fairies," Holmes replied. "And now we shall find out why."

※ ※ ※

When we roused Callow and gained entrance to the house once more the method of attack became clear. Holmes detected traces of the mechanism, which had been attached to the speaking tube from study to kitchen. A cylinder of nitrous oxide gas had been affixed to the hose and had piped the anaesthetic through to us as we studied Manchard's papers.

The kitchen door was locked but unbolted, indicating that someone had left the premises using a key; but of where the perpetrators had gone after their ruse had failed there was no indication.

Holmes was grave as he secured the house and waited for the police to come in the morning.

※ ※ ※

The Inspector of Police was a stolid, heavy-set man called Kenning. He arrived early that next morning with Mr Adley and a uniformed constable, even as Holmes was gathering the household together in the main hall to present his case.

"Ah, Inspector Kenning!" my friend greeted the new arrival. "Watson, a chair for the officer. I was just about to present some conclusions of my investigation, conclusions aided by the extraordinary events of last night."

This was the first that Adley or the police had heard of the attack upon Holmes and myself. I explained in a few terse sentences how we had been subjected to a potentially lethal exposure of medical gas. I omitted the horror I still felt at being so out of control in the face of destruction.

"That is a remarkable testimony, Mr Holmes," Kenning responded. "You might have sent for us in the night under these circumstances."

"I didn't wish anyone to leave the house," Holmes replied. "You collected my reply telegrams, Inspector?"

Kenning handed over the sealed slips that he'd picked up from the post office on his way and also passed across a rolled poster of cheap newsprint. Holmes held up a finger to indicate that we should all wait and quickly tore open each envelope and scanned the messages within.

"Hah!" he muttered once but made no other response.

I looked around the room. The Bolton girls were on the edges of their seats, wide-eyed with excitement and apprehension, subdued only a little by the sharp critical gaze of their aunt. Leah Manchard sat bolt upright with a sour disapproving expression on her face. She only endured this meeting in the hopes of news of her missing husband. Callow attempted to remain professionally aloof and failed. Stanley was pale and quiet. Adley looked worried and tense. Sarah was barely restraining her tears.

Holmes looked up suddenly. "You are doubtless wondering if I can produce a leprechaun," he told the assembly. "Be patient and perhaps I shall."

"What do you mean, Mr Holmes?" demanded Mrs Manchard. "What is this nonsense?"

"This nonsense, madam, is as clever a plot as I have met in many a month, and yet one that misfired due to the slightest chance. Allow me to present some facts to illustrate my contention."

"You know where Lionel is?" Mrs Manchard demanded.

Holmes continued in his own way. "On their first days at the Lodge, Arabella and Abigail encountered disembodied sounds and voices from beneath the old cairn in the woods. This lead them back secretly by night to encounter a blue leprechaun who gave them ancient treasure and offered to tell their uncle the future."

Mrs Manchard scowled and her gaze was frosty on Holmes and her nieces alike.

"What is not common knowledge is that Lionel Manchard subsequently also had one encounter with these fairies, and that thereafter he received communications from them via his nieces' regular night-time visits," Holmes continued.

"What kind of communications?" blurted Adley. All of this was new to him.

"What did those words mean?" Abigail Bolton asked curiously. "They made no sense."

Holmes laid a telegram on the table before him. "This communication is from a London bookmaker. It confirms that the words given to the children to convey to their uncle are in fact names. Edinburgh, Seraph's Queen, Rumbucket, Harper of India, and Effervescent are all race-horses that have run over the last three weeks. Their starting prices – the odds for them winning their races at the moment the race began – were 11 – 1, 7 – 1, 11 – 2, 8 – 1, and 14 – 1 respectively."

"The numbers in Manchard's desk," I noted.

Mrs Manchard's face clouded. "Betting? Mr Manchard would do no such thing!"

"Even on an absolute certainty?" Holmes challenged her. "That would be a sore temptation even for a lifelong abstainer of strong religious conviction. Think of the good that could be done with the winnings, if one had an absolute faith that one could predict the winners."

"At those long odds," Adley calculated, "the profits would be immense!"

"Seven, fifty-five, and four hundred guineas respectively," I speculated.

"Indeed," Holmes agreed. "I suggest that Manchard took no action on the information about the first race but was impressed enough by what he might have gained to break a lifelong abstention from gaming to venture a small sum on the next tip. Each subsequent wager was substantially larger. His latest gamble was to lay four thousand pounds on Effervescent at odds of 14-1."

"Which would win him £56,000!" I whistled.

"Lionel would never sin in such a fashion," Mrs Manchard declared, but her tone and face betrayed the nagging fear that her husband might well have fallen into such temptation for so large a sum.

"Come, Mr Holmes," Inspector Kenning chided, "you cannot be

suggesting that the missing man was receiving racing tips from a leprechaun!"

"I suggest that Manchard believed that he was," Holmes replied. "Each win made him more confident and ready to risk a larger sum, right up to his investment of whatever he could scrape together to put on Effervescent on the nose. After all he had seen fairies."

"How could the fairies – how could anyone – predict such winners at such long odds?" demanded Mr Adley wonderingly.

Holmes chuckled. "They did not," he replied. "Each of those horses lost their races, including Effervescent yesterday at Haydock Park."

"But Manchard never knew that," I surmised. "He couldn't risk a sporting paper in this house for Mrs Manchard to find. So if he was told he'd won, if he received his money…"

"Then he would never know otherwise," Holmes agreed.

"But we saw fairies," Arabella blurted. "Why can't they know the future?"

"They gave us buried treasure," Abigail argued.

Holmes produced his second telegram. "Three coins matching the date and description of the finds beneath your fairy rath were purchased at catalogue auction four weeks ago," he explained. "The buyer had the items shipped to Gainsborough."

"Fairies with cheque-books," I muttered.

"This is ridiculous," protested Mrs Manchard. Her objection was weaker than before.

"I don't understand," Arabella admitted miserably.

Holmes tempered his usual tones as he explained to the children. "If one wished to convince people that they had seen fairies then the means exist in our modern world. A speaking-tube, buried in a shallow trench concealed by long grass, coming up under the old stones, might allow for a mysterious voice to emanate from beneath the cairn. One of Mr Bell's new-patented gramophones, one of Mr Edison's phonographs, any amount of apparatus might simulate bells and pipes."

"We saw fairies. We saw Lucky," insisted Abigail.

"We felt their presence," Arabella added emphatically. "It was unmistakable."

"We felt a similar presence last night," Holmes replied. "Our experience was an intensified version of your own. We apprehended the world as if in a dream. We found everything joyous and amusing. Our cognitive state was very much impaired so that we did not properly question our behaviour." It sounded like my friend was scolding himself for mortal weakness; or perhaps some part of him was yearning for the oblivion of his seven percent solution.

"The girls were exposed to laughing gas?" I prompted to ease my friend on.

"There were traces of ammonium in a fire in the woods," Holmes told the room. "When ammonium nitrate is carefully heated it breaks into water vapour and nitrous oxide. As Watson reminded me nitrous oxide is now commonly used as an anaesthetic in dentistry and surgery. Its symptoms are those that Abigail and Arabella have described to us in their visits to the fairies. Such a gas might be piped beneath the cairn through the dug channel we found yesterday. It might induce a willingness to interpret moving lights as fairy dancers if the suggestion had already been planted. I imagine that in the darkness they would be quite convincing to people already intoxicated by the odourless influence of nitrous oxide."

"You said there were traces in the branches, Holmes," I recalled. "The broken twigs and the pocked bark."

"Traces of pulleys and threads that could hold wheels of tiny candles aloft and spin them like puppets in the darkness. Rings of fairy-lights wheeling through the air. You will recall that Lucky the Leprechaun appeared only at the end of the children's visits when the gas had cleared enough for him to safely join them without being affected."

"We were tricked?" Arabella asked, disconcerted.

"This is ridiculous," protested Mrs Manchard. Her objection was even weaker than before.

"I don't understand," Abigail admitted miserably.

"The coins, of course, might have been placed beneath the cairn at any time just before their discovery," Holmes went on.

"And what of the disturbances in the house, sir?" Callow the butler couldn't resist asking. "How could such things occur?"

"And the leprechaun?" protested Arabella. "And the fairy queen? We saw them. They were not just lights."

"And how does this relate to Manchard's disappearance?" puzzled Inspector Kenning.

"The movements in Manchard Lodge are simple enough," Holmes noted. "On some occasions night-time access might have been gained by the window which the children left open to enable their own return to their bedroom. Other times the simplest explanation is that the fairy had a key."

"Only Callow and Mr Manchard had keys," objected Adley.

Holmes dismissed this with a snort. "A wax key impression can be easily obtained in a household which has no reason to guard against it. Any staff here could gain such a thing, and any common locksmith could make copies based on it. He turned round suddenly. "Stay where you are, Mr Stanley!"

The groom went deathly pale. He glanced towards the door, but Kenning's solid constable was planted firmly by the exit.

"Stanley?" frowned Callow, wondering what this portended.

"I shall continue," Holmes announced. "Suppose that some enemy wished revenge upon Lionel Manchard. Consider that this complicated scheme seems to have been directed at defrauding him of some of his fortune; but more, it seems to have been designed to take his money from him in a way designed to make him look preposterous and foolish, to inveigle him into compromising his strong religious views, to sow discord between him and his lady wife."

Mrs Manchard looked up sharply.

"The method presented itself when Manchard's young nieces came to stay. Here were two newcomers with lively curiosity and active imaginations. It was simple enough to first ensnare them using the sounds from the cairn then bring them back by night when their senses could be dulled and they could witness the full show designed so they could see fairies."

The Bolton girls looked unhappy.

"The purpose of those early exercises was to get the coins to Manchard and convince him to come by night and experience the fairies for himself. The additional events inside the house cultivated belief in the children - and Sarah - and set the stage for Manchard's conversion."

"The milk-dish reappearing each morning in the kitchen and the problem of the locks and bolts is solved if Stanley had keys and was an accomplice," I realised.

"I'm sure there were occasions when Stanley had an alibi," Holmes responded, "but those were the occasions when a second person could have accessed the house by means of the bedroom window or by using another set of keys where Stanley had previously unbolted the door for them and later bolted it after them. Stanley's foreknowledge of Sarah's vigil to see the fairies of course assured her midnight watch would be in vain."

Stanley rose to protest. "You got nothin' on me, sir. Nothin' at all."

"All in good time," promised the great detective. "Meanwhile, Manchard was lured to the grove, to be exposed to the gas and to the whirling lights and strange voices even as the girls had been. There was no 'Lucky' this time, and no beauteous fairy queen. I take their absence as significant."

"You don't think they could have fooled a grown man as they fooled two innocent children," I surmised.

"Lucky was three feet tall, and blue!" protested Sarah, forgetting her place in her agitation, still unwilling to give up her fairies. "That's what Abigail said."

Holmes acknowledged it. "Which brings me to the night when Mrs Manchard found a stain on her china bowl which precipitated her maid's dismissal."

The lady of the house looked up sharply. Sarah winced.

"So upset was the maid Sarah with the incident which led to the breaking of the dish of milk and her subsequent dismissal that she set aside the dirty bowl on a shelf and forgot about it," my friend revealed. "Hence I was able to examine the smudge which so distressed Mrs Manchard and sent her to the kitchen to deliver her domestic reproof. I have the bowl here. Would you care to examine it, Inspector?"

Urged forward, Kenning looked carefully at the proffered soup dish. "That's a mark, alright," he admitted. Then he looked uncertainly at Holmes.

"The mark is undoubtedly a thumbprint," the great detective tutored. "Moreover a thumbprint in some greasy substance that does not easily wash from crockery in soap and water."

It was I who announced the most salient point. "A blue thumbprint, by George!"

Holmes appreciated that I'd followed his reasoning. "A blue thumbprint such as might be left by a man whose hands and face were coated with blue greasepaint, Watson. A dwarf or midget who might make himself up to present himself as a leprechaun to two innocent girls, children who were needed to inveigle their uncle into a scheme designed to rob him of his money, his dignity, and his domestic harmony. A midget who smokes the very mortal Swanson's Shag Tobacco, as I note from the traces in the clearing. A man who had received and drunk a bowl of milk in the woods and had returned the vessel to the kitchen again through the medium of his accomplice Stanley."

I noticed Stanley blanch and knew that Holmes had hit upon the heart of the deception. "The fairies were faked to get past Manchard's dour routine," I reasoned, "The objective was to steal his money."

"And to have some personal revenge for wrongs imagined or done," Holmes replied. "But superstition is hard to control. On the night after Manchard had invested so great a sum on the performance of Effervescent at the behest of the Lucky Leprechaun he was horrified to learn that his own wife had insulted the fairies by shattering their offering dish."

Adley understood at last. "He believed that the source of his fortune might vanish and his four thousand pounds be lost!"

"And so he went to the woods that night to apologise in person to the fair folk," Holmes revealed. "He went there unexpectedly, for the criminals could not have foreseen Mrs Manchard's actions. He came upon them as they prepared for their final appearance to the children – some cruel final twist to this sordid deception. He found the leprechaun greasing up, perhaps, or his beautiful female accomplice heating up ammonium nitrate for the laughing gas, or hanging the candle-wheels from the trees to make the fairies fly. Perhaps he found Professor Henshawe himself supervising the preparations."

"Henshawe?" I asked, uncertain where Manchard's rival from long-done lawsuits had suddenly entered the case.

"Come, Watson. A midget not much more than three feet tall or so is a rare thing. But you will recall the children were denied the opportunity to visit the carnival upon the common."

Holmes triumphantly unrolled the poster the Inspector had brought him. The cheap printing promised a carnival extravaganza on the common. Professor Henshawe presented amongst his other features Jack O'Leary the world's smallest man and the beautiful snake dancer Sophia.

"Professor Henshawe's Travelling Phantasmagoria!" Sarah blurted. "Tom wanted to take me there on our afternoon off!"

Stanley winced again and held his hands up. "Alright, I admit it. I 'ope as it'll do me some good in court, Inspector."

The footman's confession was brief and full. He'd not been long in Manchard's employ, and had found it far from satisfactory for a man of Stanley's lively habits, when he'd been approached by a beautiful woman offering him a chance for riches. The snake charmer at Henshawe's carnival had brought him into her master's plans, had discovered from him details of the Manchard household, and had gradually entangled him in their scheme of riches and revenge.

"Stanley was key to the plot," Holmes noted. "As a man of the world it was to him that Manchard turned for information on laying a bet. It was Stanley who made daily visits to Gainsborough where he could place such wagers. All Stanley had to do was to refrain from making the bet, take back Henshawe's seed money to pay his master's supposed winnings, and claim that the fairies' prediction had come true."

"Until Manchard made a sufficiently large bet to recover all Henshawe's set-up costs and much more," Inspector Kenning growled. "When the horse lost Manchard could hardly blame his servant for placing the bet. The fraud was complete and nobody could be held responsible for his losses but the fairies!"

Stanley nodded miserably.

"Oh Tom," breathed Sarah, her voice breaking to a sob.

"I didn't know what they was about last night, though!" Stanley defended himself. "I didn't know what they was doin' in the kitchen when they was trying to poison folks!"

"That will be for the courts to decide," Inspector Kenning said solemnly. "Thomas Stanley, I arrest you in the name of the law!"

Callow watched his footman be charged with the stoic resignation of a man who will need to engage new staff.

"But where is Lionel?" blurted Mrs Manchard urgently. "If this fantastic story is true then Lionel surprised these villains as they prepared their final tricks…"

"They was going to tell the girls that the fairies wanted another sacrifice," Stanley confessed, "and have them destroy their uncle's most precious possessions."

"But where is Lionel?" Mrs Manchard almost screamed. "What have they done to him?"

I remembered the blood on the cane, sign of a violent struggle.

"I believe they were taken unawares by his appearance and the subsequent scene," Holmes responded. "Manchard struck out at his deceivers. There was a struggle. They had no plan for that and so were forced to take him with them and keep him captive and concealed until they could make good their escape with their money."

"So Manchard is in all probability hidden at the carnival?" I realised. "Holmes, we must go there at once!"

"So that is why you asked for a pair of constables to stand watch over the showfolk on the common when you contacted me last night!" proclaimed Kenning. As always my friend had thought ahead of me.

❋ ❋ ❋

Holmes' interest waned once he had untangled the mystery to his satisfaction. He accompanied Kenning, Adley and I to Henshawe's carnival but needed to play no part thereafter. A routine search discovered Lionel Manchard trussed up in a travelling trunk while his captors still bickered about how to dispose of him. Henshawe might have brazened out some kind of defence but the Irish midget and a sweet-faced snake dancer soon confessed their parts in the fraud. Manchard's satchel of money was recovered from Henshawe's caravan.

"What possible purpose could you have for so elaborate a charade?" I wondered as Inspector Kenning made to lead "The Professor" away.

Henshawe's face reddened and turned belligerent. "That man ruined me for no reasons than his own satisfaction and overweening pride!" the showman proclaimed. "He took my livelihood, my reputation, and my happiness for his obscure religious principles. I have long waited my chance to pay him back and so I have done. He may have his money again but now he knows himself to be a fool!"

"We were fools to be following 'ye!" the midget who had played Lucky shouted to Henshawe as they were led to the police dray.

"I have been a fool indeed," confessed Lionel Manchard as Adley fussed over him and explained the full nature of what had happened. "What happens next is between me and my Saviour. And my wife."

Holmes had no interest in the domestic dynamics. Once he had confirmed what tobacco Lucky used and had examined the apparatus for the gas, the lights, and the sounds he was quite ready for an immediate return to Baker Street.

It was I who was left to resolve the aftermath in the Manchard household. I spoke with the Bolton girls, but was reassured that for all their naiveté Arabella and Abigail were sensible children who would come to no harm from their adventure; already they were planning how they would recount their summer to their schoolmates. Mrs Manchard surprised me with the charity she demonstrated on receiving her husband home. I saw in their reunion something of the love which must first have drawn these two fierce religionists together. I arranged a place for Sarah the maid in the household of Reginald Musgrave.[1]

Holmes must retain some small affection for the problem he had solved, though. As part of his fee he claimed one of the guineas that had been found beneath the woodland cairn. It remains under glass in Holmes'

---

1 Dr Watson recounts Holmes' reunion with his old university acquaintance in *The Musgrave Ritual*.

When asked by the idle and curious about the coin he sucks on his pipe and tells them it is fairy gold..

study to this day, enshrined beside memorabilia such as the mask of the Yellow Face, the photographs of Gordon and of Henry Ward Beecher, and the treasured image of the divine Irene Adler.

When asked by the idle and curious about the coin's provenance he sucks on his pipe and tells them it is fairy gold.

ON FAIRIES
AND THE STORY CONAN DOYLE COULD NOT WRITE

In 1917, sixteen year old Elsie Wright and her ten year old cousin Frances Griffiths returned from the wooded beck behind Elsie's house in Cottingley, Yorkshire, with two photographs of fairies they said they had been playing with. Frances sent one of the pictures to a pen-pal in South Africa along with a letter which casually mentioned that "Elsie and I are very friendly with the beck Fairies."

As the photographs became better known they came to the attention of the man commissioned by *The Strand* Magazine to write a Christmas 1920 article on fairies, that publication's most famous contributor Sir Arthur Conan Doyle. He borrowed the prints and began an investigation, dispatched theosophist Edward Gardener on his behalf to interview the girls, and persuaded Elsie and Frances to return to the beck and take five additional pictures of themselves playing with the fairies.

So began Conan Doyle's championing of the children's truthfulness and the photographs' veracity. *The Strand* article triggered controversy which dogged the Cottingley fairies throughout the writer's life, up to the deaths of the girls themselves in 1988 and 1986, and beyond. Conan Doyle published a book, *The Coming of Fairies*, to support the case. In 1981 the women confessed to faking the pictures using cardboard cutouts; they had maintained their charade before because they didn't wish to make a fool of the great creator of Mr. Sherlock Holmes. Frances maintained until her death that the final picture they took, showing the fairies in a sunbath, was genuine.

Even now the Cottingley fairies have their detractors and supporters. To Conan Doyle in 1920 they were an important proof of his growing spiritualist beliefs. He wrote to Gardener, "When our fairies are admitted other psychic phenomena will find a more ready acceptance ... we have had continued messages at seances for some time that a visible sign was coming through...."

It's often commented on how the creator of the archetypal rational detective became in later life such a believer – some would say credulous believer – in the occult. In addition to the Cottingley fairies he also championed the spirit manifestations of mediums Eusapia Palladino and Mina "Margery" Crandon and fell out with Harry Houdini when the great escapist denied using supernatural powers to accomplish his feats. But grieving Conan Doyle, mourning his beloved wife's death in 1906 and the subsequent loss of his brother and two brothers-in-law, suffering what we might now term clinical depression, found solace in the idea that their spirits awaited him just beyond the veil.

Conan Doyle's beliefs found their way into his fiction writing as well as his prolific essays and treatises. Professor George Edward Challenger was Conan Doyle's second-most-famous series character, an aggressive eccentric scientist and explorer. The third Challenger novel, The Land of Mist (1926), draws extensively on spiritualism and features an overtly supernatural plotline that takes Challenger away from his previous fantastic but scientifically-based adventures.

Sherlock Holmes, however, always remained in his rational world where logic pierced every shadow and mysteries could be solved by the application of intellect and expertise. Where there is a Sussex vampire or a great phantom hound over the grimpen mire there is also a jealous half-brother or tin of luminous paint to answer the puzzle. Conan Doyle had long since learned that his reading public had strict requirements for the Great Detective. Even the falls at Reichenbach could not override their implacable will.

Many authors since have found it interesting to pit Sherlock Holmes against the supernatural or fantastic. He's been placed against Dracula, against H.G. Wells' Martians, against H.P. Lovecraft's elder gods, against a demonic Jack the Ripper. In each case the tale gains its interest in juxtaposing Holmes' rationalistic worldview with the discovered truth of a more bizarre and occult creation. In the best such mash-ups Holmes and Watson's Victorian standards, morals, and intellectual capacities are respected and even profiled. In the worst Holmes is shown to be an ignorant narrow-minded fool who does not or cannot comprehend whatever greater truths the writer wishes to ascribe to his supernatural universe.

These stories may amuse and some deliver strong good stories but they rarely satisfy as Holmes tales. Airship 27's writers brief for this new generation of stories about the inhabitants of 221B Baker Street was summarised in the cover blurb for volume 1: "There are no space aliens here nor howling werewolves, simply good old fashion whodunits."

Behind that statement is an understanding that to really work, Holmes must occupy the world that Conan Doyle first placed him in right back in 1887 where he told Watson "There's the scarlet thread of murder running through the colourless skein of life, and our duty is to unravel it, and isolate it, and expose every inch of it."[2] In Holmes' world it must be the case that "when you have eliminated the impossible, whatever remains, however improbable, must be the truth."[3] – but that truth must conform to the scientific rational worldview of the enlightened Edwardian.

All of which finally brings us to The Lucky Leprechaun, wherein two young girls see fairies in the woods and an investigator from London is dispatched to understand what is happening. It intrigued me to use elements close to the Cottingley case because they are incidents that Conan Doyle could never use, in a story that he would never tell; and yet I hope they are elements that allow a traditional Holmes tale that conforms to the standards and world-limits set by Holmes' clever creator.

As Holmes himself might say, "You know my methods. Apply them."[4]

IW
Yorkshire, England (15 miles from the Cottingley Fairies), April 2010

❈ ❈ ❈

I.A. Watson never expected to become a regular contributor to Sherlock Holmes' wider canon, but he has somehow squeezed stories into the previous two volumes and hopes to baffle readers (but not Mr Sherlock Holmes) in future collections. One of his contributions to volume two, 'The Last Deposit', won the Pulp Factory's Award for Best Pulp Short Shory of 2010. His first Airship 27 novel, *Robin Hood: King of Sherwood*, was published in April 2010 and its sequel, *Robin Hood: Arrow of Justice* will be available shortly. His work also features in the anthology *Gideon Cain: Demon Hunter*.

---

2 *A Study in Scarlet*, chapter 4, "What Rance Had To Tell"
3 *The Sign of Four*, chapter 6, 1890
4 *The Sign of Four*, chapter 6

Sherlock Holmes
Consulting Detective

"The Adventure of the Mummy's Rib"

by
Aaron Smith

It was a warm afternoon in London as I returned to Baker Street after a morning out. The sky was clear, the air crisp, and a mild breeze blowing. It was a welcome relief from a spell of much too balmy weather. Uncommon for London, such heat had reminded me, and unpleasantly so, of my time in Afghanistan during my military days.

Despite the pleasant weather, I was tired, having been kept up nearly all night by the various sounds that I had come to know as the noises of Sherlock Holmes on those occasions when he fell into one of his frequent fits of melancholy moodiness. Many men fall into pits of despair when overwhelmed by work or the tasks required in daily life; Sherlock Holmes had always been just the opposite. It was the lack of work, the absence of new cases or new clients that could drive him into one of those spells of boredom, frustration, and near depression.

I had tried to fall into a state of sleep, tried to cover my ears with blankets pulled up over my head, and had even poured a mild sedative powder into a glass of water, but it had been no use. First, there had been the ceaseless tap, tap, tap of Holmes pacing back and forth across the sitting room. Then had come his flipping through what must have been nearly every book in his considerably large library of criminal histories and scientific texts. Third, and perhaps worst for one trying to find peaceful slumber on the other side of a too-thin wall, was the violin playing. Holmes has always had a unique manner of manipulating the instrument; one which would sometimes produce the sweetest, most melodic strains while at other times making noises comparable to the death cries of a cat being autopsied while still alive!

Finally, after what seemed like an eternity of such horrid sounds, it was with great relief that I heard the distinctive sound of one of the violin strings breaking! I thanked whatever deities might be within hearing distance of my prayers, and I fell into sleep.

In the morning, which came much too quickly, I had my tea while Holmes sat silently, still brooding. Finally, I could stand it no longer and I resolved to spend a few hours away from Baker Street. I dressed, muttered to Holmes that I would be perfectly willing to go out and buy a violin string to replace the one he had broken, and I left our rooms, with Holmes still not having uttered a single syllable to me.

I managed to waste several hours browsing among the shops in the streets surrounding the area of Holmes' and my lodgings. I acquired the needed violin string and stuffed it into my pocket. Seeing no point in wandering the streets any longer, I reversed my path and made my way back toward Baker Street, walking slowly, seeing no reason to hurry, and hoping that my return would find the moody detective in better spirits, though I doubted that would be the case. I knew from long years of experience that only the appearance of a new client with some intriguing riddle would bring relief to the stagnant mind of Sherlock Holmes.

As I approached the familiar building numbered 221, I could see a man leaning against the wall beside the door. From a distance, I could see that he was of average height and weight, dressed inexpensively but neatly. His casual posture was a hint to me, having learned a bit of something in my years with Holmes, that he could very well have been a non-native of England, perhaps an American. My semi-educated guess was proven correct as I neared the man and recognized him. It was an old friend and fellow physician who stood at my door!

"MacFarlane, old chap!" I exclaimed, happy that something, an unexpected and most welcome visitor, had appeared to break the monotony of my day. The man turned to look at me and matched my smile with one of his own.

"Hello, Watson. I was hoping you'd appear sooner rather than later. I tried to gain admission to your building, but that little bulldog of a landlady you have told me in no uncertain terms that Holmes was not to be disturbed today. Then she whispered in my ear that he's in one of what she called 'his dreadful fits of darkness.' I only ever met your friend briefly, but from what I recall of the intensity of his demeanor, I can see how his melancholy moments might be a bit frightening, especially to an older woman."

Having now reached a place directly in front of MacFarlane, I grasped his outstretched hand and shook it. As I greeted him, my memory flashed back to the incident which had introduced me to him for the first time.

Some years earlier, Holmes and I had suddenly been summoned to go aboard an American naval vessel which was docked near London. A dead man, not part of the crew, had been discovered in one of the ship's cabins. This man, Doctor Christopher MacFarlane, had been the ship's surgeon. He was a capable officer and physician and together he and I saved the life of the ship's third officer after he had been shot.

I was, at that moment on Baker Street, seeing MacFarlane for the first time since. He was dressed in civilian clothing now, had put on some weight, but still seemed fit, and was graying slightly at the temples.

"And what, pray tell, are you doing here, MacFarlane?" I asked my guest. "Judging by your attire, might I safely assume that it isn't naval business that brings you by?"

"That's right, Watson," MacFarlane answered. "I had my fill of boats and waves years ago, so I left the military and went into private practice in New York City. I occasionally do some work for my government; I suppose you could say they've held me in reserve for those times when the navy needs an extra man with medical knowledge. In fact, this happens to be one of those times. So, while I'm not exactly here on Navy business, it is by the request of my government that I'm in London. So, while I'm in this neck of the woods, so to speak, I felt obligated to come and visit with my old friends. It wasn't difficult to find your residence either. I simply stopped in at Scotland Yard; they seem to get a lot of people asking for you."

"Might I inquire as to what sort of business brought you here then, MacFarlane?" was my next question. "Of course, if you're not at liberty to say, that is quite understandable."

MacFarlane shook his head. "It's nothing as secretive as you might be thinking, Watson. I'm simply here to look at a very, very old corpse; a mummy actually. One of our archeologists recently unearthed a very well-preserved example from Egypt. He had it sent to New York, to our Museum of Natural History for the first official examination of the thing; an examination which I was privileged to be invited to attend. Now that, my colleague, was a fascinating experience, to look at the body of a man deceased for two thousand years!

"Well, we kept Old Ernie...that's what some of us started calling him, though I don't remember why...we kept him at the museum for a few weeks, but some bureaucrat on the board of directors accepted an offer to buy the mummy; an offer from the British Museum! I hated to see the thing sold off like that, but the board decided that new floor tiles in the lobby were more important!

"My counterpart here in London, a Professor Quick, whom I've yet to meet, was kind enough to invite me here to go over our initial findings and continue the examination with him. So, Watson, that's how I wound up in London. I arrived this morning and I'm to be at the museum tomorrow morning to meet Quick and be reunited with Old Ernie. The mummy arrived here a week before I did; I chose to travel on a more luxurious vessel than the freighter that Ernie took. I had enough of Spartan cabins and tight bunks when I was in the navy. I can afford real beds at sea now!"

I was interested in hearing more from MacFarlane concerning the mummy, as well as anything else he felt like relating to me about the years since we had last seen each other. At the same time, I thought it unwise to barge into my rooms with a guest in tow while Holmes was in such a state, so I suggested to MacFarlane that we might find a decent restaurant instead. He agreed and even insisted on paying for our meal. We enjoyed several hours of pleasant conversation on matters both medical and personal. We then parted ways for the evening, having decided to dine together again while he was still in London. MacFarlane went off to his hotel, while I returned to Baker Street to find Holmes still silent and sour-faced. I did not attempt to converse with him; I tossed the new violin string on the table and retired to my room.

❊ ❊ ❊

I awoke the next morning to find Holmes gone. I hoped he hadn't gone off in search of a supply of one of those substances, the use of which I frowned upon, but which he seemed to think gave his agile mind an advantage, like oil helps the turning of wheels. Shaking my head, I decided there was nothing I could do about Holmes' stubbornness. I sat down to morning tea, quite content to be alone for a while.

My enjoyable solitude did not last long. Mrs. Hudson gave a knock and walked in, handing me a small envelope that had just been dropped off by messenger. I thanked Mrs. Hudson, took the envelope and tore it open. Inside was a handwritten note. It had long been a joke in our profession that American physicians had the worst handwriting in the known world. That rumor was now confirmed for me, but I could, squinting, make out what MacFarlane had written to me.

"Watson, how would you like to meet the 2,000 year old man? Stop by and visit Old Ernie and me, if you feel up to it!"

I immediately jumped up from my chair, grabbed my hat, ran down the stairs and hailed a hansom cab. Within moments, I was on my way to the British Museum. I certainly couldn't pass up the opportunity to inspect an Egyptian mummy up close.

I tipped the driver handsomely, as was my habit when overly enthusiastic about where I was going, a habit my late wife often frowned upon. I flew up the museum's steps, gave my name to the guard at the door, and was led inside. I was taken down a long corridor in a part of the building that was not open to the general public, and soon found myself in a room which held a table which in turn held the ancient artifact that I had been so eager to see. MacFarlane stood beside the table with another man, an older man, bushy-haired and bearded, whom I assumed was Professor Quick. MacFarlane made the necessary introductions.

We turned our attention to the shrouded shape on the table. With the white sheet over it, it looked like any body in any morgue, but I knew that once that sheet was lifted, I would be looking at the oldest corpse, by far, that I had ever seen.

"You got here fast enough, Watson," said MacFarlane. "I only just arrived myself. Well, it's good to see Old Ernie again. Let's take a look, shall we? I want to make sure Professor Quick hasn't done any damage to my friend here."

Professor Quick, apparently not possessing a sense of humor, snorted.

MacFarlane lifted the sheet from the body and tossed it aside. I stared down at the tabletop in amazement. Old Ernie was a dried husk of a human being, dark brown, teeth bared in a ghastly death's head grimace, but still remarkably well-preserved, as MacFarlane had told me the day before. His head was bare, but his body was mostly wrapped in old, decaying bandages. On the mummy's chest, I could see where the bandages had been cut down the middle. I assumed they must have been cut and parted to examine the body, them put back in place again, perhaps held by some adhesive. By this method, MacFarlane and others could examine the specimen, and then return it, as closely as possible, to its original appearance so that it could be displayed by the museum.

At that point, and probably for my benefit, Professor Quick began to speak, launching into the tale of how the Egyptians had performed their mummifications.

"When a body was to become a mummy, most of the internal organs were first removed. Only the heart, which had great religious significance, was allowed to remain. The removed organs were placed in containers known as Canopic Jars. These jars represented the gods who corresponded to the various organs in Egyptian mythology. The brain was pulled out of the head through the nostrils. The body, now relieved of most of its organs, was covered in a substance called natron, which prevented decomposition and accelerated the process of drying. The mummified body was then wrapped in linen strips, resembling bandages, as we can see on this specimen."

I found myself both disgusted and intrigued by Quick's description. "What a wonderfully barbaric ritual!" I said. Turning to MacFarlane, and perhaps prodded on by my many years of listening to Holmes ask all sorts of questions, I inquired, "Do you know who this poor fellow was, and have you determined how he met his end?"

"No…and yes," was MacFarlane's answer. "We have no idea of his name, profession, or rank in society, as his tomb was unmarked...or at least time, the elements, and perhaps grave robbers long ago took away any identifying objects. We do, however, know what caused his death. Now we do not know if it was some accidental mishap or some manner of foul play, but he took a blow to the left side of the torso, which caused internal damage, from which he did not recover."

"Interesting," said I.

"Allow me to show you," said MacFarlane, stepping closer to Old Ernie and opening the linen strips that had been cut and then put back in place across the chest area of the ancient corpse. He placed his hand on the now visible left side of the mummy's torso.

"Good lord!" MacFarlane shouted, shock written plainly across his usually calm face. "This is not Old Ernie! This is not the same mummy!"

"What!" I managed to blurt out in response to MacFarlane's statement. It was also all that Professor Quick was capable of saying, as he exclaimed the word simultaneously with me.

"The mummy's rib; it's intact, Watson!" MacFarlane explained. "Old Ernie's left third rib had been broken. That was what had killed him. Some sort of impact had cracked the rib, sending a jagged shard of bone into his heart. This mummy has no such broken bone! This cannot be the same man!"

"MacFarlane, are you absolutely certain?" Quick asked, stepping forward and feeling the ribs himself. "Yes, yes, you're quite right, Doctor. There is no break here. Most peculiar! A previously intact mummy might conceivably sustain some damage during an ocean voyage; mishandling on ship and such, but this is the opposite situation...and a two thousand year old bone does not mend itself!"

"Professor Quick," I said, "I know that Old Ernie, or whoever this mummy is, arrived before Dr. MacFarlane. Who accepted the delivery?"

"I did," Quick assured me. "I am absolutely sure that this is the same body that was delivered to me. I hadn't checked the ribs, for I wanted to wait until MacFarlane arrived and related all that he had learned from his initial examination of the body."

While I had been questioning the professor, MacFarlane had been examining the mummy more closely, peering intently at the face, checking the condition of the limbs.

"Now that I look, Watson," he said, "I can see other differences. The face is not quite the same, this mummy is perhaps an inch shorter, and it has a few fewer teeth than Old Ernie. It looks as though a very similar mummified corpse has been substituted for the one that was intended to arrive here. Why? How? This doesn't make any sense!"

In one instant of thought, I saw how my presence at the museum could help to solve not only this suddenly emerging mystery, but also the problem that had caused me so much irritation over the past two days. I grabbed my hat, started towards the door.

"Don't touch that mummy, either of you! I shall return as swiftly as possible!"

As I left the room, I could hear Professor Quick inquiring of MacFarlane where I was running off to and why they should listen to my advice on not touching the mummy. MacFarlane's answer was precisely what I expected it to be.

"We shall soon know what has happened with our specimen, Quick, for Watson is off to fetch his friend, Mr. Sherlock Holmes!"

❈ ❈ ❈

The cab dropped me off at Baker Street. I tipped the driver well for his speed and marched up the stairs to our rooms, hoping that Holmes had returned from his early morning excursion. He had.

"And how was your trip to the museum, Watson? It was a short one."

Once again, despite years of such moments, I was stunned by Holmes' ability to deduce precisely where I had been. Instinctively, I glanced down at my shoes, expecting to see some sort of dust or powder that would only be found in a museum. My shoes appeared clean. I looked at Holmes, and he began to laugh.

"Sometimes, Watson," the consulting detective said, "the murderer does turn out to be the man holding the bloody dagger! You mustn't overcomplicate matters, or give me too much credit when very little is due. You left the note from MacFarlane in plain sight. I read it when I returned home. Where else does one go in London to visit a '2,000 year old man' than the British Museum?"

I put aside my slight embarrassment at having overlooked the obvious and announced that the need for Holmes had arisen at the museum. I hoped this new development would be sufficient to break the spell of melancholy and ennui that had taken hold of Holmes.

"Holmes, you must come with me at once!" I said excitedly. "The mummy that has arrived at the museum…is not the one that was expected. Somehow, a switch has occurred!"

Holmes closed his eyes for a brief moment. He drew in a deep breath. When he opened his eyes, the lines upon his face seemed to have grown less noticeable, as if the coming of a new mystery had rejuvenated him.

"Then we must not put it off any longer, Watson! Come!"

He grabbed his hat and coat in a blur and flew out the door, racing down the staircase two or even three steps per stride. I smiled as I ran behind him, glad to see the game afoot once more.

※ ※ ※

Holmes rushed into the museum, breezing past the guard and sped into the room where I had left MacFarlane and Quick watching over the mummy that was not Old Ernie. I followed just behind Holmes, a bit out of breath trying to keep up with the boundless energy that he possessed when excited by some new puzzle to solve.

"Hello, Mr. Holmes," said Christopher MacFarlane, but the great detective ignored him, stopped in front of the body on the table, and stared down at the mummified form. He placed one gloved hand over the mummy's chest, apparently looking for the spot I had told him about on the cab ride from Baker Street to the museum.

"Yes, Watson," Holmes said. "I can feel the place of which you spoke. This man's ribs are all intact; no signs of breakage or jaggedness."

"We've already ascertained that, Mr. Holmes," said Professor Quick. "The question now is…where has our other mummy gone?"

"I understand that perfectly well, Professor," said Holmes brusquely. "If we wish to determine where your mummy has gone, it would be wise to first determine from where this new one has come."

Holmes continued to look at the mummy, sometimes bending his tall, thin body forward to look closely at certain areas of the linen-wrapped corpse. As he examined the body, I could see also the twitching of his prominent, hawk-like nose, a sure sign that he had detected some aroma that he either recognized or was trying to place. He stood up straight again and looked in the direction of Quick and MacFarlane.

"Have either of you been smoking a pipe in close proximity to this mummy?" Holmes asked.

MacFarlane answered first, stating that he was only an occasional smoker, and limited to cigarettes, none of which had he smoked since arriving in London on the previous day.

Professor Quick was louder in his denial of such an act. "No, Mr.

Holmes, of course I haven't! The presence of smoke in the room could damage such a delicate specimen. I strictly forbid it in this part of the museum!"

"Well then," said Holmes, "if we are to assume that you are telling the truth, Professor, we have found our first clue. These wrappings contain a trace of the odor of a certain Arabian pipe tobacco, a blend that is, to my knowledge, enjoyed by very few men in London. We may then assume that the scent attached itself to this mummy in a location where it lay previous to being brought here in place of the mummy you were expecting to have delivered."

"I can't see that getting us very far," said Professor Quick, a man of seemingly little faith in Holmes' methods. "We should summon the police; put this matter in the hands of professional investigators!"

"Why Professor Quick," snapped Sherlock Holmes, his voice heavily colored by sarcasm, "that is an excellent idea! Then we can have a swarm of newspapermen following an equally annoying swarm of policemen, all of them trampling around in here, clumsily disturbing all your precious artifacts and specimens! That, Professor, would get us nowhere. We must proceed quietly and cautiously, creating as little noise and drawing as little attention to ourselves as possible."

Holmes stepped away from the mummy and turned to me. "Watson, let us leave this place for a short while. There is a man in a shop some small distance from here whom I should like to have a word with. Dr. MacFarlane, I am entrusting you to keep watch over our mummified visitor here. Good day, Professor Quick."

With that burst of words, Sherlock Holmes headed for the door and I followed close behind him.

❈ ❈ ❈

Outside the museum, we engaged a hansom cab. Holmes gave the driver an address and we were on our way. As we sped along the streets, I questioned Holmes on our next step.

"Where are we going, Holmes?"

"To find a pipe-smoking Arab with an interesting ring upon his finger," my friend answered.

"A ring," I said, surprised. "How do you know he wears a ring?"

"When those linen wrappings reach a certain advanced age, Watson," he explained to me, "they acquire a certain texture which can be imprinted with the shape of any hard object which is pressed against it with enough force. On the right forearm wrappings of our mummy, I was able to spot such an imprint. It is in the shape of a crescent and a skull. If my memory serves me well, as it does in most cases, this is a symbol worn by a certain group of men, members of a London club that consists of soldiers formerly of the Middle Eastern part of the world. Judging by the ring imprint and the Arabic tobacco, it is clear to me that a member of this club has handled our ancient Egyptian friend."

A short time later, we arrived at our destination. I had seen this place before; a small tobacconist's shop, run by a man called Redburn. There had been several occasions on which Holmes had gone to this particular shop to match some brand of tobacco to a sample he had found at the scene of some crime or another.

"This is one of the few shops in London to sell pipe tobacco of the kind I detected at the museum, Watson," Holmes said as we entered the shop.

"Why it's Mr. Sherlock Holmes...and Mr. Watson too!" said Redburn as we entered, apparently forgetting my being part of the medical profession. "Come in for a fresh supply, Mr. Holmes?"

Redburn was around fifty years of age, a fat man with a contagious smile and a friendly demeanor which grew proportionately friendlier according to the amount of money a customer seemed willing to spend.

"Actually, Redburn," Holmes responded, "I've come in the hopes of a fresh supply of answers, rather than tobacco."

He walked right past Redburn to the shelf that held many small jars, each containing a different blend of tobacco. Like a man who was a walking encyclopedia of knowledge of those substances that people liked to smoke, Holmes immediately seized the jar he sought, took its lid off and inhaled deeply of the scent of its contents.

"This blend, Redburn," Holmes asked, "how many of your customers purchase it?"

Redburn scratched his head. "Only three come to mind, sir. One is a lady who says it reminds her of her dead husband. Then there's a retired soldier with one leg. There's also a big Turk with an eye patch. I'm afraid I don't know any of their names, Mr. Holmes. They each come in only occasionally and all pay in cash; I don't have many customers whom I'm willing to supply tobacco to on credit, you see."

"Thank you, Redburn," said Holmes. He tossed a few coins onto the counter in payment for the information and marched out of the shop. I followed.

"The large Turk is the man we seek, Watson," said Holmes as we returned to the street. "A sentimental woman is probably not involved in an affair that includes stolen and switched mummies, and a one-legged man would be of little use in transporting the body in question. The hand that wears that ring, judging by the mark it made, was probably used to lift the mummy."

I nodded in agreement with Holmes' judgment. "I concur, Holmes. I believe I know the colonel. If it's the man I think, his name is Reginald Summers. I served with him in Afghanistan. I've run into him several times in London, but he refuses to acknowledge me; I think he holds a grudge over my not being able to salvage his leg. You mentioned a certain club in London. I suppose we'll go there next to look for this one-eyed Turk."

"It isn't that simple, Watson," the great detective answered. "I did not mean it was a club in the sense of a stone and glass building where men meet. I speak of a more secretive organization, one with no permanent headquarters; a group of men who meet occasionally, in varying locations. These men are of many different professions, linked only by certain similarities in their pasts and the part of the world from which they all came to London."

"So how do we find him?" I asked, hoping we hadn't reached a dead end so soon in our investigation.

"As you know, Watson," Holmes began to put my fears to rest, "Men of Arabic descents are not a terribly common thing in England. Like many non-native classes, they tend to face some ostracizing from the rest of the public. Unfamiliar appearances and traditions can cause suspicion, whether justified or not. Not only does the public make note of aliens in London, but so do the police. I'd wager a whole jar of that rather expensive tobacco that Scotland Yard has a file on this club and many of its members. As much as I hesitate to do so, it may behoove us to involve one of our occasional allies there in this matter after all."

"Lestrade, I suppose?" I asked.

"He'll do," Holmes sighed.

❋ ❋ ❋

A short time later, Holmes and I had rejoined MacFarlane and Quick at the British Museum. We sat on four chairs around the table which still held the mummy that was not Old Ernie. We waited for the arrival of a fifth man. After leaving Redburn's tobacco shop, Holmes had scribbled a short note and hired a messenger boy to deliver it to Scotland Yard, into the hands of Inspector Lestrade, a police detective who had been involved in many of the cases that Holmes and I had worked on. Lestrade had his moments of foolishness and could be an annoyance at times, but he usually meant well and could be of assistance, provided that Holmes maintained control of the situation. The note had asked Lestrade to bring us any information he had on the activities and members of that club of former Middle Eastern soldiers. Holmes and I both felt confident that Lestrade would come through and bring us the requested papers, as he was the type of detective who jumped at any chance to be part of the action.

Sure enough, the museum doorman soon poked his head into our room to announce our newest visitor. "A Scotland Yard inspector is asking to be admitted, Professor Quick."

Sherlock Holmes, not giving the professor a chance to respond, clapped his hands loudly and shouted, "Let him in my good man! We're expecting him!"

Seconds later, Lestrade shuffled in, a large, overstuffed envelope clutched in his hands, an unlit cigar hanging from his lips, his ferret eyes darting back and forth across the room, recognizing Holmes and I and sizing up MacFarlane and Quick.

"What was so important I had to be dragged away from…?" Lestrade said; stopping in mid-sentence as his eyes met the mummified man upon the table.

"What is that?"

Holmes let out a hearty laugh. Despite the way Lestrade sometimes got in the way, I always suspected that Holmes truly liked the enthusiastic inspector. "That, my good friend," said Holmes, "is a dead man; deceased for two-thousand years! But…it is not his death that we are investigating, but the reason why it is he who lies upon this table, and not another of his un-decayed kind!"

"I…I see," stammered the stunned Lestrade. "Here are the files you asked for. What does a bunch of Arab soldiers have to do with old cadavers?"

"That, Lestrade," said Holmes, "is what I hope to discover; with your invaluable assistance, of course. You know Dr. Watson of course. May I also present Professor Quick of the British Museum, and Dr. Christopher MacFarlane of the United States of America?"

Lestrade nodded in greeting to the two men whom he had not met before. He started to say something but was interrupted when Holmes snatched the envelope from his hands and pulled the stack of papers from it.

When Holmes wanted to find something, the object of his search was of paramount importance to him, and all other things became inconsequential. He began to leaf through the papers in the thick file, carelessly flinging aside each page that he deemed useless, papers falling like fluttering raindrops to the floor. After tossing aside perhaps twenty sheets, he lifted one page up for us all to see, a triumphant look radiating from his face.

"This is our man!" he announced. "Omar Kalebak, originally of Istanbul, resident of London for the past three years, six feet five inches tall, with a patch over his right eye. He works as a ship loader at the docks…and is believed to be a former professional thief, known in his home country as Omar the Spider! He has no record of ever having been arrested here in England. Watson, Lestrade, to the docks! We must find this man."

❋ ❋ ❋

We made our way to the docks as quickly as possible. On the cab ride there, Lestrade posed the obvious question. "Why would anyone want to steal a mummy, Holmes?"

"My dear Inspector Lestrade," Holmes said, "there are several reasons for such a theft. For one thing, museums and universities, as well as private collectors are often willing to pay great sums for such morbid artifacts. There are also those who, holding on to an old superstition never proved by science, believe that grinding the mummified body into a powder produces a medicine that can be used to stop bleeding and to heal wounds. I would wager that there are also those who might seek to use such specimens in rites or rituals of various occult traditions. So you see, Inspector, that we have no shortage of motives for the theft of a mummy. What we have here, though, is a somewhat different situation. To steal a mummy is an understandable crime, but what would compel one to take one particular mummy, while leaving another in its place? That is the question which we face, Lestrade!"

We disembarked from the hansom and looked around the docks. Everywhere there were men at work, moving freight on and off of ships and otherwise going about their nautical business. "And how do we begin

"My dear Inspector Lestrade," Holmes said, "there are several reasons for such a theft."

our search for one man among all these?" I asked.

"Luckily, Watson," Holmes said, "it is not an average or typical man we seek." He grabbed the arm of a stevedore who was walking past us.

"Hey, what're you doing?" the burly dock worker demanded. His whiskered face held a mouth full of yellow teeth and his forearms were heavily tattooed.

"Calm down, fellow," said Lestrade, showing his credentials. "We just want an answer to a question."

"We're looking for a certain man, a worker here like you," Holmes told the tattooed man. "He is of the Turkish nationality, he is very tall, and he has a patch where his right eye should be. A man of such distinctive appearance, surely you must have seen him here before."

"Aye, sir, I have. Hard to miss a big fella like that one; scary lookin' bloke with the patch and all that; there's a whole crew o' his kind that works together, 'bout a few hundred feet down that way is the dock they usually work off 'a." He pointed down the docks.

"Thank you my good fellow," said Holmes, giving the man a hearty slap on the back, and began to walk in the direction indicated by the answer to his question. Lestrade and I were right behind.

※ ※ ※

"Am I in some sort of trouble?" Omar Kalebak asked when we approached him. The presence of a police inspector seemed to frighten him. Despite his towering size and intimidating appearance, he had a quiet, almost gentle voice.

"At present," Holmes assured the Turkish giant, "we only wish to talk to you."

Kalebak led us to a small area near the ship his crew was busily loading. There was a table and a set of chairs where, presumably, the workers sat to eat when taking a rest from their physical labors. We sat with Kalebak and Holmes told him of our reasons for seeking him out.

"Yes, sir," Omar the Spider said, "I did carry such a thing, a dead, old Egyptian, but it wasn't any theft! I was paid for my services, all on the up and up. I'm keeping my nose clean here in England! I used to be a thief; yes I did, but not here, not no more!"

Holmes nodded. "Then tell us how you came to be employed in the transportation of such artifacts."

"It was a day off of work for me, sir," Kalebak began. "I had a bit of money left over from my last pay, so I took the chance to go and get something to smoke. There's a little shop that sells the blend of tobacco that I loved when I lived in my old country. It's hard stuff to find here, but that man's always got a supply on hand, so I went over there. I happened to see another man making a purchase of the same blend, but he was not a native Turk; he was an Englishman. I was curious, so I asked him how he came to have such fine taste in tobacco. We got into a bit of a talk and he asked if I was looking for some extra work, a way to make a bit more than I did here at the docks on most days. I told him I'd like to have some work, so he told me what I had to do.

"He gave me an envelope full of money. First, he told me he knew men who wouldn't hesitate to hunt me down and slit my throat if I tried to make off with the money. I told him he needn't worry about that, as I was just trying to make an honest living now that I'm here in London. Then he told me what I had to do.

"I was to come down here to the docks, even though I had the day to myself. I would be met by another Englishman, who would be driving a hansom cab. I found him here and he and I went over to a ship that had just come in from America. The ship's captain himself came out to meet us; he had been expecting us. I gave him the money and he led me down to the cargo hold of his vessel. There, he showed me a body wrapped in a white sheet. I picked the dead man up and carried him out of the ship's hold, put him in the cab and climbed in beside it.

"From the docks, the cab took us to a little house a few miles from there. I don't recall exactly where it was; as I didn't pay any mind to that while we rode. When we got to the house, I saw again the man who had hired me, the man I had met at the tobacco shop. He had me take the dead man out of the cab and bring it into his house. When I got the thing inside, I saw that he had another one! That one I picked up and put in the cab, trading one old, dead Egyptian for another! Once I had done that, the man gave me the money he had promised, and he sent me on my way. As I walked away from his house, I saw the cab driving off in another direction, taking the second body with it. Strange business it was, but I had my payment, so I thought nothing more about it!"

When Omar's tale was completed, Lestrade piped up. "And it never did occur to you that you might have been breaking the law?"

Holmes held up a hand to signal Lestrade to be silent.

"Inspector Lestrade," Holmes said, "Mr. Kalebak here has been quite cooperative. Perhaps it would be best to let him get back to his work. I suspect he is only a small fish in this pond into which we have been thrown by the matter of these mummies. I also suspect that he has given us ample information with which to find the much larger fish, the shark. Tell me, Mr. Kalebak, was there anything distinctive or unusual about the appearance of this man who employed you to move these bodies in and out of his home?"

"Yes, sir," Kalebak nodded. "He was a one-legged man."

"I thank you for your time and your help, Mr. Kalebak," said Holmes. "I hope you will continue to endeavor to, as you put it, keep your nose clean while here in London."

With that, Holmes walked away from Omar the Spider.

❋ ❋ ❋

We were soon in a cab once more, though we had not yet given the driver a destination. "Watson," said Holmes, "do you have an idea of where we might find your old friend, Colonel Reginald Summers?"

I shook my head. "I'm afraid not, Holmes. As I said earlier, Summers and I are not friends. In fact, the man seems to despise me." I fell silent, wishing I could be of more help. Then something occurred to me.

"Wait, Holmes. Perhaps there is a way to easily find him," I said, taking back my admission of having no means of locating Summers. "He won't speak to me for the reasons I mentioned before, but there is another old member of our regiment who lives near here; a former lieutenant who Summers had taken under his wing. Perhaps he still keeps in contact with the colonel. His name is Everett. I know precisely where he lives and works. He runs a small shop, selling rare books." I gave the driver the address of the bookshop and we were on our way.

❋ ❋ ❋

We soon found ourselves seated in the back room of Lyle Everett's book shop. He had welcomed me like an old friend and invited us all in for tea; Holmes, Lestrade and I sat together as the former Army officer told us what he knew of retired Colonel Reginald Summers.

"I haven't seen the old man for several months, Watson. We would occasionally meet for supper, talk over old times. It was a pleasant enough distraction, I suppose, until he began to grow sort of strange, as if the pain of his old wounds had finally started to go to his head, filling him with strange, unrealistic ideas and fantasies. You might say he had fallen into superstition. The last time I saw him he had come into my shop and purchased some rather odd old tomes. The books were a clear indication that his marbles had begun to roll astray. They were books on the strangest sort of occult matters; black magic and such. Unless one was a scholar of ancient tradition and superstition, I fail to see any reason one would want such books. Colonel Summers, as you'll probably recall, Watson, was not the sort to usually be interested in such things. I asked him what he wanted with the books, but he shot me an awful look, an indication that he did not welcome such inquiries. That was the last I saw of the old soldier."

"Interesting," said Holmes. He thanked Everett for the information and asked for Summers' address. Everett consulted one of his ledgers and scribbled the address on a scrap, which he handed to Holmes.

We decided to make a stop at the museum before continuing on our way to see the colonel. We wanted to inform MacFarlane and Quick of our progress in the matter of Old Ernie's disappearance.

❈ ❈ ❈

We entered the museum and made our way to the room where we had left our two companions. As we entered, we saw that Professor Quick was closely examining the mummy's abdomen again as MacFarlane watched from beside him. The expression of MacFarlane's face told us that some new discovery had been made.

"What have you found?" I asked as we approached the scene.

Professor Quick turned to face us. "Do you recall how I described the methods of the Egyptians in mummifying the deceased?"

I nodded.

"As I told you," Quick continued, "of the major organs, only the heart was left in place. Well, as I have now determined, this mummy has had its heart removed! However, it was a very recent extraction! Someone has reopened the original incision in the abdomen, taken the heart from its place, and sewn the opening closed again. It was done expertly, but a mistake was made. Whoever the culprit was, he used a type of thread that did not exist in Egypt many centuries ago!"

I looked at Holmes. His eyes were closed, a sure sign that he was busily putting various pieces of the puzzle together in his mind. He opened his eyes and spoke.

"Colonel Summers has been reading books on ancient occultism. He paid Omar Kalebak to smuggle one mummy into his home and remove another. The one that was removed from Summers' home and sent here in lieu of the one that was sent here from New York had its heart removed only recently. It is obvious that it is the hearts of these mummies that the colonel is collecting. Having taken the heart of this one, he must have had it sent here to cover the fact that he was stealing another. But how did he know of the impending arrival of Old Ernie?"

Christopher MacFarlane spoke next. "The answer to that question is quite plain, Holmes. *The London Times* ran a small article about the British Museum's acquisition of Old Ernie. Summers read about it and decided to use Ernie to get his hands on another heart. What I'd like to know is how did he get the first mummy; the one we have in front of us now?"

"Only the retired colonel can answer that question for us," said Sherlock Holmes. "We must leave at once. Watson, Lestrade, come with me."

※ ※ ※

We soon reached the address that had been provided by Lyle Everett. It was a small house, well suited to a man who lived alone in his retirement. From what I recalled of Reginald Summers, he was an ill-tempered man, not the sort who would easily attract a wife. We walked up to his front door, Holmes leading the way, Lestrade behind him, and I in the back, not looking forward to seeing a man who had an intense dislike of me. Holmes pounded loudly on the door. From within, we could hear the approach of steps, two distinctive sounds, one made by a shoe and the other by the bottom end of a crutch, a sort of step-thump-step-thump pattern. The door swung open and we were met by the scowling face of Colonel Summers. He was a middle-aged man, bordering on obesity. His hair was white and badly in need of a trim. He needed a shave also. His eyes looked tired, he sweated profusely. He was dressed in standard clothing, but his shirt was rumpled, wrinkled, as if he had not changed his attire in some time. He leaned on his crutch, eyeing us warily, his pants cut short on one side to match the length of his abbreviated thigh.

"Who are you? What do you want? I'm a busy man; I've no time for peddlers!"

Lestrade took the initiative of getting Summers to pay attention. He took out his badge and held it up for the old soldier to see.

"Hello, Colonel," Lestrade said. "Inspector Lestrade of Scotland Yard; this is Mr. Sherlock Holmes and his associate, Watson."

Summers' face flared with recognition and rage. He took an unsteady step forward, stumbling. He'd have fallen on his face had Holmes not caught hold of and steadied him.

"I know Watson," he growled, glaring accusingly at me. "He's the bloody quack who crippled me in Afghanistan!"

"Calm yourself, Colonel Summers!" Holmes commanded. "This visit has nothing to do with your past acquaintance with the good doctor. We're here on a much more current matter. May we come in?"

"No!" bellowed Summers, turning to slam the door in our faces. Lestrade put up a hand, stopping the swinging door from closing.

"I'm afraid we'll have to insist, Colonel," the inspector told him. "Now step aside!"

Holmes and Lestrade marched into the house. Summers thumped along behind them. I stayed behind Summers, knowing he could use that crutch as a weapon if he so chose.

Once safely inside, we had Summers sit down, his crutch taken away by Lestrade. I stood in the parlor, watching over the colonel, who stared at me, eyes filled with hate, saying nothing. Holmes and Lestrade began to search the house's other rooms.

Moments later, I heard the familiar sound of the voice of Sherlock Holmes, shouting "Aha!" I knew he had come across something of importance. "Blimey!" was the next word I heard, in the voice of Inspector Lestrade. I looked at Colonel Summers. He had hung his head, hands covering his eyes. He seemed to be weeping.

Holmes strode back into the room. He was holding a thick, leather bound book which looked quite old. He had it opened to a certain page; a book marker was visible, placed at that very page. Holmes began to read.

"In the scrolls of ancient Rome, many of which were saved from the ashes of Alexandria, we find mentions of yet another use for the various parts of the preserved corpses of the Nile region. It is said in legends of old that an elixir prepared from the hearts of such corpses will..." Holmes' voice trailed off at this point; he looked pityingly at Colonel Summers.

"It all comes back to the tobacco shop, does it not, Colonel?" said Holmes. "There are three people in London, it seems, who prefer a certain blend of Arabian tobacco. You are one, Omar the Turk is another, and then there is a certain lady, a woman whose husband, now deceased, once smoked that blend as well."

Summers nodded. Holmes continued.

"You happened to run into her at Redburn's shop, didn't you; just as you happened to run into Omar? She struck up a conversation with you, remarking that you reminded her of her late husband. Perhaps she was conscious of the fact that the scent of your pipe tobacco was the reminder, or perhaps that worked on a level below her awareness. Whatever the reason, you found yourself the subject of the attentions of a woman. For the first time since returning to London, bitter, angry, crippled and obese, you felt you might have some hope of finding companionship again. You were, for once, optimistic.

"Yet there was something else gnawing at your mind, was there not, Colonel? The woman seemed willing to overlook the absence of your leg…but you knew you had another infirmity, a problem that made you feel even more incomplete than a missing limb. You feared that when the time came, as you hoped it would, that you might become intimately involved with this woman, that you would be a grave disappointment and she would shun you again. So you began to search for a remedy for your infirmity. You consulted physicians, with no success. You then turned to more arcane possibilities. You consulted strange old books, looked for hope in superstitions and old wives tales. Finally, you found something in one of the books you had purchased from Lyle Everett. Here, in this old volume, is a means of making a potion that, supposedly, can make a man function in the way that you desired to function. All you needed…was the heart of a mummy!

"In the next room, from which you heard me shout in success, I found three things which completed the puzzle for me. First was this book. Second was the very old corpse for which we have been searching; I see you have not yet performed the task of cutting out this one's heart. Third was a stack of letters from those to whom you now owe substantial amounts of money. Those letters answered the question of where you had acquired the first mummy. You bought that one, probably from some smuggler, some dealer in antique contraband. That purchase nearly exhausted your finances. When the first elixir failed to work, you wanted to attempt it again, but you needed another mummy's heart.

"You could not afford the smuggler's fee again, but you read of the impending arrival of the British Museum's newest piece. You had enough money left to bribe the captain of the vessel that carried the cargo, and enough to hire Omar Kalebak to transport the thing for you! You arranged for your first mummy to be delivered to the British Museum in the place of the one that was set to arrive from New York City!

"You knew that it would eventually be discovered that a switch had occurred, but you had no reason to think that a retired colonel on a crutch could ever be suspected of stealing a two-thousand year old corpse. Perhaps you would have gotten away with it, had a certain blend of tobacco not played such a notable role in the whole affair!

"I'm afraid you've wasted not only your money, but now your freedom, Colonel Summers. The contents of this book are nonsense, superstitious rubbish. The penalties for stealing, smuggling, and destroying priceless artifacts are much more real.

"Inspector Lestrade…this man is yours!"

Lestrade escorted Colonel Summers away. Holmes and I returned to the museum, sharing a hansom cab with perhaps the oldest occupant that one had ever carried.

Doctor MacFarlane and Professor Quick were overjoyed to see that we had brought Old Ernie back in one piece, heart intact, and no worse off than he had been before his unscheduled detour. He was still dead, but that was to be expected.

As far as I know, Old Ernie and his nameless, heartless companion are still residents of the British Museum.

MUMMY AND DADDY

By Aaron Smith

One of the greatest thrills I've ever had was getting the opportunity to write a story, a story that would actually be published, featuring one of my favorite fictional characters, the Great Detective, Sherlock Holmes. Even more exciting was seeing how well received our first Holmes book, *Sherlock Holmes Consulting Detective Volume 1* turned out to be. The book sold well, almost all of the reviews were positive ones, and the overall response to the book was even better than we had dared to hope for. As much fun as I had writing my first Holmes story, I knew it would not be my last. Due to other projects, I wasn't able to get a story into the second Holmes book, but here I am, back for the third with two shorter short stories. The first of these stories, "The Adventure of the Mummy's Rib" came about as a direct result of my first Holmes story, "The Massachusetts Affair."

When *Holmes Volume 1* was about to be released, I felt the natural nervousness that any writer feels when his work is about to be judged by his readership. That's only normal. I'm glad the majority of the readers liked the story and happy that I was able, to some extent at least, to contribute to the vast sea of non-canonical Holmes stories without utterly embarrassing myself. The strange thing about having one's work published is that one of the most worrisome things is not having one's words read by strangers, but having those works read and judged by those whom one actually knows. That first Holmes tale marked the first time my family would read any of my work, on a character as famous as Holmes no less!

I'm happy to be able to report that they liked it, especially my father and grandfather, both of whom were instrumental in introducing me to Holmes to begin with. When it came to my father's reaction to the story, his first comment actually turned out to be a question. "So when do we get to read about the Mummy's Rib?" he asked me.

Sir Arthur Conan Doyle occasionally, to both the delight and the consternation of his fans, would sometimes have Watson mention a case that had not yet been related in one of his stories. Those hinted-at unpublished cases, such as "The Giant Rat of Sumatra," left readers wishing and hoping that the details of such adventures would someday be turned into yet another of the Holmes mysteries. When I was in the middle of writing my own first Holmes tale, I decided to play that little part of Doyle's game myself. Never intending to hint at a story that I would really write someday, I picked a phrase that I thought sounded like a fun title and had Watson mention "The Adventure of the Mummy's Rib."

Months later, my father had read the Holmes book, and he asked about that mummy and that rib. I was hesitant at first, but I kept thinking about how reading Doyle's little hint about that giant rat sent my brain spinning when I was a wee lad discovering the Great Detective for the first time. "Why not?" I said to myself, and I set out to turn that silly title into a decent Sherlock Holmes mystery. "The Mummy's Rib" is, in some ways, a sequel to "The Massachusetts Affair," as it brings back one of the supporting characters, the American physician, Christopher McFarlane. Once I began the story, it flowed quite naturally. The fact that I had put a mummy in the title helped, as I've always had an interest in ancient Egypt and its customs. As had been the case with the other Holmes stories I've written, going back to Baker Street was like visiting old friends. Once you have the puzzle pieces, the whole picture comes together quite naturally.

Here it is, Dad; "The Adventure of the Mummy's Rib." I hope it lives up to your expectations.

In closing, I'd like to thank my editor and friend, Ron Fortier, for giving me, once again, the chance to work with the Great Detective, one of the greatest characters in the history of popular literature. Thanks, Captain!

Sherlock Holmes
Consulting Detective

"The Singular Affair of the Sultan's Tiger"

by
Joshua Reynolds

"Watson," my friend, Sherlock Holmes, said. "We will soon be having visitors."

Having seen this trick before, I refrained from uttering a single word of disbelief. Holmes, sitting in his chair near the fire, was paging through the *Times*. He lowered the paper slightly and watched me in calm anticipation.

"I refuse to be baited, Holmes. I am well aware that you are, as ever, quite likely correct," I said, closing the book I had been perusing, my thumb holding my place. Holmes gave a snort and went back to his paper. I smiled and opened my book.

Holmes coughed. Hummed. Noises that would not have seemed out of place, had they been made by any other man. Exasperated, I closed my book once more. "Fine. Tell me, Holmes. How is it that you have come to this conclusion?"

Holmes was silent. Then, with a flourish, he stood and folded the paper. He tossed it onto his vacated seat and said, "No time for parlor games, Watson. They are here, unless I mistake my senses."

I sighed and put my book aside. Holmes smiled, a quick thing, and tapped the side of his nose. "Indulge me, Watson."

"Of course, Holmes," I said. "What was it? Stairs creaking? The clatter of a cab on the cobbles?"

"Nothing of the sort. They made an appointment earlier today. I simply forgot to mention it," he said, checking the hang of his waistcoat in the mirror over the mantle. He glanced at me. "Do forgive me."

"Why would I stop now?" I said. Holmes laughed out loud. As I rose to my feet, Mrs. Hudson, our landlady, poked her head through the partially open door. Seeing only myself, she began,

"Dr. Watson, there are some gentlemen here to see Mr. Holmes—"

"Thank you Mrs. Hudson," Holmes said, leaning suddenly around the door and waving Mrs. Hudson away. She gave an indelicate squawk at his sudden appearance and stepped aside, allowing our visitors to enter our room at 221b Baker Street with no further interruptions.

The first man was built like a terrier, with a bounce in his step that might have seemed undignified if I hadn't caught the bulge of a revolver beneath his coat. I shot a glance towards my writing desk, where my own Webley Bulldog sat in a drawer, but Holmes gave a twitch of his head and I relaxed.

The second man was quite elderly, his body trembling as if from the presence of some great weight. Dressed in stiff, starched black, he could have been an undertaker, a bank president or a particularly hygienic chimney sweep. I felt that I should recognize him, but could bring no name to mind.

Holmes closed the door behind them, after ushering Mrs. Hudson out with a request for tea. He spun on his heel as the younger man pulled out a chair for the older, brushing some of Holmes' files to the floor in the process. "Do make yourself at home," Holmes murmured.

"Mr. Sherlock Holmes?" the younger man said. His eyes were a startling blue, and his precise accent betrayed a well-to-do upbringing, though I could not place it precisely. Holmes inclined his head and gestured towards me.

"My friend and confidant, Dr. Watson."

The younger man nodded amiably, but the older man ignored me pointedly. He had a sour disposition which seemed to radiate in all directions. I judged him to be a man fundamentally unhappy with his position in the world.

"And you, of course, are Sir Richard Markesby. You made a name for yourself in India, in your youth," Holmes said, seating himself on the edge of the table and addressing the older of the two. He pulled his silver cigarette case out of his coat and proffered it to our visitors, both of whom declined. Holmes shrugged and lit one for himself, snapping the case closed with a flick of his wrist.

"My youth, and my reputation, are both long gone now Mr. Holmes," Markesby said. He had a deep voice for such an old man. It reminded me of the rumble of an elderly tiger, glaring balefully from between the bars of a cage. "And bad cess to 'em both!"

Holmes gave a bark of laughter and crossed his arms, cigarette dangling from his lips. He looked at the younger man, his eyes shrewd. "And this gentleman?"

"Ramsden," Markesby said. "My aide."

Ramsden smiled and rocked back on his heels. No part of him seemed to remain still for longer than a few seconds. Markesby, in contrast, was a stone now that he was sitting.

Holmes nodded and gestured with his cigarette. "Now that we are all introduced, may I inquire as to who you believe is intending to kill you?"

Markesby gaped for a moment, but to his credit swiftly regained control of himself. Ramsden betrayed no surprise, and my estimation of the young man's capabilities went up several notches. By this time, being quite used to Holmes' methods, I had my notebook out, and a pencil in hand.

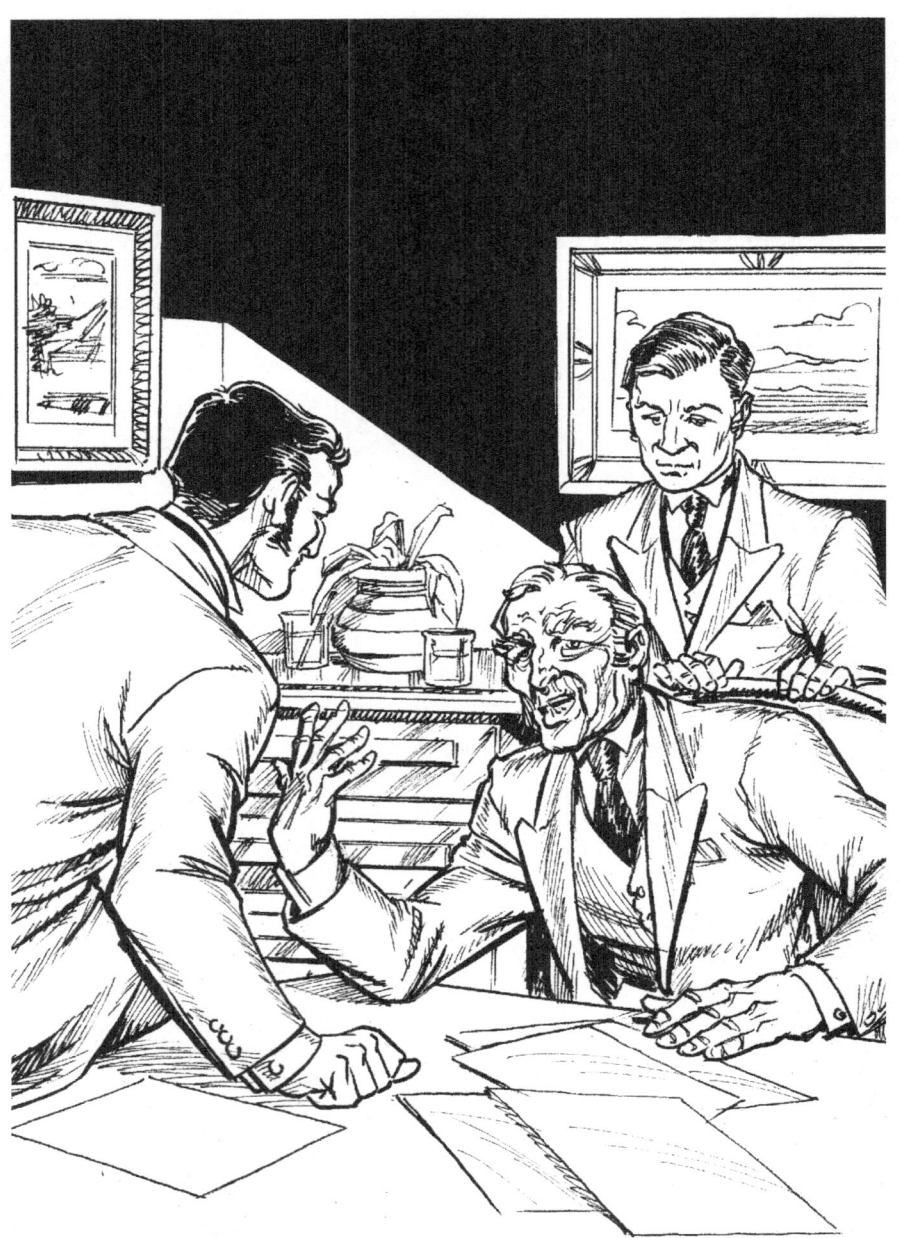

"My youth, and my reputation, are both long gone now Mr. Holmes,"

"You–how–" Markesby sputtered, fixing Holmes with a suspicious eye.

"Easy enough. You are a recluse. In fact, one of Britain's most infamous such. You once refused to leave your house when it caught fire, and stayed in your office until the blaze was under control."

"That's where I recall you from!" I said. "It was in all the papers. The Stubborn Sirdar, they called you!"

"Ha," Markesby said, glowering. "That still doesn't explain–"

"A man such as yourself would not leave the safety of his sanctum without a reason of most pressing urgency," Holmes said. "Since you are not known for being a man of business or social conduct, I surmised that the only reason would be a matter of life or death. Yours, or someone else's. Since you have no family that I am aware of, I guessed that it was yours. And since few contact me for consultation on medical matters–that being more my associate's area than mine–I made a further assumption that your life was at stake due to outside, perhaps malign, influences. An assumption only enhanced by the presence of Mr. Ramsden who, I see, travels armed."

Ramsden chuckled and patted the bulge of his pistol. Markesby took a breath. "Well. I see your reputation is deserved. Would you care to tell me what I'm about to say next, or would allow me the honor?" he said petulantly.

Holmes sucked on his cigarette, saying nothing. Markesby gave a startling growl and hunched forward. At last, he said, "It is not a person."

"Oh?"

"No!" Markesby bellowed. He began to cough and hunched even further forward, bent almost double. Ramsden crouched over him protectively and pulled a glass vial and a rag from his coat. He unstoppered the vial and poured a handful of the solution within on his rag, which he then passed to Markesby, who snatched it and pressed it to his mouth and nose.

"Breathe deep, Mr. Markesby," Ramsden murmured. He looked at Holmes, then at myself. "He's ill."

"Malaria, unless I miss my guess," I said, making to rise. "Is there anything–"

"No!" Markesby snapped, then, more calmly, "No. Thank you all the same, Dr. Watson, but I am fine." He sat up with Ramsden's assistance, and handed the rag back to his aide. "I have dealt with this for many years and I will deal with it for many more. Unless–" He paused.

"Unless?" Holmes said. Markesby frowned.

"It's the tiger."

"Tiger?" Holmes said, one eyebrow raised. Markesby's frown grew.

"Are you mocking me, sir?"

"Nothing could be further from the truth. Do go on, I implore you," Holmes said, head cocked. Markesby gave a sniff, then continued.

"I am being hunted," he said. "And gentlemen, rest assured that I know whereof I speak." He shifted slightly, his gaze falling on the closed curtain of the window on the far wall. He shuddered. "It prowls across the rooftops and through the alleyways, stalking me. Always just out of sight, but I know it's there." He tapped the side of his head with a thin finger.

"A tiger?" I said, slightly incredulous.

"The tiger!" Markesby said, eyes blazing. "The Tiger of Mysore!"

I blinked, and made to comment, but a look from Holmes stilled my voice. He turned, thumb in his waist pocket, his other hand occupied with holding his cigarette as he scanned the books on the shelf behind him.

"The Tiger of Mysore? I was under the impression, Mr. Markesby, that he was dead. Also, that he was, in fact, a tiger of the two-legged variety." Holmes stood and went to the book case. With two fingers he selected a slim volume and turned back to face our guests. "In fact, sir, it was you yourself who made such a claim in your Reminiscences of the Anglo-Mysore War 1798-1799. Or am I mistaken?"

"You are not," Markesby said. I looked at our guest again, with new understanding, and couldn't contain myself.

"You must have been but a child!" I exclaimed. Markesby laughed, a harsh caw.

"Oh, I was young. Not a swaddling babe, but not yet a man." His face darkened. "That country–that damnable country–soon fixed that however." He coughed again, but waved away Ramsden. "I was thirteen. My father– damn his heart–had bought me a commission. No grand thing, but grand enough for his purposes."

"Your father, I understand, was an associate of the East India Trading Company," Holmes said. Markesby shrugged, as if stung.

"My father built our fortune in the only way he knew how," Markesby said. "That included placing his only son into a position to eventually exert influence on future military affairs." He shook his head. "I did as I was bade. I was eager for it, in fact." He looked up, eyes bright. "India, gentlemen, was a magical land for a pretentious youth. But my love affair with it ended quickly."

"You were at Seringapatam. The last bloody stand of the Tippu Sultan," Holmes said. Markesby nodded.

"I saw things–" He paused. "What was that?"

"What was what?" Holmes said. Markesby jerked in his chair, his eyes narrowed.

"I heard it. You must have, as well. Don't lie!" he hissed.

"Heard what?" I said, rising to my feet. Markesby twisted in his seat, looking about wildly.

"The tiger!"

"Calmly, Mr. Markesby," Ramsden murmured, swiping back his coat and unholstering his pistol. I froze. Ramsden smiled slightly at my expression, but said nothing. Markesby's hand was tangled in his coat, like that of a small child clutching its parent.

"I can hear it! Hear its claws scraping the brick! Damn your ears man, is that window shut? Is it shut?! Ramsden—" Markesby said. His voice was very nearly a screech.

"Calm yourself man!" Holmes barked, his voice containing a familiar whip crack of authority. He moved to the window and ripped the curtains aside, displaying nothing but the fog and the night's usual darkness beyond the glass. "There is nothing out there not conjured up by your own fevered imaginings!"

Markesby, face pale, sagged in his seat, one hand clutching his chest. I had a momentary fear that he would die then and there, but color returned to his face soon enough. I prepared a brandy for him, even as Mrs. Hudson arrived with the tea. She shot a glare at Ramsden, who hastily holstered his pistol and mumbled an apology. Holmes, still at the window, turned.

"Thank you, Mrs. Hudson," he said, as she bustled out. The door closed with a thump that boded ill for us both come our guests' departure. Holmes smiled briefly and turned back to Markesby. "No tiger, Mr. Markesby. You are quite safe here."

"Nowhere is safe, Mr. Holmes. Damnation trails me through this forest of stone and brick." Markesby accepted the brandy from me with a brisk nod. "Thank you, Doctor."

"Damnation and danger are two very different things," Holmes said. "What makes you believe that this is both, as opposed to merely the one?"

"Noises are the least of it. Tell him, Ramsden!"

"Marks. No tracks though," Ramsden said, pouring himself a cup of tea. "Once, a clump of hair. Might have been a tiger." He took a sip. Holmes waited. Ramsden sniffed. "Never heard it, myself. But the physical evidence—"

"Is quite inconclusive, I'm sure," Holmes said, waving a hand. "Seringapatam."

"What?" Ramsden looked surprised. Holmes looked at Markesby.

"Seringapatam. Where the Tiger of Mysore, Tippu Sultan, fell at last, defending the Diddy Gateway from British forces." Holmes picked up Markesby's book again and flipped through it. "Or so you wrote."

"He died well, that little fat man," Markesby said. "No dishonor there. Not him. Not then."

"When, then?" Holmes asked innocently, still thumbing through the book. He didn't look up. Markesby stared into the middle distance for a moment. I cleared my throat, and he seemed to remember where he was.

"Later. In the Kullu Hills." He finished his brandy and gestured for another. I hastened to get it, as he continued his story.

"They call those hills 'the end of the habitable world' with good reason, Mr. Holmes. And that's where he ran. Sirdar Yar Muhammad. The Sultan's right hand. The Company put a bounty on his head that was never rivaled. Not then, not now." Markesby glanced at the window. His face twitched.

"I led the expedition to bring him to heel, of course. Me. Fresh off the siege, bloodied and eager." His eyes became slightly unfocused as he continued. "They also call Kullu 'the Valley of the Gods'. And Yar was a god of death and holy murder, as sure as I sit here." He closed his eyes. "He made those hills and valleys a butcher's corridor for us, and him with only a few men. No more than a dozen. I had a hundred men when I entered Kullu. I came out the other side with less than fifty." His eyes sprang open. "He hunted and harried us and we replied in kind."

A chill swept through me as I realized the implication of his words. I had heard of such "responses in kind" during my time in Afghanistan. Holmes must have seen the look on my face, for he frowned and said, "You took out your frustrations on the inhabitants of Kullu."

"We denied succor to the enemy," Markesby said firmly.

"As I said," Holmes said. "Please continue."

"We burned everything that could be burned that he had ever touched or slept in. We looted, plundered and I hung four men for rape." Markesby's head drooped. "It wasn't enough." He looked at me. "You were in India, Doctor?"

"Afghanistan."

"Then you understand, if Mr. Holmes does not."

"Yes," I said, after a moment's hesitation. Markesby nodded, satisfied.

"When we could not bring Yar to heel in those ways, I was ordered to be more–ah–persuasive." Markesby leaned back. Holmes' face displayed no expression.

"You used his relatives as bait," he said. Markesby coughed and shook his head.

"Not as bait. As lessons."

"You murdered them," I said. Markesby glared at me.

"I did what was required of me."

"But it was in vain, was it not?" Holmes said, before I could reply. "Yar escaped."

"The central Punjab. We were ordered on to other things. He was gone and that was enough." Markesby rubbed his face, weariness evident in his eyes. "I have not thought of those times in years."

"But now the memories return," Holmes said.

"The tiger," Markesby said, cradling his face in his hands. "After so many years. I did what I was ordered, Mr. Holmes, but that does not mean that I am absolved of guilt or memory." He looked up. "I am being stalked, even as I was all those years ago in the Kullu Hills. Yar has waited for me to become old and feeble and now he has returned to hunt me as I hunted him. I thank God that I have no family for him to slay. There is only me to harry." He lurched forward, nearly slipping from his seat. Both Ramsden and Holmes caught him before he could fall. He grabbed Holmes' coat.

"I can hear him. Hear the moan of his demon-breath as he paces. I have turned my home into a fortress, Holmes. But still, the tiger draws ever nearer!"

"Steady on, Mr. Markesby," Holmes said, removing the other man's hands from his coat. "Yar is almost certainly dead now."

"And? Death is no bar for a man like him!"

"Death is a bar for every man, regardless of his prowess," Holmes said. He stepped back. Markesby seemed to deflate in Ramsden's hands.

"You believe I'm mad," he whispered. "Overcome with guilt, eh?" He looked up, eyes dim. "I did my duty. But still, he comes for me. And when he is ready, he will take me. And my passing will not be gentle!"

"And so you fear for your life," Holmes said. "Now. After all this time."

"Yes!"

"And you wish me to–what?" Holmes said. "Hunt a tiger?"

"A demon."

Holmes seemed to consider the matter for a moment, then, "No. This agency keeps its feet firmly on the ground at all times, Mr. Markesby. I'm afraid that I must decline your request."

"You–" Markesby gaped like a fish. "You can't!"

"I do believe that I, in fact, can. Like the great chefs of the Continent, I can refuse the right of service to anyone I so choose."

"I will die!"

"All men die, Mr. Markesby. Some earlier—or later—than they should. I refuse to open this agency up to embarrassment by investigating a case of jiggery-pokery. Simple hokum, sir. From your display earlier, I have ascertained that you are, quite simply, imagining things." Holmes crossed to the door and opened it. "It is getting late, gentlemen. The Doctor and I have tickets for the Lyceum tonight. Do see yourselves out."

Ramsden helped Markesby to his feet and then towards the door. Markesby had fallen silent, and refused to look at either of us. Ramsden, for his part, merely nodded to myself and then Holmes.

"Good night, sirs," he said. Holmes stopped him with a gesture.

"Ramsden, out of curiosity, how long have you worked for Mr. Markesby?"

"Not more than four days, sir," Ramsden said.

"As I suspected. Good evening, Ramsden," Holmes said, turning away. Ramsden looked at me in confusion for a moment before quietly closing the door behind himself.

"Mr. Ramsden seemed rather relieved," I said. Holmes took a breath and nodded.

"As well he should be. Seeing as he is perhaps involved."

It took me a moment to process what Holmes had said. Then, I stared at him in shock. "What?"

"Oh yes, Watson. Ramsden." Holmes considered his cigarette, then stubbed it out on the fireplace. "Perhaps not intentionally, but there is something—" He paused and began to fill his pipe. "Could you tell what it was he used to help Markesby clear his lungs? What was on that cloth?"

"I don't know. I saw nothing on the vial to indicate what it was. I assume something to clear the phlegm—"

"Yes. But is that all?"

"What?"

Holmes lit his pipe and leaned an elbow on the mantle, puffing contentedly. His eyes were half-closed and he appeared deep in thought.

"Holmes?" I said.

"Your impressions, Watson," he said.

"Of Ramsden? Or Markesby?"

"The latter."

"He's guilt-ridden. Eaten away and through by old ghosts," I said. Holmes gave a quick smile.

"Very poetic. And quite apt." He looked at me. "His book reveals nothing of those events he described, of course." He waved a hand at the volume. "Nonetheless, he has a bad reputation among men of character, but is humored due to his advanced age."

"He must be nearing a century," I said. Holmes nodded.

"Yes. Senility setting in now would surprise no one. Least of all those who might be inclined to investigate his claims."

"I wondered why you had ushered them out so rudely," I said. Holmes tapped his head.

"It wasn't too obvious I hope? There is something more going on here."

"So you are intending to investigate, then."

"Of course," he said, plopping himself down in his chair, one leg cocked up over the arm rest. He pointed the pipe at me. "Ramsden."

"He seems competent. Markesby was quite taken with him."

"Mmm. A rock of stability in a sea of chaos." Holmes puffed on his pipe, eyes narrowed to slits. "Unimaginative and steady."

"The perfect valet."

"Yes. Perfect." Holmes looked at me. "And the story?"

"Of a spectral tiger stalking him? Twaddle."

"Don't hedge, Watson. Give me your true opinions, I insist," Holmes said, smiling.

"It's tosh. Utter codswallop." I rose and stoked the fire furiously. "I don't deny that someone may be playing on his guilt, but—"

"A tiger loose in London. Yes. It is preposterous. But not impossible." Holmes pressed his fingers together in a pyramid and leaned back. "You recall, of course, the affair of the orangutan and the riding crop?"

"But a tiger? Even allowing for a trained animal, surely it would be noticed in the city. If Markesby lived anywhere else, I could see the possibility, but—"

"No. No, Watson, once again you've hit the nail on the head." Holmes stared at the fire as it flared to life. "There is no devil here, no beast, save man. But who, where and why?"

"Revenge?"

"Possible. But unlikely," Holmes said. "No. Vengeance is rarely deferred. Not for this long. Almost a century?"

"Then what?"

"Money, perhaps. Invariably, money plays some role in these schemes."

"Then what is our course of action?" I asked. Holmes smiled and closed his eyes.

"Well, first, a trip to the museum."

"The museum?"

"Yes." Holmes said nothing more, and after a moment, I retired to bed, knowing that he would most likely remain in his chair for the rest of the night.

My dreams were unsettled to say the least. Markesby's story had unearthed bad memories and I can say that I awoke with no little relief the next morning at the touch of Holmes' gloved hand.

"Up, Watson. I wish to break our fast sometime before lunch, if that is quite all right with you."

"Holmes, I doubt very much that the world will end should we indulge in late morning meal," I said, rising to dress. Holmes laughed.

When I left my room, he was already at the morning paper with an empty plate before him. I ate quickly as he scanned the headlines.

"Anything of interest?" I said, swallowing a last morsel. He tossed the paper aside with a snort and rose to put on his coat.

"It is all interesting, in the proper context. A robbery, most likely conducted by Drury Septon, an upper-story man of my acquaintance. The death of a government official, undoubtedly the work of an intruder. And, of course, the absence of the idle scion of a wealthy family from his club for the past four mornings, leading to suppositions on his welfare which are clearly overwrought considering that he's still in the city." He knotted his scarf at his throat and gave a disgusted sigh. "Still, Watson, we must concentrate on nothing else save for the affair at hand. It will, I fear, prove to be, in the end, more than engrossing."

"You've not figured it out then?" I said, brushing crumbs from my cravat. "I'm shocked." Holmes grunted.

"I have the pieces, but not the shape of the puzzle." He gestured to the floor. "When Ramsden was applying that mysterious tonic to the rag for Markesby, some spilled on the floor. I noted it, and collected a scraping after you retired for the evening."

"And?" I said, shrugging into my coat as we left our rooms.

"Distillation of Amanita. Aminata Muscaria to be precise. Found mostly in the Northern Hemispheres, it is used to great effect in certain rituals practice in Siberia, as well as India."

"India," I said. "Coincidence?"

"Perhaps not. I cannot say for certain, though I am tempted. Are you familiar with its effects?"

"It's a hallucinogen of some type, isn't it?" I said, trying to recall what

I knew of fungi. Holmes nodded. It was cool and crisp outside, with a hint of a wet winter. Holmes pulled his scarf tighter as we walked.

"One of the oldest such, in fact. The effects vary from person to person. Some individuals have even been known to die." He raised his cane and flagged down a passing hansom cab.

"Ramsden is dosing Markesby with a hallucinogen then. Do you think he realizes?" I said as we climbed into the cab. Holmes shouted a destination, then turned back to me.

"Which? Ramsden, or poor Markesby? Perhaps, to the former, certainly not, to the latter. No. On its own, the concoction I studied last night would not cause strong hallucinations. Rather, it would put an individual of a sufficiently weakened constitution into a more receptive state of general paranoia and fear. Sounds and hints would become portents."

"Malaria would weaken his constitution," I said. Holmes clapped me on the shoulder.

"As ever, Watson, you anticipate my query. Yes, it is as I suspected." He sat back in the cab, leaning his chin on the head of his cane. "But why? What is there to gain?"

"Perhaps it's even as you said. Wealth. Markesby is rich, is he not?"

"As we would think of it, yes." Holmes frowned. "But, who benefits should he die? More information is required. First, however, the museum."

We arrived at Somerset House soon after. Somerset House was the home of the South Kensington Museum, the site of art and cultural works from around the world, including, as Holmes informed me, those items once housed in the now-defunct East India Company Museum. It was one of these orphans that Holmes had brought us to see—namely, Tippu's Tiger.

Crafted at the behest of the Tippu Sultan in the years prior to the fourth and final Mysore War, it was a marvel of wood and clockwork, cunningly (or perhaps maliciously) devised in such a manner as to resemble a tiger mauling a European soldier. While the victim's red coat spoke to his probable British origins, his other accoutrements—those that were visible beneath the garish tiger's bulk—were of various national origin.

"French shoes and a Dutch hat to go with his English coat and bright German buttons," Holmes said, as we gazed at the apparatus, surrounded by other patrons. "Do you think its creator was making a statement, Watson?"

"Something of the sort," I murmured. Truly Tippu's Tiger, as it was called, was a hideous marvel. Cunningly crafted, it contained an organ, as well as devices which allowed it to mimic a death-struggle between man and beast. "Why did you wish to see this ghastly thing, Holmes?"

"Do you recall the phrase that Markesby used to describe the sound of his nocturnal stalker, Watson?"

"I–" I frowned. "Now that you mention it, no."

"He said that it moaned. The exact phrase was–ah–'the moan of his demon breath', I believe," Holmes said, falling into an approximation of Markesby's raspy voice that startled me. "Odd phrase that. Tigers growl. Or roar. Or, even hiss. But moan?"

As he said this, Holmes reached out with his cane and tapped the handle set into the tiger's neck. I very nearly leapt out of my skin as a dolorous moan issued forth from some hidden agency within the contraption. Several other patrons stepped back, and one woman looked ready to faint then and there.

"Good God," I said. Holmes laughed.

"It was, I gather, intended to be an approximation of the intermingled cries of the dying man and his savage killer. Made by a set of bellows and carved pipes."

"You think that this is the sound that Markesby heard?"

"As I said, it was an odd phrase to use in conjunction with a tiger." Holmes leaned on his cane, keen eyes studying the automaton. "Perhaps it is nothing. Coincidence."

"You don't believe in coincidences," I pointed out. Holmes gave a quick flash of a smile.

"Ha! No. No, I do not." He turned away from the display and set off towards the museum exit. "Come, Watson. We have business to attend to."

Our business, as Holmes put it, proved to be with a man named Prendrick. He was a procurer for the Royal Zoo, who, Holmes informed me, also supplied the needs of wealthy individuals on the side.

"No tigers, Mr. Holmes, Indian or otherwise," he said as we sat in a Kensington pub. "Don't deal in them. Can't trust a tiger, sir. Can't trust them." Prendrick was a thick–set man with too many chins and too few eyes. One was a white marble swimming in a sea of flesh, a gift, he said, from an irate American Grizzly Bear.

"I wasn't aware that any species of predator was what one could call trustworthy, Mr. Prendrick," Holmes said. "Tiger or no."

"Ha! And that's the truth. But tigers are particularly nasty. No social graces, as it were." Prendrick took a sip of his drink and laughed. "Sebastian Moran could tell you that, I warrant. If you hadn't locked the bugger up, that is."

"Yes," Holmes said, face going stiff. Moran was a touchy subject for my friend, having almost killed him on two separate occasions. Despite his being locked away, I knew that the thought of the murderous old shikari was still enough to put a chill up Holmes' spine. "Are you aware of any other procurers who would be willing to do so?"

"In London? No. This is my ground, Mr. Holmes. My territory. Them other lads they know it, as is good for them." Prendrick slapped his fat hand on the table. "No sir! No!"

"Good," Holmes said.

"Eh?"

"Nothing. Watson, I believe we have an appointment to get to," Holmes said, rising to his feet.

"Do we?"

"Quite. With another associate of mine. Mr. Prendrick, I bid you good day." Holmes gestured impatiently and I stood. Then, Holmes stopped and turned. "Mr. Prendrick. Do you happen to use artificial animal calls in your–ah–line?"

Prendrick rubbed his chin. "Strange you should ask. Quite often, yes. Helps us keep the buggers calm."

"Have you ever crafted a tiger call?"

"I–no. Never. Told you sir, I don't mess with them buggers, no I don't." Prendrick cocked his head. "Why do you ask?"

"No reason. Come, Watson!"

Prendrick waved a paw at us as we left.

"Holmes, what–"

"You have your revolver, Watson?"

"Ah, no. I wasn't aware that–"

"No matter. We shall muddle through as best we can." Holmes set off, and I followed. We hailed another cab, and when Holmes indicated for this one to take us to the Rookery of St. Giles, I suddenly mourned the absence of my revolver.

The Rookery was one of the worst areas of the city, a haven for the lowest of the low, and a home to every wretched creature that could not bear the light of London's day. Thieves, pimps, prostitutes and peddlers of every vile peccadilloes rubbed shoulders in the overcrowded slums. I had seen worse places in my time, but not many.

"Holmes, are you sure–" I began, as we clattered along. He swiped the air with a hand.

"Surety doesn't come into it I'm afraid, Watson. Necessity does. I need evidence, and I cannot risk alerting our opponent that I am on to his game."

"What game? Are you so certain that you know what's going on?" I said.

"As I said, I have the outline—the shape of the thing—in hand, but to fill in the details, I need more information. Information that we can only gain from the Markesby residence."

"Then why not simply go there? Mr. Markesby would be glad to see you—" I stopped. "Ramsden. Of course. You are convinced that he would take any investigation amiss?"

"Indeed. More than that, it is curiosity that stays my hand. Ramsden is almost certainly involved, as I've said, but is he the only one? Or are we engaged against an as yet hidden opponent, for whom Ramsden is only a pawn?" Holmes sat back, rubbing his hands together. "Too, there's the reason behind this whole business. Markesby is terrified, but to what end?"

"I see your point. But, then, why are we heading into the Rookery, if your intention is to burgle Markesby's residence?"

"Who said I was going to burgle anything?"

"Holmes, do give me some credit, I implore you," I said, feeling slightly insulted. "You will recall our dealings with Charles Augustus Milverton several years ago? Or the affair of the Bohemian letters?"

Holmes laughed and thumped his cane on the floor of the cab. "Ha! Watson! Yes, I admit to a bit of house-breaking, but this time I believe we need to employ the services of a professional."

"A professional?"

"Drury Septon. You heard me mention him earlier this morning?" Holmes said slyly.

"Yes," I said.

"Well. I happen to know where young Drury is hiding in the bowers of the Rookery. And, the scalawag owes me a favor."

"Oh?"

"Yes. Or, rather, he will, when I inform him that I know the exact circumstances of the robbery he committed last evening." Holmes sat back, a self-satisfied smile on his face. I couldn't help but give a grunt of disappointment.

"Holmes, that is blackmail!"

"Yes. In the service of preventing a murder," he said calmly. "In any event, we're here. Driver!"

I was forced to pay the driver an exorbitant fee to wait on us within the crooked street we found ourselves in. I was reminded of Hogarth's satirical painting *Gin Lane* as I looked around, keeping a wary eye out for trouble.

The Rookery was much like I imagined the inside of a honeycomb to be, with perforations in the form of numerous blind courts and alleyways with no other outlet than a grim, grinning entrance. Everywhere there were wretched hovels with shattered, gaping windows patched with old, yellowing news sheets and filth ran freely in the gutters. Lines and poles of barely clean linen flapped in a cool breeze, obscuring the sky from the sight of those standing below.

Unnerved, I followed Holmes into one of the slumped, sagging houses, where grubby children streamed past us and out onto the streets. Some cried out to Holmes in a familiar manner and I knew at once the method by which Holmes had ascertained Septon's whereabouts.

Holmes glanced back at me and smiled, as if reading my thoughts. "Information, Watson, is worth its weight in coin."

"Then where is he?"

"Upstairs. Waiting for us, I'll be bound." Holmes gestured with his cane. "If he isn't attempting to escape."

"Shouldn't we hurry, then?" I asked, concerned.

"No need Watson. Those youths who scampered past are watching the street for me. Luckily, I can pay more handsomely than young Mr. Septon." Holmes started up the stairs and I hurried after him.

On the second floor of the hovel, inhabitants watched us through partially opened doors, slamming them whenever I looked at them directly. All except for one. Holmes held a finger to his lips and waited. Then, at the sound of glass breaking, he stepped aside and swept his cane out.

"Watson. If you please."

Keeping hold of my hat, I put my shoulder to the door, snapping the rusty lock with ease. I nearly tumbled to the floor even as a thin, raggedly dressed youth whirled, fingers darting inside his coat. Holmes swooped past me and thrust his cane out with all of the grace of a champion fencer. The end smacked into the youth's wrist with a loud crack and he yelped and fell back onto a sagging mattress. Clutching his injured limb, he cursed us both roundly until he saw Holmes' face full on.

"You!" he shouted. Holmes kicked the door shut and bent forward, pressing the head of his cane to the center of the young man's breast bone.

"Me. Hello, Mr. Septon. I see the wainscoting has defeated you yet again," Holmes said, gesturing with his free hand to the broken window.

"It's me curse," Septon said. He looked past Holmes and bestowed a gap-toothed grin on me. "Bad with window locks."

"An unfortunate affliction for such a noted second story man to have, I've always said. Hence your continued–and distinctive–use of a lady's stocking filled with powdered brick when the locks get the best of you." Holmes sniffed and poked Septon hard. "Brick which bears the distinctive characteristics of being from this area, might I add."

"So that's it then. I'm nicked. I'm for the boat, then." Septon held up his hands as if awaiting a pair of shackles. He was still grinning cheerfully, and I couldn't help chuckling at his expression. Holmes stepped back and leaned on his cane.

"Not yet, Mr. Septon. Perhaps not at all, if you agree to the proposal I intend to put forward to you," Holmes said. "A task of little difficulty for an experienced individual such as yourself."

"Well, now you're just flattering me." Septon reclined on the bed, his fingers interlaced over his belly. "Anything for you sir, anything at all as long as it keeps me out of the dock."

"I hoped you'd be amendable," Holmes said. He sat on the window sill and pulled a slip of paper out of his coat pocket. "This is the address of a certain house belonging to a certain man. I wish you to employ your skills and enter the house. Take what you please, but don't be greedy."

"What?" Septon's look of confusion mirrored my own. Holmes made an impatient gesture.

"Even as I said, Mr. Septon. Break. Enter. Burgle. Pilfer. Snatch. But take care not to be caught."

"I think I can manage that, yeah," Septon said, rubbing his chin. "And I keep what I steal?"

"Yes. You will pass along information as to what you stole to one of the boys outside, who will then deliver it to me. I wish for you to keep an eye out for anything…untoward, Mr. Septon."

"Like?"

"Anything that pricks your thumbs, sir," Holmes said. He stood and tapped his cane on the floor. "Now. We'll be off. I look forward to your report no later than mid-week."

Septon watched us go, bemused. I waited until the door had closed to round on Holmes. "Holmes! What was that–"

"Calm yourself, Watson. All will be revealed in time." He held up a finger and waited. From inside the room came an oath. Holmes smiled and pointed towards the stairs with his cane. "Now we can go."

"Are you going to tell me, or must I puzzle it out?" I said. Holmes smiled.

"So that's it then. I'm nicked. I'm for the boat, then."

"By all means, try, Watson. But, as yet, the puzzle is incomplete. We must visit Markesby's home."

"I thought you said—"

"Not Markesby himself, Watson, but his home. I need to see it." Holmes climbed up into our cab. "Or, rather, its surroundings."

I sat beside him, puzzled. Markesby's residence was located in Kensington, I discovered. Surprisingly near the museum, in fact. I refrained from asking Holmes about it, and instead settled for watching him watch the street, which was, in many respects, an important activity in and of itself.

Not simply because I, in some ways, relied on Holmes to supplement my meager income as a medical practitioner, but, it was truly something of an educational experience. Watching Holmes at the hunt was an opportunity to study one of the finest brains in creation as it was bent to an often impossible task.

He hunched forward, his beak of a nose nearly parallel with the ground, his eyes fixed on the house with an intensity that never failed to disturb me slightly. It was a feverish thing, bright and sharp and as clear as diamond.

Markesby's residence sat on the corner of the street and was connected to other homes in such a way that made it seem as if they all were one great edifice. Holmes assured me that Markesby owned the entirety of the corner domicile, including the basement and attic flats.

"He is a thrifty soul, our Mr. Markesby," Holmes said. We stood behind an ivy-covered iron rail across the street from the building. "He bought those flats nearly sixty years ago, and has, according to most sources, not changed them one iota since the day he moved in."

"Is that relevant, you think?" I asked. Holmes said nothing. I popped a leaf from the ivy and flicked it away. "Holmes, what are we—"

"Hsst." Holmes held up his hand. "There." I followed his gesture, and saw, to my amazement, the narrow shape of Inspector Lestrade!

The beady-eyed inspector from Scotland Yard was standing on the stoop nearest Markesby's residence, lighting a cigarette and berating an underling.

"Holmes! What is Lestrade doing here?"

"Ha," Holmes said. "Watson. I wish you to go down the street and purchase a paper."

"What? But—"

"A paper, Watson. Please. Make sure it's the *Times*."

"But Holmes, you've already read the—"

"It's for your benefit, Watson. Not mine," Holmes said, fixing me with a steady gaze. "Go. Please."

I went, finding no good reason to argue further. As I walked, however, I felt a prickle of worry crawl up my spine. I stopped and turned, but saw nothing.

By the time I had returned with the paper, the prickle had all but vanished. I mentioned it to Holmes, who frowned.

"Have no fear of your senses, Watson. It is as I suspected. You'll forgive me, but I had to know."

"What do you mean? Forgive you for what?" I said, confused. Holmes tapped his lip with a stiff finger.

"Bait, Watson. I dangled you before the tiger, and it obligingly revealed itself." He took the paper from me and traced the lines of print with the head of his cane. "Here. Look."

My mind whirling, I looked at the paper. "Yes. The break in you mentioned earlier. The one you claimed Drury Septon was responsible for. But what has this to do with anything?"

"The address, Watson. Look at the address!"

I looked, then blinked in surprise. "Why, it's right next door to Markesby's residence!"

"Yes. And this," Holmes said, flipping the page.

"The article about the government official being murdered–hunh. It doesn't say what his job was exactly. Or his name. That's odd." I paused as something caught my eye. I looked up. Holmes nodded.

"Yes, Watson. The address of the murder? Right where Lestrade is standing. Undoubtedly, that poor constable he's berating was sent to request our presence."

"What? Why?"

Holmes stuffed the paper into the ivy and began to walk briskly towards where Lestrade stood. I hurried to keep up. "Holmes!"

"In a moment, Watson. Inspector Lestrade!" Holmes called out, raising his cane. Lestrade turned and saw us, and his eyes seemed to bulge slightly.

"Mr. Holmes?"

"Lestrade, we came as soon as we heard!" Holmes said, pushing past Lestrade and heading for the open door. "I assume the body has already been moved, of course. No matter, as I said to Watson earlier, we shall simply muddle through as best we can. Where is the scene of the crime? Upstairs? As I suspected! Come Watson!"

"Doctor? How did–" Lestrade began, looking befuddled. I clapped him on the shoulder as I followed Holmes.

"We're here, Lestrade. Leave it at that," I said. Lestrade followed me, tossing his cigarette aside.

"Yes, but how did you know?" he said, slightly petulant. But only slightly. Much like myself, Lestrade had grown used to Holmes' methods. "I only just sent a man out."

"Serendipity, Lestrade," Holmes said from somewhere up the stairs. "Merest happenstance, I assure you. Ah!" Holmes stood in what was obviously an office, cane held lengthwise across his back, head bowed as he examined a stain on the wooden floor. "This was where the murder took place?"

Lestrade nodded. "Yes. Never knew what hit him, looks like. Poor bugger."

Holmes knelt abruptly and ran his hand along the floor. Then, still crouching, he waddled towards the far wall. "Cause of death?"

"Revolver of some type." Lestrade glanced at me. "Though if Dr. Watson would like to take a look–"

"No need! No need." Holmes waved a hand. "If one cannot trust the body-men of Scotland Yard, after all." He ran his hands across the wall for a moment, before stopping, turning and extending his cane. He frowned. "The window is broken."

"We think the thief broke it trying to get in. Noise must have alerted the–ah–resident and he came running." I looked curiously at Lestrade. He had quite deliberately not spoken the name of the dead man. Holmes didn't seem concerned.

"There have been a series of break-ins, then?" Holmes said. "In the neighborhood? On this street?"

"One last night. Around the same time. We're thinking a gang hit the area looking for swag. Probably not local. I've got men down near the docks, looking into things."

"Mmm," Holmes said. "Then how did the glass become so scattered?"

"What?"

"The window, Lestrade. Do pay attention," Holmes said, stretching out and tapping the window with the end of his cane. "Glass on the floor and on the sill. The window was broken, then fell apart after it was opened. Meaning…" He paused, looking at me.

"That the…resident–" I said. "Was shot through the closed window, prior to the thief entering."

"But–"

"Ha!" Holmes said, whacking the wall with his cane. He pulled a small clasp knife from within his coat and began to dig at the wall. In moments he had pulled a deformed pistol ball free. He held it up for us to see between his thumb and forefinger. "Watson, go to the window and tell us what you see."

I did as Holmes bade. "A courtyard. The block of flats curve around it, containing it."

"And directly across from the window?"

"The back windows of Markesby's residence!" I said. I turned. Holmes bounced the bullet on his palm.

"See anything familiar about this scenario, Watson?"

I snapped my fingers as a flash of memory took me. "An air-gun!" I said. "Like the one Colonel Moran used."

"Quite so," he said, tossing the ball to Lestrade, who caught it awkwardly. "What was taken, Lestrade?"

Lestrade looked at me, frowning. Holmes made an impatient sound. "We don't have time for this Lestrade! I understand the order of secrecy you were placed under but the time for that has passed. What was taken?"

"Certain papers. Notebooks," Lestrade began hesitantly. Holmes' face was a mask.

"I had hoped that they would have been disposed of properly."

"They were written in code, y'see," Lestrade said. He shrugged. "They thought—"

"To break the code and thus puzzle out the information contained within. I assume my brother refused?"

"So he did, sir, and rightly, I thought. But there was as them higher than me who—ah—thought that information should be known." Lestrade looked shamefaced. Holmes patted him on the shoulder.

"Do not bear the guilt of others, Lestrade. It is a useless thing. But, now we find ourselves in a quandary. Luckily, I anticipated this. Come, Watson. We have done all we can here. Lestrade, I shall prevail upon you to be at Baker Street tomorrow morning, sometime after dusk. Bring four of your stoutest men."

"Why?" he said.

"In order to resolve this situation in the most amicable manner possible, Lestrade. With no embarrassment to either yourself, your superiors or anyone else involved."

"Mr. Holmes? Embarrassment?" Lestrade said.

"Trust me, Lestrade." Holmes left the room, and I followed, bursting with questions. I prudently waited until we were out on the street before I burst out,

"Holmes, what was that about?"

"I was wrong, Watson. This case does have to do with ghosts. But not Mr. Markesby's. Mine." Holmes didn't look at me. "You recall when Professor Moriarty's organization was dismantled?"

"How could I forget?"

"Yes." Holmes smiled bitterly. "Well, Moriarty's holdings were raided, and a number of papers were found. Lists and ledgers. Account books. Names, Watson."

"Good God," I said, stopping on the street. Holmes stopped and turned. "You mean to say–"

"Yes. Moriarty's tendrils extended even into Whitehall. It was assumed that–for the good of the nation–those papers would be contained and that no attempt to crack the code they were written in was to be made. So my brother was promised."

"But now, we find that someone has been attempting just that," I said. "If those books were ever translated…" I could not complete the thought, so staggering were the implications.

"The Lion and the Unicorn, Watson, are terrible foes though they both serve the Queen. Any advantage, no matter how distastefully gained, is eagerly sought." Holmes sighed. "I suspected, and have for some time, that this would happen. Men are too easily tempted, I fear. Ambitious men especially. I even considered theft as a way of removing their malign influence once and for all, though Mycroft talked me out of it. Truly Watson, there is no grimoire or demonic tome more dangerous to our fair isle than the anal scribblings of that fiendish star-gazer, James Moriarty."

Those were strong words for Holmes, an indication of his seriousness in the matter. I knew then that this case had moved from the realm of the diverting to the personal.

"What is our next step, then?" I said. "Do we wait for Septon to report?"

"Septon? Watson, I thought you realized," Holmes said, looking at me. "Septon is involved in this affair from his smile to his shoes, Watson."

"What? But–"

"As is Prendrick, of course. You recall how he made mention of Moran of abominable memory? Prendrick was a former acquaintance of Moran's and a tool of Moriarty, as was Septon, though to a lesser degree."

"Prendrick?" I shook my head, trying to process this new information. "Then why–"

"I am playing the long game, Watson," Holmes said, leaning on his cane. He looked up at the buildings surrounding us. Behind those windows, the mighty of London went about their business, unaware of what transpired within their very midst. "Not so long as some, but longer than others. Two games, in fact."

"Two," I said. I looked back at the Markesby residence. Something glinted in one of the upper story windows. "Holmes," I said, a chill flashing through me. A chill, in fact, identical to the one I had felt earlier. We were being watched, and not by friendly eyes.

"I see them, Watson. They will not fire. Not here. Not now, with the police so close and the sun in the sky, illuminating their crime for all to see." Holmes spoke with a confidence I could not share.

"You sound sure of yourself, Holmes," I said.

"When have you ever known me not to be, Watson?" Holmes shaded his eyes with his hand. "I wanted them to see us. I wanted Prendrick to know we were curious about tigers. I wanted Septon to know that we suspected something was amiss with Markesby. And now, Ramsden has seen us here."

"All three of them?"

"Oh yes, Watson. A criminal triumvirate." Holmes lowered his hand and started back down the street. "I still lack a number of facts, but the story is beginning to take shape."

"And what story would that be?"

"A black one indeed," Holmes said softly. He glanced at me. "I believe we are facing the genesis of darksome force, Watson. And I intend to stop it before it goes any further. But if you wish to bow out, I–"

"Holmes," I said. "I have faced air-guns before. And in the hands of more deadly men than these, I'll wager."

"Perhaps. But not by much." Holmes turned away.

"What of Markesby?" I said.

"A pawn. Less, perhaps. I believe that his part in this is minor, at best, and fast coming to an end."

"They intend to kill him, you mean."

"Possibly. But not yet." Holmes raised his cane, flagging down a cab. "And not at all, if I can prevent it."

We rode back to Baker Street in companionable silence. I could practically hear the gears turning in Holmes' mind. I knew that he was examining the problem from multiple directions, trying to plan for even the slightest of possibilities. If it had been anyone else, I would have thought them doomed to failure.

"Mrs. Hudson!" Holmes called as we entered. "We will be dining in tonight!" As we climbed the stairs, he continued, "Watson, as soon as we are inside, close the shades and curtains both in every room and pocket your revolver. We will need it before the night is out, I warrant."

"You believe they'll come for us?"

"I certainly hope so!" He shook his head. "I've put much effort into ensuring that they would."

Not knowing quite what to say to that, I remained silent. Holmes looked at me. "You understand my reasoning, of course?"

"No, I cannot say that I do."

"Think, Watson," Holmes said, crossing to a window. "They must deal with us before they deal with Markesby. He is their security. We two are far more dangerous to their nascent organization. And they know that we are on their trail. Thus, they must deal with us first."

"You mean, then, that this entire day was spent–"

"Baiting the tiger. Or tigers, rather. Yes." Holmes edged back a curtain with a finger and glanced out. "You see the copy of the *Times* there?" he said, pointing at the folded paper on the table.

"Holmes, I think I have little need to look at it again," I said, retrieving my Webley and checking the ammunition cylinder. Holmes laughed.

"But you do. In order to know the true face of our enemy." He picked up the paper and folded it to display an article concerning a missing member of the gentry. I took the paper as I dropped my pistol into my coat pocket.

"This is the young man you said ran off to avoid his debts," I said. Holmes tapped the artist's rendering.

"Is it? Look closely. Imagine him without a mustache. With artificially lightened hair."

"I–" For the third time that day, a sensation of dread spread swiftly through me. "Holmes, this is Ramsden!"

"Not his real name, of course," Holmes said. He lit his pipe, and tossed the spent match into the fireplace. "Like many before him, gambling proved a hard vice to shake for our Mr. Ramsden, as he now calls himself. I would wager that he's been a bad egg for quite a while, before slipping into this identity. You recall, of course, the affair of Mr. Neville St. Clair and his alter-ego, Hugh Boone?"

"But St. Clair was hardly a criminal, despite his ill-advised play-acting," I said. "Why would he–"

"Money, Watson. Money to clear his debts, or to simply indulge his vice.

Or, perhaps, during a game of chance, he discovered something which sparked a cancerous creativity in his soul. Idle hands turn to evil swiftly, Watson." Holmes sat down in his chair, his face wreathed in smoke. "Regardless of the cause, he has become a far deadlier creature than he once was."

"You sound as if you believe Ramsden to be in charge," I said, sitting down across from him. "Is not Prendrick a more likely candidate? You said yourself he was a former compatriot of Moran."

"No. Prendrick, much like the beasts he sells, is a brute and no more capable of complex planning than a leopard is of changing its spots. And Septon, despite his abilities, is a petty thief. No, it's Ramsden who drives these men." Holmes leaned back, his face grim. "And it's Ramsden who will lead them here tonight. Though in what form their assault will take—" Holmes waved a hand.

"But why?" I said. "Why do this? Why the charade with the spectral tiger?"

"Simplicity," Holmes said. He stood and tapped out his pipe on the mantle as Mrs. Hudson arrived, carrying a dinner of cold cuts, bread, butter and cheese. "Ah, Mrs. Hudson. Would you do me the favor of leaving the front door unlocked this evening? I am expecting callers."

"Callers? Mr. Holmes you try me," she said, sounding slightly exasperated. "Still, I suppose I can trust your judgment."

Holmes took her hand and bowed his head. "Mrs. Hudson, you are a treasure. What would Dr. Watson and I do without you?"

"Starve, most likely," Mrs. Hudson said, as she swept out of the room, closing the door quietly behind her.

We moved to the table and ate in silence as the sun set. Some time later, Holmes continued as if there had been no interruption.

"Markesby's residence provided an ideal location from which to plan the theft of Moriarty's papers—something which I believe to be the central matter of this affair."

"Then what of the robbery Septon committed?"

"Ah. That is where things become interesting. When I recognized Ramsden from the paper, I immediately rushed to my files to see what I knew of his former identity. His was a sorry case, but one all too common. A man driven from his usual haunts of gentleman's clubs and social functions to seek game of chance further afield, where his markers still had worth. I had made note of his involvement in several minor scandals, including an interesting case of blackmail which apparently had neither victim, nor perpetrator." Holmes smiled ruefully. "A bad egg, Watson, as I said."

He sat back in his chair, his eyes far away. "I believe that Ramsden encountered both Septon and Prendrick at a fateful game of cards not long ago. Between seven and eight days, no less, though perhaps more." Holmes rubbed his chin. "Both are devoted chancemen, and Prendrick was a known acquaintance of Sebastian Moran. I believe that Ramsden had made Moran's acquaintance prior to the death of Ronald Adair. They were members of several of the same clubs, including the Anglo-Indian Club."

"Ramsden was looking for them, then?" I said. Outside, the gas lamps lit up the street with a weird glow.

"Perhaps. It is likely that, knowing something of Moran's illicit dealings, Ramsden sought to kindle a relationship with those who might benefit him in a similar manner and learned of Moriarty's legacy through application of drink. It is equally possible that Ramsden knew of the attempt to decode Moriarty's notes prior to his meeting with the two." Holmes held up a finger. "This is all supposition, you understand, but I believe that one of the two theories is correct. In any event, once contact was made, a plan was formed.

"Markesby would have been known by reputation to Ramsden, and he could easily have ferreted out the truth of things with a few simple questions to the right people. And it would have been a simple matter for a man of Prendrick's experience to fabricate the evidence to fool the senses of an ageing man like Markesby, who had faced tigers before. And Septon would be an ideal candidate to place that evidence where it would be sure to reach its target."

"But why bother convincing Markesby he is the target of spectral vengeance in the first place?" I said.

"To place him in the position of requiring an aide, Watson," Holmes said. He pulled a cigarette out of his case, tapped it once on the lid, stuck it between his lips and lit it. "A protector. Ramsden. Ramsden who would, in turn, let his accomplices into the house. And Ramsden who would dose poor Markesby with the distilled hallucinogen in an attempt to keep their unknowing host docile. Thus giving them the time needed to plan their theft of Moriarty's papers. Once again, Septon was an integral part of that plan."

"They intended to merely steal it, then? And not murder the man attempting to decode it?" I said, my disbelief obvious even to me. Holmes nodded, unsmiling.

"Yes. But, I believe Septon had his own plans. If we were to inquire, I further believe we would discover evidence of robbery in nearly every house on that row. Unfortunately, Septon's weakness with window locks once again reared its head, necessitating his use of his trademark tool." Holmes smiled. "In a way, we have Septon to thank for alerting us to the true nature of the goings-on."

"Septon?"

"Yes. If he hadn't given in to his lower impulses, I would never have begun linking the disparate parts into a whole–"

"I shall bear that in mind for the future," Ramsden said. I rose from my chair with an oath I shall not repeat here, and clawed for my pistol.

"I hope you don't mind, but we let ourselves in as quietly as possible. Wouldn't want to awaken your landlady." Ramsden stepped out of the doorway, hands behind his back. Prendrick followed him in, holding an air-gun which was pointed at Holmes. "Calm yourself, Doctor," Ramsden said, smiling faintly as he looked at me. "We don't need any accidents this close to the end of the game."

"I concur," Holmes said. He glanced at the window. "Feel free to come in off the ledge, Mr. Septon. You must be quite uncomfortable."

I am not ashamed to say that my jaw fell as Drury Septon raised the shade and slid in through the open window, smiling cheerfully. "What was it then, Mr. Holmes? No troubles with the locks, I swears to you," Septon said, seating himself on the sill. Holmes laughed.

"No, Mr. Septon. I noticed your shadow lingering at the top of the shade as the sun finally dipped below the horizon. One can but admire your ability to perch for what must have seemed an inordinately long time."

"And yet you said nothing," Ramsden said. He sat down in my vacated seat. I stepped closer to Holmes, my eyes locked on the weapon in Prendrick's hands.

"What was there to say?" Holmes said. He leaned back, puffing contentedly on his cigarette. "Now you are here and it is all out in the open."

"Yes. Mr. Prendrick?" Ramsden said, raising a hand. Prendrick laughed and raised his air-gun. I tensed, but Holmes merely chuckled.

"You won't shoot me, Mr. Ramsden. In fact, I daresay that you need me. Us." Holmes interlaced his fingers and squared his shoulders. Ramsden frowned.

"Oh?"

"Yes. Or have you managed to crack the code those papers you stole were written in?"

"Ha," Ramsden sat back. His face betrayed nothing. "No, as a matter of fact, we haven't."

"Don't tell him that!" Prendrick snapped.

"And why not? If there's a smarter man in London since the good Professor kicked off, I don't want to meet him," Septon said. "He won't play us false, not with his friend the Doctor here." He gestured to me and I stiffened, but said nothing. The pistol was heavy in my pocket. If I could but reach it, I was certain that I could render Prendrick, at least, harmless.

Ramsden sat silently for a moment, then slapped a hand down on the table. "Ha! Fine." He reached into his coat and pulled out a thin notebook. He tossed it to Holmes. "This is what I have so far. If you can crack it, I may let you live."

Holmes flipped open the notebook and paged through it, one thin eyebrow quirking. "Quite impressive. You've made more progress than I thought possible in such a short amount of time."

"Some of it was already done for me, I must admit," Ramsden said. "I simply built on what had already been teased loose."

"Still. A mind like yours is wasted on criminal pursuits, Mr. Ab–"

"Don't," Ramsden said. "My name is Ramsden." His hand closed into a fist and Holmes smiled briefly.

"Of course. How thoughtless of me." He snapped his fingers. "Watson, a pencil if you please."

I turned and snatched a pencil off of my writing desk. I handed it to Holmes and caught a glimpse of an odd mathematic scrawl on the pages before him. "Holmes, those look like coordinates of some kind."

"Indeed, Doctor," Ramsden said. "They are theoretical calculations of the Earth's proposed rotation in a given span of years."

"Very good, Mr. Ramsden." Holmes tapped his lips with the pencil. "You'll recall, Watson, that Moriarty was an astrophysicist of some note before his turn to the bad. No wonder the fellows from the government were having such a time of it."

"This is foolish. One of the other papers undoubtedly has the answers we need, Ramsden," Prendrick said. He was seated on the arm of the couch, the air-gun resting on his knee, the barrel aimed in a general fashion at us. "We should kill this bastard now."

"It is entirely likely that Moriarty kept the secret of the code in his head," Holmes said without looking up. Ramsden nodded.

"Prendrick. Settle down."

"No! We've come too far to–" Prendrick raised the rifle, his dead eye glinting dully. Ramsden's hand flashed quicker than the eye could follow and not half a second later, he was aiming a revolver at his compatriot.

"We've come too far not to go further. I want those notes. I want those names. I want everything," Ramsden said, his voice a menacing purr. "Now. Calm down."

"You—" Prendrick said. But he sat back, apparently cowed. I eased my hand into my coat pocket as I stepped behind Holmes' chair. Septon was occupying himself with the remains of our dinner, slathering butter on a chunk of bread. Ramsden, unnaturally still, watched Holmes.

"I must commend you on your loyalty, Mr. Ramsden. A lesser man would have dispensed with Mr. Prendrick long before this," Holmes said, making a few notes on the page in front of him. Prendrick stiffened, his good eye narrowing.

"Oh?" Ramsden said. He had a slight smile on his face. His pistol was on his lap, his hand over it. Holmes wet the end of the pencil with his tongue and smiled.

"Yes. Once he had created the materials you used to convince Markesby that he was being haunted, and obtained the air-gun there from whatever cache it was languishing in, I would imagine that his usefulness decreased significantly."

"Use and worth are ever-changing variables, Mr. Holmes," Ramsden said. "For instance, your own worth teeters on the cusp of irrelevance as we speak."

"Ha," Holmes said. "I doubt that. You are gifted, Ramsden, but your brain is crooked and stunted in the necessary areas." He pointed the pencil at the other man. "Else, you would have predicted Mr. Septon's continued endangerment of your activities."

"Here now," Septon said, chewing a slice of salami. "That's uncalled for."

"Perhaps. Then, you had an inkling prior to his slip-up, I think," Ramsden said, ignoring the glare Septon threw him. Holmes inclined his head.

"Your mistake."

"The Amanita," Ramsden said, leaning back in his chair. Holmes sniffed.

"That and the fit it caused. I knew that there was no physical threat then. No mysterious stalker. Thus, it had to be something else."

"Yes. A mind like a difference engine," Ramsden said. "I've noticed that you've stopped writing."

"I am merely pondering," Holmes said, settling back, legs crossed, fingers pressed together.

"What, exactly?"

"Your motivations."

"Ramsden," Prendrick said. Ramsden gestured irritably.

"Quiet! My motivations?" he said, addressing the last to Holmes.

"Yes. If you break the code, what then? Moriarty's organization has been dismantled. Most of his support structure has long since been imprisoned. Only those on the fringes, such as Mr. Prendrick, have escaped the gaol or the noose. What is there to gain? Blackmail material, perhaps?"

"Among other things," Ramsden said. "Besides, with the proper plans, a fallen structure can easily be rebuilt."

"Ah," Holmes said. "Hubris."

"Confidence," Ramsden said. Holmes clapped his hands together and gave a bark of laughter.

"Wonderful! Marvelous! You are a treasure, sir," he said. Ramsden looked momentarily puzzled.

"What?"

"Doctor, what time is it?" Holmes said, glancing at me. I checked my pocket watch.

"Nearly half eleven."

"Lestrade should be here within minutes then, I think," Holmes said, turning back to bestow a beaming smile on Ramsden. The young man lunged forward, grabbing the notebook and pulling it towards himself. His face went pale with fury and he shot to his feet.

"Prendrick!"

"Now, Watson!" Holmes said, grabbing the edge of the table and flipping it upwards into both Ramsden and Septon, the latter of whom crashed into Holmes' desk. I spun on my heel, my hand—and the pistol it held—coming out of my coat pocket. A whistle of air caressed my cheek and then my revolver roared dully.

Prendrick gave a great cry and fell backwards, his shoulder gone red. He staggered forward, swinging the air-gun at me like a club, and forcing my retreat. A wild swipe sent my Webley flying from my grip and left my hand throbbing painfully. Ignoring the pain, I stepped into his blindspot and drove a fist into his side. My second blow caught him on the chin and he fell forward with a groan. His arm hooked my leg and I stumbled, bringing both fists down on his back. He fell flat and did not move.

"Watson!" Holmes cried. I turned and threw myself to the floor as Ramsden's pistol spoke. Something on the mantle shattered, and I scrambled for my pistol where it lay. Ramsden fired again, gouging a chunk out of the couch.

"Yes. If you break the code, what then? What is there to gain? Blackmail material, perhaps?"

I swept up the revolver and rose into a crouch. My shot tore a flurry of splinters from the doorframe even as Ramsden ducked through it.

"Holmes," I said, turning to see my friend take hold of Septon's arm, even as the latter made a looping punch, and throw him over his hip, face-first into the upended table. Septon hit with a tooth-rattling thump and fell noodle-limbed to the floor.

"Ramsden is fleeing," I said, heading for the door. "We must go after him!" Holmes grabbed my arm.

"Careful, Watson. Remember his revolver."

"We can't simply let him go!"

"And so we won't. I merely wish you to exercise caution. If we die here, Ramsden walks free. A new name, a new face, with Moriarty's legacy to guide him and he will have accomplished all that he has set out to do. We are all that stand between him and the realization of that savage dream." Holmes gestured to the landing beyond the doorway. "Go. But be careful. I will take a different route. Perhaps we can catch him between us."

"Different route?"

"No time to explain, Watson. Go," Holmes said, turning towards the window. I stepped towards the door, my pistol at the ready. I stepped out onto the landing, my senses stretched to their utmost. Beneath my foot, a board creaked.

A bullet plucked at the banister beside me and I flung myself against the wall.

"Doctor?" Ramsden's voice floated up to me. I did not answer, and he laughed. "Yes. Of course it's you. Where is Mr. Holmes, I wonder?"

I crouched and waddled towards the banister. I thought I could make out Ramsden's shape just inside the curve of the stair.

"Seeing to the others, perhaps? Sending you out to draw my fire?" Ramsden continued, his voice mocking. "Where are the police, Dr. Watson?"

"On their way, I assure you," I said. Ramsden fired again and I fell back, splinters digging into my face. I could feel blood trickling down my cheeks and I heard a thump behind me.

I rolled, narrowly avoiding the thudding boot that slammed down where my head had been. Prendrick snarled down at me and swept back his coat, revealing a khukuri knife sheathed across his chest. He unsheathed the angled blade and lunged at me. I threw myself backwards, nearly falling down the stairs to the second landing as the blade chopped into the banister. "Ramsden!" he cried.

"Kill him, Mr. Prendrick!" Ramsden crowed. I fired my Webley wildly and Prendrick gave a hideous scream as the bullet caught him high on the face. Clutching at his cheek, he hacked at me again. I caught his wrist on the downward stroke of the blade and forced his hand to the wall. He toppled onto me, bellowing. I brought the Webley crashing across his face and he slumped to the side. I shoved my way out from under him, and got to my knees.

Ramsden stood below me, face serene, the barrel of his pistol aimed unwaveringly at my face. "Goodbye, Dr. Watson," he said. In that moment, I saw my death. Not for the first time, but, I thought, almost certainly the last.

But, before the pistol could sound, salvation arrived. Ramsden was unaware, until the very last second, of the approach of Sherlock Holmes, who flew upon him seemingly out of nowhere, slapping the revolver from his hand and sweeping his legs out from under him. Holmes swung Ramsden to the ground, and, crouching over him, struck him twice, swiftly, once on the sternum, then on the throat. Ramsden curled up into a ball, making gagging sounds deep in his throat. Holmes snatched up the man's revolver and stepped back, seating himself on the bottom stair.

"Holmes, how did you–" I began, climbing to my feet. Holmes glanced at me over his shoulder and smiled, a trifle wearily.

"The window, Watson. I merely climbed down, dropped to the street, and came in through the front door. Once I saw that Ramsden's attention was sufficiently diverted–"

"By me, you mean?" I said.

"Well, yes," Holmes said. He had the good grace to look ashamed for a moment. But only for a moment. Then, smiling, he turned back to look at Ramsden. "I believe I hear the distinctive tread of the Peelers, Watson."

Ramsden snarled and uncoiled, springing up and diving for Holmes, murder in his eyes and a thin blade in his hand. Holmes barely moved. He simply raised the pistol and coolly fired, knocking Ramsden's leg out from under him. The man fell heavily, squalling like a wounded animal.

Holmes shook his head. "I had such high hopes for that young man, Watson. Such intelligence is rare, you know."

"Yes, lucky for us all," I said.

"Ha!" Holmes stood, pulling his pocket watch out of his waistcoat even as the front door opened and Lestrade stepped inside, followed by several men.

"Ah, Mr. Holmes. We're here as you re–" Lestrade stopped dead as he caught sight of Ramsden on the ground, clutching his leg. "What?"

"Your murderer, Lestrade. As I promised. And, I believe I know the location of the missing papers as well." Holmes put his watch away and handed the pistol to one of the policemen. "You will find his accomplices upstairs, I believe."

"How–what–" Lestrade took off his hat and rubbed his head. "We'll need to sort this out at the Yard."

"Of course, of course, wouldn't hear otherwise," Holmes said, slapping Lestrade on the shoulder and then turning towards the stairs. "Tomorrow though, I believe. Tonight, I must rest. It has been a trying evening, has it not, Watson?"

It took less time than one might expect to remove the three men from our residence, and from our lives, save for one occurrence, of which I will relate more in a moment.

In the morning, Holmes and I visited Markesby in his home, and related to him the true events surrounding the singular affair of the sultan's tiger. Markesby was silent through much of it, and spared us not one word of thanks. We left him there, sitting in his parlor, face unreadable.

To this day, I believe that what I saw there, on that wizened countenance, was disappointment. Disappointment that it was not, in fact, spectral vengeance come to claim its due. Markesby had desired death at the claws and fangs of a demon–tiger, a death to assuage the guilt that had eroded his personality down the long tunnel of years since his ride through the Kullu Hills.

It was not to be. In the end, Markesby died alone, in his bedroom several months later, his face contorted not in a rictus of horror, but in a grimace of resigned frustration.

Ghostly retribution, deserved or not, is the province of fairy stories, it seems.

Ramsden's room was in the attic, and was a small, spare space, completely devoid of all personality. As we searched the room, I could not bring myself to blame Markesby for his attitudes, and I said as much to Holmes, who merely shook his head.

"Stoke the fire, Watson," he said. "I'd hate to catch a chill."

We found the papers beneath a false board in the floor, wrapped in a waterproof oilskin. Holmes sat for some time, paging through them. Then, with barely a flicker of emotion, he tossed them one by one in the fire I had just finished bringing to life.

"Holmes, what are you doing?" I said.

"What I should have done in the first place, Watson. A man lost his life thanks to these scribblings. They are far too dangerous to leave intact." Holmes finished and stood, his face tight. He looked at me. "Come, we must pay a visit to Lestrade."

In the end, Prendrick went to the gallows for the murder of the government official. Septon, slightly more lucky, was sent to Newgate, for the assorted robberies. I have had word that he is as amiable and cheerful as ever. Ramsden, for his part, was sentenced to transportation, thanks to what I suspect were his family connections.

In any event, he never made it to Australia.

It was some time after the trial, at which both Holmes and I were obliged to give testimony, that we returned back to Baker Street from an evening out to find Lestrade waiting for us, a grave look on his face.

"He scarpered," he said, without preamble.

"What?" I said. Holmes gave a snort of laughter and threw his hat across the room as he plopped himself down in his chair.

"Ramsden, Watson. He's escaped."

"You expected this?" Lestrade said.

"No. But I did suspect. What happened?"

"He dove off the boat before it left London, irons and all. We're dragging the river, but—"

"You won't find him," Holmes said, confidently.

"You believe he escaped?" I said. Holmes lit a cigarette and smiled.

"Of course. He could do nothing else. Even as he could not resist confronting me here. Or resist the lure of Moriarty's legacy. No. That boy is a born criminal, and a magnificent one at that. An escape in broad daylight? In chains, no less? Ha!" Holmes jabbed at us with his cigarette.

"I told you that I had high hopes for him, Watson." Holmes leaned back in his chair. "High hopes, indeed." And then he laughed again, louder this time, and as clear as the peal of a church bell.

A SUCKER MOVE –

Right, so, sorry. The preceding story had absolutely nothing to do with either a sultan or a tiger, except in the most tangential sense. It was a sucker move, and I apologize.

Still, it was fun, right? And what about that history lesson? Tipu's Tiger is real, by the by. I've seen it.

Right.

I've always thought that Arthur Conan Doyle created Professor Moriarty as an afterthought. He was a tool, used and discarded once he'd done the deed. But he lingered. Like all good villains, his presence was felt all the more strongly once he'd given up the stage.

But a man like Moriarty—well, he was Holmes' flipside, wasn't he? A man like that wouldn't have gone into the night quietly. No, his fall should have shaken London down to its rotten foundations.

But it didn't.

No mention is made of Moriarty's organization, beyond an aside to the effect that the lower orders are being rounded up. But Moriarty couldn't have functioned as he did with only stranglers, gamblers and thieves as his tools. He'd need 'gen'lmen what have influence' as well.

That's where this story came from. I wondered what happened to the higher-ups that Moriarty had had in his tweed pockets. Were they forcibly retired? Exiled to the fringes of the Empire? Or was it all shoved under the rug?

Well, if you read the story, you know which one I went with. Perhaps my view of the Victorian-era English government is a bit murkier than Doyle's.

At any rate, I also figured this was a chance to add a bit to the Holmes mythos. Moriarty's death left a vacuum, and Nature abhors those things. Or so I'm told. Somebody would be looking to step into Moriarty's shoes, and who better to create that somebody than me?

Well, obviously Conan Doyle, but we don't always get what we'd like, do we?

So there you have it. Ramsden (not his real name) is out and loose in the world, and Holmes couldn't be happier. Will they cross wits again? Who can say?

Only me, and I refuse to tell.

I hope you enjoyed the story, despite the lack of sultans and tigers.

❄ ❄ ❄

JOSHUA M. REYNOLDS – is a freelance writer of moderate skill and exceptional confidence. He has written quite a bit, and some of it was even published. For money. By real people.

Feel free to stop by his blog, Hunting Monsters [http://joshuamreynolds.blogspot.com/] and cast aspersions on his character.

Sherlock Holmes
Consulting Detective

"The Adventure of the Injured Inspector"

by
Aaron Smith

"**G**ood lord, Holmes!" I shouted as we sat at our breakfast with the morning's newspaper open upon the table. "Inspector Lestrade has been shot!"

"Is he dead?" Holmes asked, somewhat coldly, as if his question was guided by intellectual curiosity rather than concern for a man who had often been our ally.

"No," I answered, reading the article and paraphrasing its contents. "The bullet struck him in the shoulder. He's recovering in hospital, expected to recuperate fully."

"And has his assailant been apprehended?" Holmes inquired next.

"Apparently not," I said.

"Well then," Holmes announced as he began to rise from his chair, "We shall begin our day with a visit to the wounded policeman."

❃ ❃ ❃

We found Lestrade sitting up in bed, his shoulder heavily bandaged, with a sour expression on his face.

"Are you in much pain, Inspector?" I asked.

"Not so much pain, Watson," the wounded policeman answered, "as anger. It just isn't right, you know, shooting a man down from where you can't even be seen! It's the act of a spineless coward, I tell you! Truth is too, I wish I could say I had some faith in my own department to catch the scoundrel... but I don't. Is that why the two of you are here? Are you plannin' on goin' on the chase then, Holmes? A month's pay I'll give you if you bring the bastard in!"

Holmes looked down at the bedridden figure. A rare look of sympathy crossed Holmes' face. He spoke to Lestrade in a gentle but firm tone. "Inspector, you have been of assistance to me on many occasions, even if you have frequently crossed barriers and intruded more than I would like into my investigations. Despite your shortcomings, I have always judged you to be an honest man and a hardworking policeman. I shall look into this matter free of charge, provided you are willing to answer any questions I may have with nothing short of absolute and complete honesty."

Lestrade nodded. "Thank you," was the only phrase he could seem to bring himself to utter.

"Now, Inspector Lestrade," said Holmes, "I want you to tell me everything you recall about the incident, in your own words, from your point of view, that of the victim in this case."

Lestrade began his narrative. "I was done with my shift for the evening. It had been an uneventful day, mostly devoted to writing reports and other such busywork. It was nearly ten o'clock at night when I left The Yard and began my walk home. I don't often take a cab home at night, as I find I sleep more soundly after a long stroll. It was dark, but I know my way around those streets after walking them so many times before. Oftentimes I stick to the main streets, but I sometimes take advantage of a particular shortcut, going through a courtyard that lies between the back sides of two buildings, each of three floors. The courtyard makes a nice way to get where I'm going a bit quicker. So I got off the main street and took the courtyard route. As I crossed the courtyard, I heard an odd noise, a scraping sound, so I paused on my way and took a look around. Next thing I know, there's the sound of three shots—one of them hits me in the shoulder—and down I go!"

Holmes held up a long finger to stop Lestrade for a moment.

"Three shots, Lestrade? Are you certain?"

"Yes, Mr. Holmes," Lestrade went on, "I know for sure there were three shots, for as I lay there bleeding, I remember thinkin' to myself that it must be an awful poor marksman that takes three shots to hit one man in a little courtyard! And he only hit my shoulder at that! If I were in his place, Holmes, I'd have aimed at my head!"

"As would I, Lestrade, as would I," said Holmes, in a way that made me chuckle, though I was not sure if Holmes had meant his remark to be humorous. "Watson and I shall return in several hours," Holmes told the inspector. "We shall make an examination of the scene where you were shot. We shall then return here, where I will doubtless have some questions for you to answer."

Holmes turned and left the room. I went close behind him, turning back to give some doctor's orders to Lestrade, it being my habit to bark such commands.

"Rest, Lestrade. Try not to tire yourself too much. Take care with your stitches."

❋ ❋ ❋

The Adventure of the Injured Inspector

Holmes and I reached the place that Lestrade had spoken of. It was just as he had described it; a round courtyard, hidden from the street by its placement behind two buildings which contained apartments. The courtyard could be seen from the rear windows of both buildings, both of which were three floors tall. The courtyard was nothing extravagant, just a round area with cobblestone paving, several trees off to the side. It looked like a good place for children to play or for the elderly to sit and read or play chess, out of doors but isolated from the bustling streets on the other side of those two buildings.

The courtyard, at the point when Holmes and I arrived, was far from as empty as it had been when Lestrade had been attacked. It was now positively crowded with activity; policemen looking over the place in a noisy, confused circus of constables trampling all over the place, probably foolishly demolishing any evidence which might have been there waiting for the attention of Holmes' thorough eyes.

Holmes let out a sigh and drew in a deep breath. When the direction of that intake of air was reversed and Holmes let it out, it was accompanied by an incredibly loud shout, the great detective's attempt at getting the attention of every man in that courtyard.

"Who is in charge of this pandemonium?"

At the sound of that voice, full to the top with intensity and authority, every policeman in that courtyard, uniformed constable and long-coated inspector alike, stopped what he was doing and turned to look at its source. They were all speechless for several seconds, until one lone voice broke the silence.

"That would be me, Mr. Holmes." It was Inspector Tobias Gregson, an inspector whom Holmes and I had worked with before, though not as often as we had found ourselves accompanied by Lestrade. Gregson was among the more intelligent of Scotland Yard's inspectors, which Holmes would say was not such a great accomplishment, but he did possess some skill in his profession. He was also a cold-hearted sort of man, not as jovial and likeable as Lestrade. Still, it was good to know that a man who had worked with us before had been placed in charge of the scene of Lestrade's assault. This could only serve to make the situation easier for Holmes and me.

"Inspector Gregson," said Holmes as the plainclothes policeman walked over to meet us, "I am surprised and sorely disappointed! I would have expected you to exert more control over your men than to have them wildly trampling all over this area, an area which doubtlessly contains...

or did contain…vital evidence! For the sake of justice and for the sake of our success in discovering who nearly killed your colleague, I demand that you clear this area!"

Gregson knew that Holmes was right. He loudly blew his whistle and waved the large contingent of men out of the immediate vicinity. Within a minute or two, only three of us remained; Holmes, Gregson, and myself.

"A few moments of peace, if you don't mind, Gregson," Holmes requested. "Watson and I shall examine the area." Gregson knew better than to argue with Holmes; he stepped to the side, found an upside down wooden crate, sat on it and lit a cigarette.

Holmes walked to the center of the circular courtyard. I went along, right beside him. We looked down at the spots of blood that had dried on the cobblestones.

"We know that the bullet struck the inspector in the front of his shoulder, Watson," said Holmes. "The bullet did not pass through, but remained in his shoulder until extracted by the surgeon. That would indicate that Lestrade was facing in this direction when he was struck." Holmes stood where Lestrade had stood, facing one overlooking building, and his back to the other.

"Inspector Gregson," Holmes called out to our Scotland Yard ally, "Have you determined where the other two bullets went? Lestrade recalled having heard three shots."

Gregson answered from his perch, hesitant to approach Holmes after the scolding he had received. "That's the peculiar thing, Holmes. The shot that hit him came from the direction you're facing, but another came from behind him! It looks as though the shot from behind sailed right over his head and struck the ground. It was not the same type of bullet as the one they dug from his shoulder either. We haven't yet located the third bullet."

Holmes spun around where he stood. He looked up at the windows of the building that had been behind him a moment before. He pointed up at one at one of the windows.

"Up there, Watson! That window has been shattered! Come!"

Holmes raced into the building. Gregson got up from his makeshift seat and followed Holmes, as did I. We made our way to the third floor of the building and into the room that had the shattered window.

The room was unoccupied. Inside, we found shattered glass upon the floor, accompanied by some drops of what appeared to be more dried blood. Holmes knelt down to examine the broken glass.

"Look, Watson, Gregson," announced Holmes, "the glass, when

"Look, Watson, Gregson, the glass, when shattered, fell into the room rather than out."

shattered, fell into the room rather than out. Clearly, this window was shattered from outside, perhaps by our missing third bullet. Note also how it was shattered when the window was partially open. The shot also appears to have struck the occupant of the room, although not injuring him seriously enough to prevent him from fleeing the scene!"

Holmes bent down again to examine the floor. "Judging by the layer of dust here, this room had been unoccupied for some time. Here the dust has been disturbed…and it appears that a large man's shoe was the disturbing force. So the shooter who fired from behind Lestrade was a large man, he is wounded, and his was not the bullet which punctured Lestrade's shoulder. Now we must inspect the building that looks down upon the courtyard from the other direction."

We made our way down to ground level again and crossed the courtyard. Holmes dispatched Gregson to inquire of the landlord which rooms were not presently rented. When he returned, it happened that there were three such rooms, but only one above the first floor, that one being on the third. We quickly made our way to that room.

Inside, we found a room that was empty, much like the first. This one was just as dusty, but contained no shattered glass and no blood. Holmes went over to the window, which was still partially open. He examined the sill.

"Here, Watson, we have a slight dent in the windowsill, a groove." He pressed down on the groove with a finger. When he lifted his finger, small particles of wood clung to it. "The bits of wood that came loose as the barrel of a gun was pressed down on the sill and fired have not yet been either blown away or moved aside when the sill was dusted. I believe this to indicate that the gun was fired from this window very recently. Note that the gun fired from the other window was not laid upon the window frame in this way. That may show that this shooter was not as strong as the other, perhaps smaller." He bent down to examine the floor. "Also, the footprint left in this room's dust is a smaller one, a slimmer one. The shoe that made it had a pointed toe. This shooter may very well have been a woman!"

"Ha!" laughed Tobias Gregson suddenly. "You mean to tell me that the great Lestrade was shot down by a woman? He'll never be allowed to forget that down at the Yard!"

A stern look from Sherlock Holmes made Gregson cease his bragging instantly.

"Inspector Gregson, I thank you for your assistance," said Holmes. "We shall be contacting you quite soon. Watson, let us return to the bedside of our fallen friend."

❋ ❋ ❋

As Holmes and I rode back to the hospital, he repeated what we had ascertained so far.

"Lestrade stood in that otherwise empty courtyard. Two separate people waited for him to arrive in that spot, one in each overlooking building, and each on the third floor of their respective buildings. The shooter in the building which Lestrade was facing, the woman, fired two shots, one of which struck Lestrade in the shoulder, and one of which shattered the window in the opposite building and struck the other shooter. The second shooter, in the building to Lestrade's back, was a man. He fired one bullet, which missed Lestrade entirely, striking the ground. He then fled the scene after being wounded by the shot that had also shattered the window in front of him, a window which was partially open to allow him to fire his sole shot."

"Incredible," said I. "Lestrade managed to survive despite having not one, but two people trying to kill him at the same time!"

"No, my dear Watson," said Sherlock Holmes. "I do not think that was what happened at all."

That remark certainly aroused considerable curiosity in me, but Holmes offered no elaboration. He simply sat back, closed his eyes, and fell silent for the rest of the ride.

❋ ❋ ❋

I soon found myself standing beside Holmes, looking down at Lestrade. The injured inspector was sitting in bed exactly as we had left him. He looked at us as we entered.

"You weren't gone long, Holmes. What did you discover?"

"Tell me, Lestrade," said Holmes, "how long have you been working undercover on your investigation under an assumed identity?"

Utter shock and dismay came over Lestrade's face. Had he not been in bed already, he surely would have fallen over.

"How'd you know about that, Holmes?" Lestrade asked, nearly shouting enough to rupture his sutures. "No one's supposed to know about that except for me and the superintendent of inspectors!"

"Yes, I thought as much," said Holmes calmly. "That is why I did not mention it in front of your fellow inspector, Gregson. By the way, Lestrade, you owe a somewhat unusual sort of debt of gratitude to the person who shot you. The one who fired the bullet that pierced your shoulder certainly did mean to injure you, but not to kill. In doing so, she also saved your life!"

Lestrade's look of shock grew even more amazed, to the point that it approached comical heights. "Just how much do you know, Holmes?" he asked.

"That, Lestrade remains to be seen," Holmes replied. "Let me relate what I think I have pieced together, and then you shall tell me how correct I am."

Lestrade nodded and Holmes began to relate his tale.

※ ※ ※

"At some point in the past two months, perhaps several weeks ago, perhaps more, your commanding officer at Scotland Yard asked you to participate in a certain investigation. Such an assignment would involve you assuming a false name and perhaps making use of a disguise of some sort. You would assume your alias and infiltrate one of London's criminal organizations, probably one that is run by a specific family. You would attempt to gain their trust and gain employment within the organization. Once you had firmly secured a position there, you would pass on information to your superior at The Yard.

"You did well in your assignment and soon came into the presence of the head of the organization itself. You gained his trust. You would spend much of your time in your disguise, while occasionally reverting to your true identity in order to visit Scotland Yard and pass information on to the superintendent.

"While in the company of this certain family of criminals, you managed to catch the eye of a certain young lady, probably the daughter or perhaps the niece of one of the members of the organization. You became entangled with this woman in what seemed to be turning in the direction of possible romance."

Lestrade's mouth was agape with surprise at Holmes' accuracy. Holmes continued.

"You thought you had safely concealed your true profession from those people you sought to bring to justice, but you had miscalculated. Something you did or said, some subtle hint which you inadvertently dropped alerted them to your presence as a spy among their kind. A member of the organization was dispatched to follow you, a surveillance which you failed to notice. This person saw that you tended to follow a particular route home after your visits to Scotland Yard. He made note of the quiet, concealed courtyard through which you often walked.

"Plans were made, Lestrade; plans for your assassination! A marksman would wait in the third floor window of one of the buildings that overlooked the courtyard. As you passed under his watchful eye, late in the evening on your journey home, you would be shot dead!

"However, another pair of ears caught word of this plan. Those ears belonged to the young lady with whom you were on the edge of a budding relationship. She experienced, at that point, two conflicting sets of emotions. On one hand, she was appalled and furious at the thought that you were a Scotland Yard spy and that any feelings you may have expressed for her were but a sham. On the other hand, she truly cared for you and could not bring herself to allow you to be killed. I must also assume that she had kept your relationship a secret from the older male relative who was part of this clique of crime.

"The night of the scheduled murder arrived. The appointed marksman took his place in the vacant third floor room. He waited for you to cross the courtyard, his weapon pointed out the window, just enough to take adequate aim, but not enough to be easily sighted from where you would pass.

"Across the courtyard, the young lady awaited, possessing a gun of her own. Because she knew what to look for, she could spot the position of the male shooter across the yard. I assume that she had grown up in this family of crime, for it is unlikely that a young woman who had not grown up in such an environment would know how to shoot so well. Still, despite her skill with guns, she was small, slight of figure, and had to lean the gun barrel on the window sill to take proper aim. Like her counterpart across the way, she waited for you to arrive on the scene.

"Shortly before ten o'clock on that fateful night, you were on your way home after reporting to your superior. Not expecting any danger, your guard was low and you were in a relaxed mood, perhaps quite tired. You took your usual route, including the shortcut through the courtyard. As you crossed the courtyard, the man high above you took aim, probably at your head, as he was a professional murderer with intent to kill.

"Across the courtyard, in the other window, your young lady saw the marksman's gun take aim. She doubted she would have time to shoot him before he fired at you, so she pulled her trigger, probably at almost precisely the same time as the man pulled his. If you recall the position in which you stood when you were shot, Lestrade, you will remember that you were several paces closer to the building in front of you than you were to the one behind. That placement is the sole reason why you still live.

"Recall, if you will, that I said that your young lady had very mixed emotions. She wanted you to live, but she was terribly angry at you. She satisfied both those emotions when she pulled her trigger. She hit your shoulder with her shot, wounding you, as she wanted to do, thus gaining a bit of revenge for your subterfuge. The impact with your shoulder knocked you down…just as the bullet from the male marksman whizzed over your descending head; the head which would have been shattered by hot lead had it not dropped at that very moment!

"The marksman was stunned by the fact that he had missed you…and by the fact that someone else was shooting at his target. Due to this shock, he pause momentarily, trying to get his bearings, trying to figure out what had just occurred. That was when your lady friend decided to take her second shot. She raised her gun and fired into the window across the way. The window's glass was shattered and the marksman shot, though not in a way that killed him. He was merely wounded and quickly fled the scene. The female shooter left her building at the same time, both snipers fleeing into the London night, leaving you prostrated on the cobblestone, bleeding but not fatally injured."

Lestrade was speechless, which was an unusual condition for him. After several moments of alternately shaking his head and nodding to himself, his ability to put thoughts into words came back to him.

"Well I'll be!" the shocked inspector muttered. "You put the whole thing together, Holmes, you certainly did! The person who shot me saved me from being killed by the person who didn't shoot me! Absurd, absurd, absurd! I'll tell you, Holmes, if I ever see that girl again I won't know whether to kiss her or wring her pretty little neck!"

※ ※ ※

One hour after our second visit to Lestrade's hospital bed, Holmes and I were seated in the office of Scotland Yard's Superintendent of Investigations, Sir Charles Richmond, an older gentleman, several years past standard retirement age, but showing not even the slightest signs of senility or frailty.

"I'd like to thank you, Mr. Holmes, for putting together the pieces of what happened to Inspector Lestrade. That being said, I have work that must be done now. Good day, Mr. Holmes, Dr. Watson."

"I beg your pardon, Sir Charles," said Sherlock Holmes, "but I believe that I may be of further assistance to you. I should like to see those responsible for Lestrade's injury brought to justice."

Sir Charles was not prepared to simply let Holmes proceed. "I have men who are perfectly qualified to continue this case where Lestrade left off…"

Holmes, never one to place too much importance on rank or position, interrupted the superintendent. "Sir Charles, it takes a great amount of skill and experience to infiltrate the more proficiently run crime syndicates of the London underworld. You have some well-trained detectives on your force, but they are sorely lacking in the requisite talents for a job such as this one. I am offering my services, Sir Charles. Accepting my offer may very well prevent another misfortune such as the one that has befallen Lestrade."

The debate continued for several more minutes as I sat in the corner, listening, waiting for the inevitable victory of Holmes. As I knew he would, Holmes eventually won the argument and Sir Charles agreed to let him enter the affair.

"It was the organization of Nathaniel Cross that Lestrade was involved with, Holmes. I'm not going to tell you much more than that; I'll leave you to your own devices. I truly hope I'm not making a mistake by allowing you to interfere in this matter."

Having accomplished our objective, Holmes and I left the office of Sir Charles and made our way back to Baker Street to make certain preparations.

※ ※ ※

I sat down to finish reading the newspaper that I had put down that morning after reading of Lestrade's injury. As I read, Holmes went into another room, from which he shouted to me to explain certain things about the matter in which we were now involved.

"If you are not familiar with the name, Watson, though you should be, Nathaniel Cross is the head of a large organization of those who participate in various criminal enterprises here in London. Smuggling, robbery, blackmail, and assorted other misdeeds can often be traced back to his orders. He rarely deals in murder, but I suppose Lestrade's intrusion into his business pushed him beyond some of his usual boundaries. Now that I know exactly who it is that Lestrade was dealing with, my task is made easier. I do, of course, know some of the details of Cross's life and organization. It should be no difficult task to find both Cross's daughter and the man who Cross ordered to kill Lestrade."

"Surely, Holmes," I shouted back to him, "you're not just going to go and ask Cross who the man was!"

"I certainly hope you don't take me for such a fool, Watson," said Holmes as he emerged back into my sight. Had I not known that it was indeed Sherlock Holmes reentering the room, I'd have thought a stranger were present. The man before me appeared to be about fifty pounds heavier than Holmes, although of approximately the same height. His hair was a lighter shade of brown than was Holmes' and he had several scars upon his face, one on his chin, one on his forehead, and one running down the length of his left cheek. His nose was somewhat more bulbous than that of Holmes.

This "stranger" walked over to one of the room's several cabinets, opened it, and took out a pistol, one which I had never seen Holmes use before.

"Watson, I shall, I hope, return here before morning. If I should fail to do so, please inform my brother Mycroft that I have encountered some difficulty. He has resources that I trust far more than those of Scotland Yard."

With that, Holmes, looking very much unlike himself, marched out of the room and down the stairs. Outside the window, dusk was beginning to settle over the city. I sat up and waited for him to return.

❋ ❋ ❋

It was nearly five o'clock in the morning when I heard Holmes' footsteps coming back up the stairs. I had dozed off once or twice, but had remained alert through most of the night. Holmes strode in; carefully placed the pistol back in its cabinet, then began transforming into himself again. He tore the padding from out of his shirt and trousers, tossed aside the false nose, and began to peel the artificial scars from his face. Once he was Holmes again, he sat down, looking somewhat tired, and lit his pipe.

"Well Holmes," I inquired, "did you succeed?"

"That I did, Watson, that I did," he assured me, and he launched into his rather dry retelling of what had transpired that night.

"The face you saw me wearing when I left here hours ago and when I returned just now is one that is not unknown in the London underworld. It is the face of one Billy Barlow, a man who is known to be what you might call a 'hired gun.' I have assumed that guise on several previous occasions, never resorting to violence, but building a reputation for such acts. Barlow's reputation is a sterling one in his gruesome profession; he is a man who criminals like Nathaniel Cross often employ, especially when they do not wish to sow seeds of discontent within their own organizations.

"Dressed as Billy Barlow, I went right to Cross. I made a claim of having heard that a certain underling of his had sorely disappointed him by failing to fulfill an assignment. I offered to, for a fee of course, make this man pay for his failure. By doing so I was able to learn the name of the man who had tried, and failed, to kill Lestrade. It was an easy matter to find out where this man had gone into hiding, fearing Cross's wrath. I found him, a man called Frazier. The wad of bandages that made a lump in his left sleeve confirmed that he was the man who had been wounded by the young lady's second shot.

"When Frazier saw me he flew into a panic, afraid that I, for he believed me to be Barlow, would kill him. With his injured arm, he would be unable to adequately defend himself. I did not kill him, obviously. Instead, I interrogated the man, gaining information that Nathaniel Cross would not have so willingly divulged, such as the likely location to which Cross's daughter, Helena, would have gone to avoid her father's anger at her interference in his planned assassination of Inspector Lestrade. Once I had what I wanted from Frazier, I placed him into the hands of Gregson, who I had summoned and left waiting outside.

"After seeing that Frazier had been properly apprehended, I turned my attention to finding Miss Helena Cross. Frazier's information proved to be accurate and I located Miss Cross at the home of an aunt, one who she trusted to refrain from revealing her whereabouts to her father Nathaniel until such time that his anger cooled. It was now growing late and the lamps in the downstairs portion of the home had been extinguished, I could tell from the windows.

"I had arranged for Gregson and two of his men to wait outside the house, carefully concealed amid some bushes. I then picked the house's locks and made my way inside. I crept up the stairs to the room where the girl was sleeping. I had determined that it was her room by the size and shape of her silhouette in the window, eliminating the possibility that her aunt occupied that room due to the fact that her aunt was quite obese.

"As quietly as possible, I went over to the girl's bed and placed my hand over her mouth, simultaneously waking her and assuring that she would not scream. To put it mildly, I scared her senseless, as she immediately assumed that I had been sent by her father to kill her.

"When I determined that I had frightened her sufficiently, I raised my arm in a previously agreed upon signal which Gregson could see through the window. At my signal, Gregson and his men beat down the door of the house, stormed in and 'rescued' the young lady. She all too willingly ran straight into Gregson's arms as his men 'arrested' me. After that, Watson, we all took a leisurely cab ride down to Scotland Yard. I was placed, for the sake of realism, into a holding cell while Miss Cross was taken into an interrogation room by Gregson, where she would soon meet our friend Sir Charles Richmond.

"Miss Cross was given a choice. She could stand trial for the charges that could easily be filed against her; she had, after all, put a bullet into a policeman! Her other option was to provide Scotland Yard with every piece of information she knew about her father's little empire of crime. In exchange for this cooperation, she would be given a certain, fairly generous sum of money, and sent to Australia, where she would be free to start a new life, under an assumed name, out from under the shadow of the family business. This part of the deal would be overseen by my brother, Mycroft.

"Miss Cross, not being an idiot, chose the second option. Once Sir Charles is satisfied that she had told them everything she knows, Mycroft will have her safely smuggled out of the country and off to new frontiers. I predict, Watson, that the next several weeks' newspapers will chronicle the gradual collapse of Nathaniel Cross's organization. The credit will, of course, be claimed by Sir Charles, Inspector Gregson, and various others at Scotland Yard."

The story told, Holmes leaned back in his chair and closed his eyes. I should have let him drift off to sleep, but I had an urge to make one further questioning comment.

"Holmes, does it never bother you to see others receive all the credit for your work? I know you won't accept Lestrade's offer of a month's worth of his pay and I doubt Sir Charles will reimburse you for your efforts."

"True, Watson, true," said Sherlock Holmes without opening his eyes, "But there shall come a day when we must ask a favour of either Lestrade or Sir Charles. I foresee them being a bit less hesitant on at least the next occasion."

❊ ❊ ❊

As Holmes had predicted, the newspapers were soon stuffed full of news of the end of the Cross criminal empire. The failed assassin, Frazier, was sent away for a long prison term. Various other lieutenants of Cross's were arrested and tried for assorted offences. Nathaniel Cross tried to flee by sea, but was stopped at the docks by a fully recovered Inspector Lestrade. Cross was eventually convicted of a long list of wrongdoings. His jail term was shortened considerably by a sudden, fatal stroke.

At some point, Helena Cross must have learned who that scar-faced man in her bedroom had really been, for two years later we received a letter from Australia. It was a wedding invitation, of all things, from a bride whose name we did not recognize. We declined the invitation, but passed on the other enclosed message, an apology from the young lady, and the hope that Lestrade's shoulder had not developed a tendency to ache when the weather was bad.

AARON SMITH – a veteran writer of mysteries and pulp fiction, has written stories featuring such characters as Sherlock Holmes, Dan Fowler: G-Man, Wild Bill Hickok, the Three Mosquitoes, and the Black Bat. He is (as far as he's been able to find out) the first author to write a novel featuring Doctor John Watson without Sherlock Holmes (*Season of Madness*). He holds a position as a staff writer for the Pro Se Productions line of pulp magazines. He has also written a science-fantasy novel, *Gods and Galaxies*. Characters created by Smith include Hound-Dog Harker, the Red Veil, and Detective Lieutenant Marcel Picard.

Aaron Smith counts among his biggest influences as a writer Sir Arthur Conan Doyle, Roger Zelazny, JRR Tolkein, HP Lovecraft, Stan Lee (and all his collaborators), Bram Stoker, Gene Roddenberry, Ian Fleming, and many others.

He is currently working on a long horror novel that will probably offend as many people as it entertains.

Sherlock Holmes
Consulting Detective

"The Adventure of the Towne Manor Haunting"

by
Andrew Salmon

Never let it be said that the journey along the Gravesend road out of the village of Upper Higham is not without its distractions. As I was scrutinizing a profusion of wild flowers from the wagonette this drowsy summer afternoon in early July of the year 1887, the gentle stillness was shattered by a piercing shriek. I threw my head about in search of the source of the exclamation but none revealed itself to me. The shriek was repeated at the same instant an arched gate appeared ahead on the left. A path stretched under the arch, and I observed that it led to a rather modest though no less ostentatious estate of striking white gables, slanting tiled roofs and clapboard porticos with a widow's walk dominating all. The presence of a halted ramshackle wagon heaped with all manor of foul-smelling detritus and a sagging mare feasting on the mid-summer grasses beside the gate offset the otherwise immaculate scene of rolling hills and wild flowers bowing their heads against the light breeze.

"Thief!" sounded the shriek a third time. In this instant so close as to compel the driver to bring his horses up short. The wagonette jerked to a halt close to the gate. I turned and gazed along the length of the path towards the house. To my surprise I spotted a most singular shape shambling down the path towards us. A rotund, aproned cook gave chase with surprising agility, exposing linen turned the colour of old bone by wear. As this strange scene played itself out before me, I concluded that the shrouded, grotesque, hulking figure would reach the offensive wagon and make good his escape before the waddling maid could gain ground.

I sprang off my seat and blocked the entrance to the estate grounds which proclaimed in weathered iron the family name of Towne. Here I paused to beckon the driver to join me in preventing the shambling flight of the fleeing figure but he was having none of it. I dashed through the gate alone, placing myself between the wagon and the approaching figure. As it neared, I could make out nothing of its features or form. It was cloaked, head to toe, in what appeared to be soiled burlap. The size of the figure gave me thoughts of my revolver but the rapid staggering gait of the fugitive seemed somehow lacking in menace thus I was confident I could restrain the figure until help arrived.

Suddenly the figure bounded over my head as I attempted to encircle it with my outstretched arms. So smoothly was this leap accomplished that I scarcely heard the faint impact of the form behind me. I whirled to see the

"Thief!" sounded the shriek a third time.

cloaked figure hop up into the wagon, seize the reins and, with a coarse click in its throat, spur the mare into a canter. The wagon rolled away at a good clip. I took two steps in the direction of the road so intent on taking up pursuit of the dwindling wagon that I did not, at first, notice that my driver and the conveyance from which he derived his title, were receding in the opposite direction. Having no stomach for a fight, the man had tossed down my bags and deserted me.

By this time the maid, panting like a steamer, was beside me, thrusting her red face in mine accusingly.

"You let 'im get away!" she bellowed.

"Not through lack of effort, ma'am," I countered.

She gazed at me sidewise. "If I'd not seen yer come in that wagon, I'd think yer was in league with that vagabond!"

"As I am not native to the region I can hardly lay claim to any acquaintance with its inhabitants."

She eyed me suspiciously. "Might I have yer name, sir?"

"It's Watson. Dr. John H. Watson."

A great smile suddenly split her crimson visage. "Bless me! It is! Dr. Watson hisself! Them pictures they put with yer stories don't do yer justice. That said, they must catch yer right enough for me to recognize yer."

Grinning from ear to ear, she slid an arm plump and round as a salami in mine and guided me up to the house, talking a mile a minute. From this monologue I gleaned that the scene which had just played out was not uncommon here at Towne Manor and this served to confirm that I had, indeed, reached my destination. My presence there on that sweltering July afternoon could be attributed to my good friend, Mr. Sherlock Holmes, from whom I'd received the following missive the previous morning:

Watson,

We have work. I have learned from one Donald Towne, a traveling companion here in France, that Towne Manor in Higham requires our attention. Look into it. The master of the house, and I, shall join you in two days time.

S. H.

The absence of details in the note was deliberate but only to the extent that I approach the case free from any preconceived notions save that a mystery was afoot that had so captivated Holmes as to inspire the letter now resting in my pocket.

"What was all that about?" I asked, when the cook paused for breath.

"The devil!" she fairly shrieked. "That hulk's been skulkin' round for years, digging up the vegetables or messin' the bins about for scraps."

I soon ascertained that her name was Patricia Grant and she'd been employed as a cook at Towne Manor these last three years. I gleaned nothing further for the moment as Mrs. Grant recovered herself sufficiently to recommence interrogating me.

"Why, Dr. Watson!" she exclaimed as though just becoming aware of my presence. Her large hazel eyes widened comically. "What brings you to Towne Manor? Surely not the haunting!"

We stepped into the kitchen and I was struck by the haste she employed in locking the door.

"I received a message from Sherlock Holmes, instructing me to pay a call here at the request of your master. The two have struck up a friendship while abroad and Holmes will be accompanying Mr. Towne here upon his return. As I understand it, I am to await their imminent arrival."

"Sherlock Holmes! Coming here?"

I nodded in the affirmative.

The news flustered Mrs. Grant no end and she pulled and smoothed her dress as if Holmes were presently coming up the path. As the afternoon was waning and Holmes had asked me here to work, it was time to begin my investigation.

"I am sure this haunting you mentioned would be of great interest to him," I began. "I should like to provide him with some details about it upon his arrival."

Her primping ceased instantly and the care lines barely discernible in her moon face suddenly etched more deeply into the soft flesh and rheumy green eyes.

"It's 'orrible, Doctor! And there's no doubt. If the master had not saved the life of my dear departed Harry, I should have packed up and left long ago. But I pays my debts, Doctor, and here I stay."

My heart went out to the woman upon hearing the anguish in her tone, but, at last, we were on to something. "If it is not too unpleasant for you, I would ask you to give me the history of the haunting."

She agreed with some hesitation and I learned that Donald Towne was a widower and that his beloved wife, Evelyn Towne, formerly Lady Evelyn Howard, had succumbed to an overdose of laudanum within these very walls not six months ago and that, in his grief, Towne had taken to journeying abroad. Jewels and other valuables had also gone missing over the years, leading up to and proceeding Lady Towne's passing. At first believed to be the work of servants with sticky fingers or of that wretched, thieving brute, Mr. Towne had fortified the house, installing stout locks and barred windows more suited to a prison than a country estate. Yet with all these precautions, the thefts continued unabated. No witnesses, no suspects – only a parade of dismissed servants branded as thieves before being ordered off the premises. Not one of the stolen items had ever been recovered. This explanation shed some light on Holmes's interest and I determined to retrieve the gauntlet my friend had thrown down and solve this baffling case before he arrived.

"I dare say this is a most singular situation. I wonder if I might have a tour of the manor and grounds," said I.

"Yer needs Jakes fer that!" Mrs. Grant explained. "Perhaps e's outside with ol' Perkele, the gardener, searching the grounds in vain fer the hooded thief. 'Ave a look for 'im, if you please. If you don't find 'im, give a knock. Otherwise, Jakes has the keys."

I inclined my head in thanks and stepped out into the summer heat. My brief exposure to the kitchen had been one of cloying stuffiness, a shut up, oppressive air quickly alleviated by the country air outside. The door closed behind me and I heard the bolts shot home. I sought the elusive Jakes.

I chose a circuitous route around the house in order to examine the grounds privately. The search yielded nothing of interest save for the presence of stout iron bars on all the windows. A low hill dotted with the odd cottage here and there faced the serpentine road from the village. The rears of these homes looked down on Towne Manor, the grounds of which were substantial. Stands of trees and grass meadows stretched to a property line etched by a distant fence overhung with swaying branches from tall bordering oaks.

My course brought me to the rear of the manor and I beheld a kitchen garden set some distance from the house partially shaded by a large willow tree. Beneath said tree two men made a half-hearted show of examining a portion of the garden. One was of average height with short black hair and chiselled features and held himself with a singular rigidity as though standing at attention. The other wore overalls and a wide straw hat under which I beheld a somewhat satanic visage emphasized by the remains of a jet black goatee that was growing out and deeply sunburned skin. I called out to them and received scowls by way of reply. A stranger suddenly come upon them after what had just transpired no doubt coloured their reaction until they realized how unlikely it was that I was the bandit whose work they had been examining. I introduced myself and learned that the shabbily attired man was named Timothy Perkele and the other was the man Mrs. Grant had sent me looking for, David Jakes. Jakes sent Perkele back to his gardening duties, then turned his deep set, discerning blue eyes on me. I explained how I came to be there before turning the conversation back to the matter at hand.

"I'll have that thief one of these days," said Jakes, venomously. "Look at his handiwork."

We bent to examine the garden patch and saw where carrots had been torn from the ground. Tomato plants also lay broken and crushed into the loamy earth. Turning my gaze back to the house from this spot, I noticed that the view of the manor was obscured by the overhanging branches of the willow and therefore this section of the garden was also invisible from the house. The cunning thief had exploited this blind spot.

"Have you considered pruning back these branches or allowing this section of the garden to lie fallow?"

"Of course!" he responded with some ire. "Master won't permit it. It's the missus, you see. May she rest in peace." Jakes gazed up at the swaying branches. "This was her favourite tree. See that bench?" Here he moved stiffly to one side to reveal an off white stone bench behind him. It was placed near the trunk of the tree and had clearly not been used for some time. Moss grew up the sides of it and the seat was carpeted with dead leaves. "Quite devoted to Lady Towne he was and her passing hit him hard."

We returned to the house. Jakes had a stout, iron ring of keys in his pocket and used one to open the door to the sun porch. He closed and locked the door, then reached up awkwardly to trip a switch near the upper hinge.

"If you don't mind my asking, what are you doing there?"

"The Master ordered bells installed on all the doors and windows. I set them with a trip wire and if anyone tries to open the door, the wire goes with the bells not far behind. I disarmed this one when Patty hollered and exited to render aid."

I inquired if I might have a demonstration. Jakes opened the door and this action set off a terrible clanging of bells over the door. Jakes silenced the racket and reset the switch.

"And this security measure has been in place since the thefts began?"

Jakes indicated that it had, leaving me at a loss to hazard a guess as to how the thefts were pulled off. Reluctantly I stepped back into the stale air and Jakes closed and locked the door behind us. The only breath of fresh air entered by way of the tiny cracks around a small hinged panel at the base of the door. It was some seven or eight inches high and perhaps six inches wide. I was about to ask Jakes about it when Mrs. Grant appeared to inform us that the maid had taken my bags upstairs and a room had been prepared for me while dinner was on the stove. All but gagging on the fetid air, I thanked Mrs. Grant and followed Jakes along a narrow, panelled corridor to the living room and the bedroom stairs beyond that.

My room prepared, I took my leave of Jakes, advising him of my desire to freshen up after the road and that, upon completing my ablutions, I should like a tour of the house and, of course, would very much like to hear about the supposed haunting. Alone in my chamber, I sat down to quickly jot some notes concerning what information I had gathered since my arrival. I stepped out and spied Jakes coming out of a bedroom at the opposite end of the hall.

"Is everything satisfactory, Doctor?"

"I shall be most comfortable. Although I must admit to it being a bit close in the house."

Jakes nodded with resignation. "I do beg your pardon for that. It's master's orders that the place be shut up at all times. There are small air shafts cut here and there and, as the nights can be chilly, you'll find the place cools off for sleeping. Periodically the maid opens doors to change the air. If you still want that tour, I'll tell you how Towne Manor came to be shut up as we walk."

For the sake of brevity, I shall summarize the tale related to me by Jakes as he showed me the house:

Through shrewd business dealings, Donald Towne had elevated himself in society and met Lady Evelyn Howard – one of two living heirs to the now defunct Howard ship building concern. Immediately smitten with the young lady, Towne eventually won his heart's desire, purchasing the manor and furnishing it before bringing his new bride home with the hopes of starting a family. Jakes was particularly vague in some of the details of Towne's early life and the whirlwind romance which culminated in the death of Evelyn Towne six months previous to my being there. The omissions were telling in their absence but, for the moment, I was content not to press the matter.

The tour of the house was illuminating in itself. The shut up rooms, although decorated tastefully and hung with art selected by a keen eye, seemed steeped in melancholy and shadow. The entire house needed airing out and I suspect the men and women trapped within its walls might also do with some fresh air – both in the physical and metaphoric meanings of the term. Every window was double-locked with crisscrossed bars across it, the exits were of strong oak and festooned with bolts like a dungeon. I learned from Jakes that every door and window was to be checked and double-checked before the house retired for the evening and no one was allowed outside after dark for any reason – these measures were in addition to the bells Jakes had demonstrated. The indisputable testaments to the security of the house strengthened the haunting claptrap prevalent amongst the inhabitants of the region. How else were the thefts pulled off? What stranger could bypass the alarm from outside? How could the thefts continue unabated for years with no one living in the house, ever seeing anything untoward? It was clear that no one could come and go without tripping the alarm. No one that is, save Jakes.

These considerations ran through my thoughts as we headed upstairs to inspect the upper chambers. There was the master's bedroom in which Lady Towne had passed, several nondescript guestrooms, Jakes quarters, two sitting rooms and a billiard room, all of which were as barred and sealed as the rest of the house. One door next to the master bedchamber had escaped Jakes's notice, whether deliberately or not, I could not say. At my request, Jakes opened the door then stood stiffly to one side as I entered. The room was of substantial size, decorated with pink frills and lace, which culminated in a lavishly decorated crib with satin sheets. The room was meant as a suite for a little girl – the child the Townes would never have. The defining feature was a veritable battalion of dolls. There were dozens, if not hundreds, of the things sprawled on the crib, packed on to the wall shelves and perched eerily on the little white rocker decorated with pink horses heads.

"The master had wanted a daughter and he created here what he thought was a proper room in which a girl could grow into womanhood."

"How sad."

"The master comes and sits in here when the mood is upon him."

The abandoned nursery was unnerving in the shadow of late afternoon and the eyes of the doll army glistened, seemingly following us about the room. Eager to quit the place, I turned and noticed another of those small, hinged flaps at the base of the door. As this one was only the latest in several I'd seen so far, I took this opportunity to raise the matter with Jakes.

"Of what use are these tiny doors?" I asked, indicating the panel to Jakes.

"The master had them cut out for Rascal."

"And who might Rascal be?"

"He was the missus's cat, Doctor."

"I see. Then this flap, like the others scattered all over the house, permitted the cat to come and go as it pleased?"

"That is correct."

"Where is Rascal now? I've seen no cat on our tour."

"Dead. The cat was found poisoned three days later after we came here."

"I see. Has this, too, been attributed to the Towne Manor ghost?"

Jakes paused before answering. "I don't know what to think anymore. At first I believed it to be the work of a thieving domestic prompted by motivations of malice."

"And now?"

"And now, Doctor, the missus is dead and a pall hangs over us all. The thefts continue though the house is shut up like a gaol and the remaining staff are utterly loyal to Mr. Towne. In plain, truth, if it's not a ghost, I'm at a loss to furnish an alternative."

At this point, the maid joined us outside the nursery with news that dinner was ready. We went down to dine and the rest of the evening consisted of a fine meal, good cognac and cigars enjoyed between fielding questions concerning the adventures of Sherlock Holmes and the miracles they might hope to expect when he arrived. These I answered as best I could before retiring early to bed on the claim of weariness from the road.

I did not sleep, however. First I recorded the scant details Jakes had provided concerning the history of Towne Manor in my notebook. The work finished, I sat ruminating on the strange mystery before me.

Who was behind the thefts? Why had Towne Manor been selected for these tragedies? Was it fate? Or chance? A curse? Perhaps it all came down to crooked staff members who threw the objects out a window to a waiting accomplice. Perhaps it was Jakes himself as he had the keys. The staff struck me as beyond suspicion however, ruling out this half-baked theory. Could it have been Mrs. Grant or the maid quitting the grounds under the ruse of running errands, their pockets stuffed with stolen finery? This, too, seemed improbable unless my conclusions about the staff were completely wrong. My eyes grew heavy, my thoughts muddled and I took myself to bed. Having invoked the name of my dear friend over dinner, I fervently wished Holmes was present that I might learn what his considerable intellect made of it all. I doused the light and settled in for sleep.

I awoke to some commotion the next morning. The tread of feet upon the stairs and quick, hushed voices reached me where I lay. Jumping from the bed I dressed quickly and stepped into the hallway to see what was the matter.

"There has been another theft," said Jakes simply.

I followed him into the master bedroom where the maid, a dark-haired waif, sat crying softly at a side table. Jakes proceeded directly to the preserved dressing table of Lady Towne. There he placed his hand on an oblong wooden box. The box was a foot high and looked to be a foot and a half long. The wood had been polished to a high lustre. There was a keyhole at the centre point on one side.

"Last night," recounted Jakes, "someone entered this room, opened this jewel box and made off with two pairs of black pearl earrings."

Recalling the bastion-like state of the manor, this seemed extraordinary. "Has a search of the house been conducted? Perhaps the thief left some evidence behind."

"All of the doors and windows remain locked. The bells have not been tripped on a single exit."

"Incredible!"

Well versed in Holmes's methods, I launched a fact gathering campaign upon the spot. "If you could please relate to me precisely what transpired."

"For all the good it will do," said Jakes, shaking his head in disbelief. "Miss Duval, here," he indicated the maid, "entered this room as she does each morning in her daily routine. She dusts and makes up the bed when Master Towne is at home. She is also to open missus's jewelry box to ensure that nothing is missing and to polish those items that need it. She opened the box – "

Seeing the state of the poor girl, I asked, "Is the girl capable of relating what happened next?"

The maid looked up at me expectantly. She nodded quickly.

"You are sure you're up to it?" Jakes asked and received another quick nod.

I learned that her full name was Kelly Duval and she was of French descent, then continued with the matter at hand. "Now Miss Duval, was anything amiss when you entered the room?"

"N-Non, sir. It was as when I come yesterday."
"Nothing out of place?"
"Non."
"The box was locked?"
"Oui."
"Who has the key?"
"I do, Docteur."
"It is the only key," Jakes added. "She wears it about her neck, removing it only to sleep."
"Under my pillow, I keep it," added Miss Duval.
"That is where you found it this morning?" I asked.
She nodded with some vigour.
I glanced about. "Is anything else missing?"
Here Miss Duval sprang up and looked over the dressing table of Mrs. Towne. Her manner indicated that she was confirming, for my benefit, what she already knew. Namely, that nothing else had been taken. She shook her head meekly, her large brown eyes brimming with fresh tears and resumed her seat.
"Thank you, my dear." I turned to Jakes who told the poor girl she could leave. She exited with only the faintest rustle of her house dress. When Jakes and I were alone, I resumed the investigation. "Have we reason to suspect her?"
"Kelly Duval grew up under the Master's care," said Jakes. "Her father was a good friend to the Mr. Towne. The man was a trapeze artist in Paris. That was where they met. He fell to his death when Kelly was but a toddler. As her mother had died in child birth, Master brought the girl to England to live with him before he settled here at Towne Manor."
"Very noble. They get on well?"
"Reasonably so. Master views the arrangement as an obligation to a friend rather than any paternal impulses. There has been no trouble from the girl and she harbors the greatest respect and gratitude towards him. Her tears were for Master's well being, I suspect. This has been a trying time."
As this avenue of inquiry seemed blocked, I chose to set it aside in order to inspect the grounds. I indicated this to Jakes who accompanied me to the main door, disarmed the alarm, and opened it. We stepped out into the morning air, humid with the rain which had fallen in the night. I tested the grass bordering the walking path with the toe of my boot and the earth yielded readily. Perhaps the thief in his flight had left tracks.

Jakes re-locked the door and we made a circuit of the grounds. My hopes for telltale footprints were soon dashed as not a single track we uncovered. The path skirting the manor was shale, which does not take impressions even when wet. However the path up from the front gate was earthen and might yield something of interest. An inspection revealed the muddy conditions I had hoped for, but no footprints. Somehow the thief had trespassed onto the grounds, entered the house without tripping a bell, stole to Mrs. Towne dressing table and removed two pairs of earrings from a locked jewelry box, then extricated himself leaving no evidence behind. How was this done? The foolishness of a ghost within the walls of the house began to seem more and more possible to me and I wished Holmes was here to make some sense of it all.

Jakes strode towards the gate in the vain hopes of discovering something of use, while my thoughts carried me off the trail and into the trees, grasping at explanations for this strange mystery. It was while we were so situated that a mail wagon rattled up the road. I could just make out the thing through the intervening branches. The driver hauled back on the reins and the wagon stopped at the gate. From my concealed vantage point, I saw the mailman doff his hat to Jakes and bid him good morning. These pleasantries, however, were cut short for there was a man sitting next to the postman and the black scowl on his fleshy features, along with gnarly-fingered hands clasping bony knees, revealed his agitation and anger. He raised one of the crab-like appendages and stabbed a knobby finger at Jakes.

"I'll have a word with you, sir!" he spat in a gravely voice.

Jakes cast his gaze about and I realized he was ascertaining if I was in earshot. I ducked down behind a rhododendron bush.

"I've got money coming to me!" the man continued. "And I'll have it from you if that mealy-mouthed master of yours can't pay what he owes!"

"Master Towne is not at home, Bradbury," said Jakes by way of reply.

"Fitting! And maybe you've convinced his creditors in the village of that." I peered through the branches and saw Bradbury withdraw a fist full of telegrams. He shook them at Jakes. "Or maybe you haven't! If these are any judge."

"You are close to a thrashing, sir," said Jakes, through clenched teeth, his already stiff, awkward posture even straighter. "I have no money to give you. You may settle up with Master Towne when he returns. Now give me the telegrams at once or I'll have them by force."

Such vehemence from Jakes was startling as I'd had found him to be of a more sublime nature. His response astonished the telegraph officer as well who leaned back on the bench, finally at a loss for words. The postman sheepishly handed the regular mail to Jakes who never took his eyes off Bradbury clutching the telegrams. Seconds ticked by, then the man blew air out of his blubbery lips and flung the telegrams at the feet of Jakes.

"I'll even up with this house," Bradbury vowed, jabbing a thumb at Jakes. "Mark my words."

With that the wagon trundled off. Only when it was out of sight did Jakes stoop to retrieve the scattered missives, which he thrust into the inside pocket of his coat. As he turned back to the house, I spied one telegram that had become separated from the rest, landing beneath the bush I crouched behind. As Jakes would be searching for me, I had scant seconds in which to act. I thrust my hand through the branches and seized the envelope. I tucked it into a pocket and trotted towards the spot where Jakes and I had parted company, hoping all the while that the trees obscured what I was doing. There was a bend in the path to the house. I chose this moment to step out from the trees and call to him. He whirled to face me as I caught him up.

"I had the fool notion that the thief might be using the tree branches as a means of escape," said I. "I must be getting soft in the head."

Jakes seemed to take some comfort in my presence and relaxed his stiff posture a fraction. He sighed. "Don't trouble yourself, Doctor, We at Towne Manor have had years in which to consider and have attained the same results as you."

"A good breakfast will set us right, I dare say."

He nodded and we headed up the path together. I had already decided that I would make no direct mention of what had transpired at the gate, allowing him to raise the topic. Although a little prodding might prove necessary. On a quiet country road, sound travels and I did not want to arouse suspicion by not saying anything about what had happened.

"I thought I heard voices a few minutes ago but could not make out what was said. Are there visitors to Towne Manor?"

He paused before replying. "No. It was the post."

The dining room was a scene of tense silence as the breakfast was served. The pall so prevalent over the house seemed heavier in light of the latest robbery. Jakes was lost in thought throughout and my mind harkened back to the confrontation at the gate. Jakes did mention, towards the end of the meal, his intention to head into the village to report the stolen earrings as they were worth some £200 a pair and a claim must be made for insurance purposes.

The meal completed, I retired to my room while Jakes sought Perkele so that the wagon could be prepared for the journey into the village. I turned my attention to the telegram I had recovered. The envelope has been dampened from its brief contact with the wet grass and the sealing glue had weakened. I carefully opened it and read the contents. The telegram was from the insurance firm of Saylor and Wallace and concerned an outstanding premium of £30 payable immediately under threat of revoking the policy. Here was concrete evidence to back up the telegraph officer's claims that the house of Towne was hard up. The number of telegrams the man had hurled at Jakes set me to wondering if most, if not all, of them were from bill collectors. Jakes's desire to keep the incident from me was perfectly understandable on the surface as he wished to preserve his master's privacy, But was there more to his secrecy? Was Towne Manor on the verge of financial ruin? Had the thefts been engineered from within as a way to cash in on the insurance payout? This last caused me some uncertainty as Towne could merely sell what valuable items were in his possession for ready cash. Unless, by orchestrating the thefts for insurance purposes, Towne was claiming the insurance while also arranging to sell the purloined items as well – doubling the capital for each piece. To this thought I added Jakes's run of the house, the keys in his possession and the duty of arming the bells, and suddenly I was possessed of a burning desire to accompany him to the village.

Quickly I folded the sheet and returned it to the envelope. I sprang out of my chair and seized up my medical bag. From it I removed a vial of spirit gum and used a portion to reseal the envelope. Jakes was outside and might leave at any moment, thus I threw on my jacket and slid out of the room, the sealed envelope in my pocket. On tip-toes, I proceeded to the study of Donald Towne where, sure enough, the telegrams were amongst the mail Jakes had left for his master's attention upon his return. I added the telegram to this pile. Beating a hasty, silent retreat, I hurried downstairs in the hopes of catching Jakes before he departed.

To my relief I found him outside where he was finishing with the team. I asked if I might accompany him to the village as I had letters to post. I watched him carefully to read his reaction to a travelling companion but he did not seem disturbed at the idea. The team harnessed, I swung aboard and we were off.

Some time passed on the road during which we had only our innermost thoughts to occupy us. The breeze warred with the heinous sun for our comfort until we ran into a stretch of road shaded by tall trees casting cool, dark shadows.

"Is this trip not premature?" I asked at last as we turned off Gravesend Road onto Telegraph Hill. "After all, it will be necessary to return tomorrow to retrieve your master and Sherlock Holmes. Surely filing the claim could wait until then."

Jakes nodded, glancing to his left at Gad's Hill Place, the final home of the late, venerable author Charles Dickens, just visible through the swaying trees. "Master has ordered the thefts be reported immediately and here we are."

"He strikes me a most singular fellow. I am looking forward to meeting him. Perhaps you can provide me some insight into his character."

"Well, he looks after himself."

"Have you worked for him long?"

"All my life."

"Really?"

"I never knew my parents. Mr. Towne took me in, gave me work."

"Much like he did with Miss Duval, then."

"Yes, Doctor. Life has not been easy for Mr. Towne, and he wished no ill on those what suffered along with himself."

Ah, here was my first glimpse past the armour Jakes had surrounded his master in with regards to the past. I groped for a subtle question to mine deeper this vein, but in my moment of silence, Jakes asked me about Holmes, who was as much a stranger to him as Towne to myself. I was obliged to answer. Unfortunately this topic carried us from St. John's road past the soaring steeple of the church to School Lane and into Lower Higham and I was unable to return the conversation back to Donald Towne. Up a wooded side street, we rolled until Jakes pulled the team to a halt outside a small red brick building.

"After I have reported the theft and filed claim," said Jakes, "we'll swing round the train station and see about the arrival time from London for Master Towne and Mr. Holmes. Will that be all right?"

I gave my consent and we climbed down. Jakes and I entered the office of the local constable. The sergeant recorded the details in a perfunctory manner, presented Jakes with a copy of the form duly notarized and we were back on the street in ten minutes. From there we walked three doors down to the offices of Saylor and Wallace. Jakes went inside while I remained outside. I had not seen much of the village upon my arrival thus

"He strikes me a most singular fellow. I am looking forward to meeting Mr. Towne."

I took a moment to drink in the lush greenness of the place. Mosquitoes from the marsh hungered for my blood as I gazed around at the narrow streets with the odd wagon trundling past, the quaint brick buildings with roofs of straw and wood here and there. Jakes joined me on the street a moment later and we climbed aboard the wagonette.

"In all these years, the police have turned up nothing?" I asked when we were underway.

"It's a dead end to them, I'm afraid," said Jakes, scowling. "They have hauled in what unsavoury characters the village possesses but no charges have stuck, no suspicions realized."

Fixing my eyes on Jakes lest I miss some subtle expression play across his features, I said, "Surely the thief must be local. He must have criminal connections through which he converts what he steals into cash. Perhaps we might inquire in some of the shadier corners of the village. If you could direct us – "

Jakes stiffened proudly, his chin defiant. "I have no clue, Doctor. Now, please, let us check the railroad timetable and be on our way."

"I meant no offence, sir. My thinking was merely that in a village of this size, there would be few, if any, secrets and that you would be aware of what seedy hangouts there might be about."

By this time we had come down the gentle hill leading to the small clapboard train station where the ticket agent confirmed the arrival of the express from London at 6:50 the next morning. As we exited, I heard the distant shriek of a locomotive whistle. I turned to Jakes, my eyebrows raised questioningly.

"Has to be the London freight," he replied to my silent query.

The train was screeching to a halt as we went round to where the horses were tethered. Jakes worked loose the knot, then we both climbed aboard. Our route took us past the station entrance and I saw the thick plume of black smoke from the train's stack rising above the station. A sudden downdraft and the cloud shrouded the station, making us turn our heads against the noxious fumes. It lifted and we faced forward, much relieved. To my shock and disbelief, a familiar figure stood framed in the doorway, just visible through the dissipating smoke.

"Why, it's Holmes!" I blurted.

"What's that?" asked Jakes.

"Sherlock Holmes, as I live and breathe." I jabbed a finger at the station. By this time Holmes had been joined by another man.

"And that's Master Towne," said Jakes.

They made a singular duo coming down the station steps. Towne was dressed in a conservative charcoal travelling suit. He was a tall, slightly stooped man with sharp features and close-cropped iron-grey hair. He held a black top hat in one hand and placed it on his head as they reached the bottom of the steps. Curiosity would normally have fixed my gaze on Towne, however travel had done much to alter the appearance of Holmes. My friend was draped, head to toe, in bright Burberry tartan, which took the form of a deerstalker cap with the ear flaps buttoned on top and a great duster. Such a sight was Holmes that many a head turned to stare in his direction and he fairly withered from the attention his attire garnered.

Chuckling at my friend's obvious discomfort, I waved my hand. "Here, Holmes!"

He heard me and strode to the wagonette with his customary long stride. Towne, seeing my friend's target, recognized Jakes and brought up the rear.

"Dear Watson!" Holmes cried. "You are a saviour." He turned to my travelling companion. "David Jakes, I presume? Permission to come aboard?"

Jakes nodded, his eyes on Towne who greeted his servant coldly. I quitted my post to allow Towne to sit up front and joined Holmes hunkered down in the back after taking the hand of Towne in greeting. Towne inclined his head to Jakes who took his meaning and the wagonette resumed its course. We soon left Lower Higham behind us.

"I am most delighted to see you both," said I. "But what are you doing here a full day ahead of schedule? Has something happened?"

"Put it down to good fortune," said Holmes. "We hit London and learned of the freight proceeding to Higham within the hour. It seemed logical to forgo the comforts of a passenger coach to save a day wasted knocking about the city."

"Mr. Holmes can be most persuasive," added Towne, flippantly, though the look in his eyes as he turned back indicated that he did not share Holmes's offhand dismissal of creature comforts.

Immediately upon our departure, Sherlock Holmes set to prattling on about his time abroad in a most uncharacteristic fashion. I took his meaning and knew with utmost certainty that Holmes sought to avoid any discussion of the case until such time as we were afforded privacy for candid disclosure. Playing along, I found myself expressing profound interest in the Parisian weather and the best tourist lodgings and restaurants. After some thirty minutes of this nonsense, we found the wagonette pausing at the border of the Towne property while Jakes hopped down to open the gate.

We stopped at the front door of the manor and dismounted. A slight restraining hand from Holmes on my arm kept me from following Towne and Jakes up the path.

"Pray, let us hang back," said Holmes sotto voce. "I should like to see how Towne is received by his staff."

Holmes made a show of re-adjusting his colourful garb which had become twisted while reclining in the rear of the wagonette. I lagged in handing him his traveling case. Our companions were at the door, a key in Jakes's fist. Holmes kept his eyes riveted on the door as we continued our charade lest they glance back.

"You seem to have done well for yourself in the finer shops of Paris," said I, not being able to resist poking fun at Holmes's travelling attire.

"Pshaw, Watson!" Holmes replied, his eyes never leaving the door. "I had the great misfortune of rendering aid to a Parisian official who had misplaced spectacles vital to a soiree that very night. Once the spectacles were found, he insisted on bestowing on me this country outfit by way of thanks. I believe his idea was that a consulting detective was a hunter of men and should be so attired."

"What possessed you to wear it?" I asked, enjoying my friend's discomfort.

"He ambushed me as we left the hotel and would not be put off. To add insult to injury, the devil had a photographer at the pier! Come! We must join the group."

With his bag in his fist, Holmes proceeded slowly up the walk, his eyes glistened as the door yielded before the ministrations of Jakes who stepped aside to allow Towne to enter. The master of the house did so and the servants were lined up in the foyer to bid him welcome. It was a most formal reunion. Towne inclined his head to each in turn and they whispered curt greetings. By the time Holmes and I were at the threshold, Widow Grant and Miss Duval had been dismissed to return to their duties. Perkele remained in the shadow before Towne. At the sound of our approach, Towne whispered quickly to the man and Perkele quickly thrust his floppy hat on his head and scurried off with Jakes.

"Welcome to my home," said Towne to Holmes. He faced me. "I extend a belated welcome to you as well, Dr. Watson. I trust everything has been satisfactory?"

"Without question."

"Very good. Mr. Holmes, I am told a room has been prepared for you."

"Excellent," said Holmes. "With your kind permission I should like to get squared away before we begin."

"By all means." Towne turned his ferret eyes towards me. "It is the room adjoining yours, Doctor. Can I impose upon you to escort our mutual friend there?"

As I had a great deal to discuss with Holmes privately, I agreed readily and we went upstairs. Towne closed and bolted the front door, then quitted the foyer no doubt eager to reacquaint himself with the goings on under his roof.

I directed Holmes to his room and we both entered. Holmes set his bag down near the hearth and roughly threw off the flamboyant cap and duster.

"Is that any way to show one's appreciation for such a generous gift?" I asked.

"They will be the death of me," replied Holmes. "The Frenchman vowed to send us a print of the photograph! I sidestepped by neglecting to provide our address. Egad! What if he should send it to the magazine printing your little tales? Should the artists illustrating your scribblings clap eyes on it, they might be convinced that I habitually wear such garments and so depict me so attired. I shudder to think of the implications to posterity." Holmes paused. "Perhaps I am overreacting. Surely they will realize that no proper gentleman would go stalking through the London streets in country attire! Preposterous. Still I shudder at the very thought of such misrepresentation."

"Well," said I, "if you were not so averse to having your picture taken, there would be a wealth of reference material from which illustrators might derive an image of your true self."

"You are right, Watson," said Holmes with a faint smile. "I am a victim of my peccadilloes. As are we all. It is good to see you, old friend."

We shook hands and that finished the matter for both of us. The hungry look in my friend's eyes and the high colour that had come to his normally pale face had nothing to do with the warm weather. There was work to be done and it was time we were at it. I set about filling him on what I had learned from the incident at the gate, to the loss of the black pearl earrings and how we came to be in the village upon their arrival. Holmes had thrown himself into a chair and steepled his fingers as his machine-like intellect absorbed my words. He did not interrupt and I spared no details. His only reaction consisted of a slight raising of the eyebrows at mention of the theft that very morning.

"A most interesting sequence of events," said he when I had finished my recounting. "I will admit to being greatly relieved that Towne and I were able to secure passage a day early."

"Yes, about that," I began, then stopped. "What? Relieved? Whatever for?"

"I feared for your safety, dear Watson. Distance left me quite helpless and the thought of you ignorant of the peril I had placed you in was sheer agony."

I was deeply moved by this singular admission but adhered to the matter at hand. "Surely you don't mean the haunting."

"It is precisely that to which I refer."

"Really! It is stuff and nonsense, I dare say. Or, perhaps, you learned something from Towne to indicate otherwise."

"Not directly, no."

"Then what?"

"A theory. Nothing more. Donald Towne is a most reticent man. Cold, distant, and tight as a clam."

"Really? Jakes speaks highly of him and one can't forget what he has done for the orphan French girl."

"Yes, he has taken her into his home. Yet he has not provided her with an education or means to elevate her station. Rather, she is condemned to the life of a servant to his property. Spare me any noble sentiments with regards to Donald Towne. He is a vain, selfish man. I learned that much from my time with him. As to the goings on here, I maintain that he is half-convinced his home is beset by supernatural forces."

"Do you believe it?"

"I believe everything. And nothing. Right now the scale is level. We shall meet the staff, tour the grounds and, in the process, toss pertinent facts on one end or the other, tipping the balance. Then we shall have our answer. Why, have you an explanation for the events?"

"I suspect Jakes is behind the thefts by order of Donald Towne. You heard me speak of the debts of Towne Manor. I believe Jakes has been taking the items and selling them to a fence squirreled away somewhere in the village while his master has been collecting insurance recompense on the purloined items."

"Extraordinary. What evidence have you?"

"The very impossibility of the crimes throws guilt upon Jakes once we have thrown out the silliness of a haunting. Jakes is in sole possession of the keys to every locked door and window and may come and go as he pleases. He has his master's trust and confidence as well. I say they are in league together in an attempt to save the estate."

"Why, Watson, you have been busy, haven't you? Bravo! And who knows, perhaps you are right after all. However your reasoning does not cover every aspect of the case."

"What does it leave out?"

"The murder of Lady Towne. The murderer is still within these walls, I fear. This was the danger to you which prompted my speedy voyage here."

Had I not been familiar with the vast intellect of my friend, I should have been duly shocked by this admission. Instead, I pressed him for more information. "You believe her overdose was not accidental."

"I do."

"On what do you base this extraordinary assumption?"

"The very same theory I alluded to earlier. A theory we must set about proving or refuting. Talk, and what I have seen thus far, have accomplished only so much. It is time for action."

With that we returned to the main floor, each of us motivated by our own curiosity. For Holmes, it was the mystery before him and the burning desire to see his theory proved out one way or the other. For myself, I was all but certain of my conclusion and was eager to see how Holmes would interpret the evidence I had collected these last few days.

Now it has been my experience with Holmes to always expect the unexpected and yet so certain was I that, with a murderer about, he was prepared to launch a lengthy investigation and interrogation of the staff that we would be up half the night on our mission. What followed could not be further removed from my expectations. Holmes did indeed submit to a tour of the rooms which I narrated to the best of my abilities. We lingered in the child's room, Holmes scrutinizing the dolls while I prattled. We saw the dressing table from which the earrings had been taken. We examined the spot near the torn up garden where Mrs. Towne took her leisure. However we spent so little time in each of these locations that it hardly seemed worth the effort.

Holmes spoke to the staff as well and it was here that I thought some truth would be rooted out. Again I was mistaken as he spoke briefly to each of them, asking the most mundane questions. I shall record here only the ones which struck me as particularly odd.

He began with Miss Duval, covering only the theft, and receiving the same information as I had learned.

Of Mrs. Grant, Holmes inquired about her late husband. We learned that his name was Walter Grant and that he had stood six foot three, weighing a whopping twenty-one stone.

We encountered Jakes who informed us that dinner was not far off. Convinced Holmes would press Jakes along the lines I had laid out earlier, to my surprise he merely asked Jakes for his full name, finishing up the interview with a request that Mr. Perkele be sent in so that Holmes might have a word with him. Jakes moved to fetch the gardener, but Holmes put a restraining hand on his arm.

"One last thing," said Holmes. "Do you happen to know how Mr. Towne acquired so many dolls for his child's bedroom? Did your master buy them all at once or piecemeal?"

"They all came in at once."

Holmes released the man and Jakes went off in search of Perkele. In the short time it took for the request to be fulfilled, I racked my brain as to the singular approach Holmes was taking towards the case and could come up with no explanation. The interview with the gardener only deepened my confusion. The man entered, burned red by the sun despite his customary wide-brim hat, which he did not remove. His black goatee glistened with perspiration.

"Ah, Mr. Perkele," said Holmes warmly. "Thank you for joining us. I shan't take but a moment of your time."

"That is all right," Perkele replied in his sing-song voice. "I can help?"

"A question, if you please."

"I am ready."

"Excellent. Here it is. What nationality are you?"

"Olen Suomalainen," said he proudly. "I am Finnish."

"Thank you, sir. That is all."

It would be gross understatement to say that I was utterly flabbergasted when Holmes indicated to me that he was satisfied for now and that we should dress for dinner. So distracted was I that I do not recall how I managed to dress myself and take my place at the table.

Towne awaited us there and his already pinched face seemed more careworn than when we had last seen him. Recalling the telegrams, I had a good notion as to the cause of his worry. However he greeted us politely, inquiring as to our comfort. The talk turned to general matters of country and government while we supped on succulent lamb. Towne came across as somewhat stiff in his manners though correct in every aspect. It was over the custard that he raised the subject of our visit.

"Sir," said he addressing Holmes, "again I cannot express my gratitude for accepting my request for aid. These last few years have been a burden. To say nothing of the last few months."

"How could they not?" observed Holmes. "It was my intention to ease your mind once and for all."

"To that end, I eagerly await a report on the status of your investigation."

"I can offer no conclusions," said Holmes. "To be utterly frank, I am at a loss to furnish any explanation whatsoever for what has transpired here these last few years. Due to this failure, Watson and I must return to London for the present. I think the matter might be better served when I am once again back in familiar surroundings. Perhaps then there will be some hope of making a breakthrough. For the moment, I can render no comfort to you."

I did not hear the reply Towne made to this remark as, taken off guard by this bold move of Holmes's, I was choking on my custard. I recovered with a discreet cough and tried to fathom what my friend was up to. Did he suspect Towne had murdered his wife? Had she discovered his playing fast and loose with the family fortune and had to be silenced? And how could London trap Towne if he was guilty?

I had made no progress with these burning questions by the time Holmes and I boarded the train to London the next morning and was at a loss to comprehend how such a trip could shed light on the mystery of Towne Manor. Well it had been said by some that there was madness in Holmes's methods and, until now, I had never been more inclined to agree. The train lurched and we were on our way out of Higham. Holmes stood to open the window and allow fresh air to enter, then resumed his seat, sitting in a half-turned posture in order to gaze out the window. I fidgeted in my seat, the events of the last two days spoiling my comfort.

"Before I tell you why we are London bound," said Holmes, aware of my inner turmoil. "I should like to ask you if you still see Jakes for the thefts."

"You mean Towne is not the focus of our attention?"

"Whatever gave you that idea?"

"Your boldface lie about the status of our investigation."

"I did not lie, Watson. I told Towne that I could offer no explanation at this time. That is complete and utter truth. I have a theory without facts. Thus I have nothing concrete to report."

"Then why bring up Jakes?"

"It is you who have cast the aura of doubt upon him."

"Well, until dinner last night, I could think of no other explanation for the thefts. The telegrams from debt collectors were my main evidence."

Holmes nodded. "In that you are quite correct. Towne Manor is on the brink of ruin. Though this has nothing to do with the thefts. Insurance fraud is not the motive here."

"What other motive could there be?"

"What indeed?"

"Well?"

"Who murdered Lady Towne? Jakes? Or Towne himself?"

"I wouldn't believe it of Jakes for a moment."

"Correct, Watson. Towne, then?"

"You know him more intimately than I, what do you say about him?"

"He is innocent. Of murder, at least. What of the hungry raiding brute you encountered?"

"I have given the matter much thought but am at a loss to explain him. If you are claiming that he murdered Lady Towne, then I would ask you how he managed to do it. Other than that I believe the brute has no bearing on what has transpired within the walls of the estate."

"By that do you mean to say that you are convinced that both crimes were committed by someone inside Towne Manor?"

I nodded my agreement, then sat back somewhat satisfied.

"Watson, I applaud your reasoning. There are certain aspects of the case which you have deduced precisely and I commend you for it. However in others, I believe you to be in error." He held up his hand as I began to speak. "Please, permit me a question. Why do we travel to London?"

"I have not the foggiest notion," I replied.

"Very well. It is clear that there are a number of points about the case in which we are not in agreement."

"Regretfully, I have to admit as much myself."

"Then let us mine the depths of our discrepancies and see if we can come to a mutual understanding. First of all, we are heading to London to see Joseph Merrick. I have it on good authority that he is recently returned to London from the Fawsley Hall estate, Northhampshire where he has spent the last few weeks visiting."

Had Holmes named the Queen herself I should not have been more surprised. Poor Merrick, dubbed the Elephant Man by the press, was an invalid at the London Hospital, Whitechapel. We had made his acquaintance after the plea to raise funds for his care had appeared in the Times. Holmes had hit on the idea that we volunteer a sum of £50 par annum for Merrick's care under the alias of Mr. Singer. The proposal was accepted by the hospital and Holmes and I had had opportunity to visit Merrick on occasion though we had never let on that we were his unseen benefactors. I found Merrick to be an intelligent, pleasant man despite his horrific deformities. However I did not see how he could possibly assist us with the case and told Holmes this.

"Oh, it is a long shot, I know," Holmes agreed. "But such people tend to be extremely tight-lipped with regards to outsiders. Also, the recent change to the laws forbidding their livelihood in this country have scattered them to the four winds. Merrick is the only one we have established an intimacy with."

This explanation, rather than clearing up the matter, so clouded my thoughts that I did not know what to make of it. "Confound it, Holmes!"

"Forgive me, Watson. Perhaps we have gotten ahead of ourselves. I thought, as a medical man, there was no need to cover the ground leading me to Merrick."

"What the devil are you talking about?"

"You are not aware that David Jakes has three arms?"

"What!"

"One left, two right? The extra limb is vestigial but clearly present to those who have eyes to see. Did you not notice his stiff posture?"

"I did. It was my assumption that some ailment of the spine or accident as a child was the cause."

"Watson, you are a credit to your profession. No, the stiff posture of Jakes is caused by his keeping the withered limb tight behind his back, much like a soldier standing at ease. This requires a slight arching of the back to pull off."

"How were you able to detect it whereas I was not?"

"There are two components to my answer. The first is that I endeavour to remain free of assumption in all things. You met Jakes under genial conditions in the country. The man is bright, capable – any unpleasant examples of human endeavour would understandably be the furthest thing from your mind."

"I will accept that though I do not understand it fully. What is the other?"

"You'll recall we loitered at the wagon upon my arrival."

"I do. You said you wished to observe Towne's interaction with his servants."

"And so I did. But I also sensed the tension in Jakes, not learning from you until later the cause. The tension manifested itself in Jakes not only through increased severity in his posture, but also, as he had his back to us at the door, an almost imperceptible clenching and unclenching of the atrophied fist at his lower back, as though a tarantula lay beneath his coat."

"Your deductive powers are sound as always," said I. Holmes inclined his head in accepting the compliment.

"And now you see why we must go to London."

"From this visit you hope to solve the mystery of the Towne Manor haunting."

"Solve it? No. I already have a theory as to that. Our mission to see Merrick is undertaken in the hopes of proving the theory valid or invalid dependant on what the man can tell us."

I desperately wanted to question Holmes on a number of points but knew from past experience that he was reluctant to elaborate on things which had not been verified to his satisfaction. Seeing as Merrick was potentially conducive to this end, it was pointless to pursue the matter at this time.

The train deposited us at Victoria and we flagged down a hansom for the long journey to Whitechapel. The noise and teeming of the great city was a welcome and familiar sight after the stifling conditions at Towne Manor. The chaotic coming and going echoed my clamorous thoughts.

Our previous visits to see Merrick, plus the slight notoriety we had gained through the accounts of our adventures I had written up for publication made us instantly recognizable to the hospital staff and we were granted access to Merrick's room which was at Bedstead Square on the hospital grounds. A narrow, brick passageway led us to his door. We knocked and heard Merrick bid us enter. The room was bright, made cheerful with flowers, books and pictures. High windows allowed sunlight to enter. We found Merrick in a chair by the window where he had been working on one of the lovely models upon which he exerted tremendous energy to create. These he bestowed as tokens of gratitude to those who had shown him kindness. Constructed solely with the use of his left hand, the right being useless to him, they were wonderful recreations of some of the great buildings of London.

When in the presence of Joseph Merrick, one is immediately struck by the foul, uncontrollable odour emanating from his misshapen form. While this assailed our olfactory senses, the quaint comfort of the room put one at ease. Merrick himself was a dichotomy in human form. Never in my medical experience had I encountered a man so afflicted by disease. Some in my profession believe it to be Elephantiasis but I did not concur with this diagnosis. His condition seemed to me to be more a case of von

Recklinghausen disease. And yet, trapped in a twisted deformed body reposed the most intelligent, soft-spoken, charming individual one should be fortunate enough to meet. Given the squalid conditions of his earlier years, the man was, to be frank, a wonder to behold.

Holmes and I greeted him warmly and clasped his rather delicate left hand in friendship.

"I am honoured to have such renowned personages pay me a visit," said Merrick in his mild, lisping voice. "Most kind. Are you on some bold new adventure?"

Holmes chuckled, nodding his head in the affirmative. "We'll make a detective of you yet, my friend. Yes, Watson and I are investigating a matter and are in great need of your assistance."

Merrick's eyes widened in their bulbous pits and he would have smiled if his deformed lips were capable of doing so. "Capital! What can I do?"

"Joseph," said Holmes. "I am sorry to say that we have need of your intimate knowledge of the carnival sideshow."

A brief shadow clouded Merrick's eyes, but he blinked away unpleasant recollections impossible for you or I to guess at, and raised his gnarled head a fraction of an inch. "All right, then," said he.

"Does the name Donald Towne mean anything to you?"

"Not at all, Mr. Holmes."

"What about David Jakes?"

"Jakesy!" Merrick slurred. "I knew a David Jakes once."

"This man had three arms? One left, two right?"

Merrick inclined his ponderous head. "We were shown together for a time in Blackpool. 'Goodness Sakes Jakes' they called him. Could arm wrestle himself and such stuff."

"Watson!" Holmes cried, his eyes flashing. "We're on the right track. Joseph, can you make anything of the names Harry and Patricia Grant, or Timothy Perkele?"

"I knew a strong man named Henry Grant," said Merrick, "But I could not tell you if he was married. There was a Tim Perkele who performed as the Scandinavian Devil in Brighton. Is this the man you mean?"

"He was given this title due to a somewhat satanic appearance?" asked Holmes.

"That and the horns growing out of his head."

I recalled then that Perkele neglected to remove his floppy hat indoors save in the presence of Donald Towne and that the gardener had quickly donned the covering when Holmes and I had approached. Holmes, on the other hand, had immediately caught the gesture and the motivation behind it.

"Mr. Merrick," said Holmes with mock formality, "you are a godsend. And yet you are sure you have never heard the name Donald Towne in connection with the sideshow circuit?"

"That is correct."

"Do you recall if you met Grant, Jakes and Perkele in one particular show or did your encounters with them occur individually?"

"The former, Mr. Holmes. Oh, yes, it was one of the biggest curiosity shows around then. I was with the show only a short time however."

"Who owned or operated the show?"

"Mr. Barker did. I do not recall his Christian name."

Here Holmes described Donald Towne to Merrick in precise detail.

"That sounds very much like Mr. Barker, although I cannot say for certain."

"Progress, Watson!" Holmes fixed Merrick with his piercing gaze. "Sir, do you know anything of Mr. Barker's history?"

"Only the general scuttlebutt at the time. There are no secrets in such places."

"Please recount what you know."

"Oh, it was a great romance! Barker had grown rich from the business and had met Miss Amelia Wood – a contortionist and acrobat or some renown. They were to be married but he broke off the engagement after selling the concern for great profit. Barker disappeared, never to be seen on the circuit again."

"What became of Amelia Wood?"

"I'm sure I don't know. She had a sister in the show, I recall."

At this point Dr. Treves entered and greeted us in a professional manner though he was present as a friend to Merrick and not his doctor. Genuine concern for his friend prompted Treves to ask that we cut the interview short for fear of overtiring Merrick. Although I could see that Holmes bristled with questions unasked, we were well aware of Merrick's tenuous health and acquiesced to Treves's wishes. We made our goodbyes and soon found ourselves back on the bustling street.

"We have scored a breakthrough, Watson," said Holmes.

"Hardly. All we have established is the reason behind the occupants of Towne Manor's reluctance to speak of their collective past. How this solves thefts and murder from a barricaded home is lost to me. What is our next move?"

"Mr. Merrick," said Holmes with mock formality, "you are a godsend."

"Why we need to see the land titles for Higham and its environs. I should think that would be obvious."

Within minutes we were at the Land Claims Office but soon learned that residential titles outside the major cities were handled regionally. Copies of all deeds were to be filed in London but rarely were and inaccuracies abounded. Holmes shook off his frustration on the office steps and was again flushed with the thrill of the hunt.

"Back to Higham, dear Watson," he announced. "And an end to the Towne Manor haunting."

I pressed Holmes for clarification on the train back to Higham but he begged off, stating simply that the claims office would reveal all. Frustrated, I settled back in my seat and consoled myself with gazing out the window at the turbid Thames. When at last we reached our destination, we proceeded to the Village Hall where land deeds were stored in a much disused basement. As the deeds were a matter of public record the clerk left us at the musty cabinets.

"I beg your indulgence, Watson," said Holmes. "But would you be inclined to hunt up the deed to Towne Manor and see in whose name the property is entitled while I search elsewhere in this mess?"

I agreed readily and we began. We had been told that the office would be closing in one hour which proved to be sufficient time for our quest. Forty-five minutes later I had the deed to Towne Manor before me and said as much to Holmes.

"Splendid. In what name is it?"

"It is made to the order of Donald Towne."

"And no other?"

"Just Towne."

Holmes made no comment on this as a moment later he found whatever he had been searching for and triumphantly brandished it over his head after but glancing at it. He slid it back into the cabinet and declared our work there completed, banging the drawer shut.

"Come, Watson! Enough of this dismal place. We have business at Telegraph Hill."

"What have you found?"

"A key. Pray, hurry, my friend. I wish to turn it."

We enlisted a wagonette and, to my surprise, it was owned by the same man who had abandoned me outside Towne Manor three days previously. The man mumbled an apology while endeavouring to appear sheepish but I was having none of it. Holmes and I climbed aboard, he in great excitement, myself shooting daggers at the cowardly driver.

Telegraph Hill was known for the country bungalows atop the gentle rise. We had passed the place several times coming and going from the village and I had noticed the splendour of the surroundings. Holmes gave the driver explicit directions and fifteen minutes later the driver stopped the wagon outside one of the modest homes. The grounds were immaculate, the walks swept, uniform profusions of flowers on either side. The walk ended at a stout oaken door with a rounded arch which gave the property a gnomish aspect. Holmes instructed the driver to wait for us before alighting and I added a heartless glare at the man to drive the point home, then stepped down to join Holmes on the path.

My friend's knock brought the maid and Holmes asked the tall, spindly woman if the lady of the house was at home. We were told she was and were beckoned into the foyer. The maid disappeared and a moment later a petite, strikingly beautiful woman of some thirty summers greeted us warmly. She announced herself as Mrs. Rosetta Dunhill and bade us enter. The introductions dispensed with, we stood with our hats in our hands fairly drinking in the uncommon beauty of the woman before us.

"How may I be of help?" she asked, her voice as lilting as a summer breeze.

"We are investigating the rash of thefts which have occurred at Towne Manor these last few years," said Holmes. "Know you anything of them?"

Mrs. Dunhill shook her head. "Only what has been going around the village."

Holmes glanced about the gloomy room. "Please forgive my insolence. But might we continue our conversation in a more pleasant part of the house? For the doctor's sake. He was injured during the war and it acts up when cold works on him."

"By all means. There is a solarium at the rear of the house. If you will accompany me there, we may continue."

A moment later we were all seated in the solarium. It was unbearably humid and difficult to see as the sun shone directly through the glass panels. Tea was sent for and Holmes resumed when the maid left us.

"This is a most charming room in which to enjoy the beauty of Nature. I commend you on the view."

Squinting into the sun, I barely discerned a number of estates dotting the valley stretching out beneath us.

"Yes," Mrs. Dunhill agreed. "It is my favourite room in the house. I often come here to think. Now, Mr. Holmes, how precisely may I be of service to you with regards to Towne Manor?"

"Frankly, madam, we are at our wit's end," said Holmes. "So much so that I have resorted to interviewing the residents of Telegraph Hill merely because the homes here look down on the valley. Is that not Towne Manor directly below? To the right?"

Mrs. Dunhill did not turn her head before replying. "It is."

"I thought so. I am wondering if you or your husband recall seeing anything untoward from this vantage point?"

"I have seen nothing."

"Your husband, perhaps?"

Mrs. Dunhill lowered her gaze. "I am a widow."

"Forgive me. It's my hope that you and he had many wonderful years together."

"We were together only a short time. Roddy was a much older man and married late in life."

"I am most sorry to hear it."

"My husband left me well taken care of. I want for nothing. I am one enamoured of solitude."

"Ah, but the heart can make sport of our certainties. Is that not so?"

"The secrets of one's heart are private, Mr. Holmes. I believe it was Towne Manor you wished to speak to me about."

"Yes. Now you claim to have seen – "

"I do not claim anything. I state a simple fact. I'm not in the habit of spying upon my neighbours."

"Of course."

The tea was brought in and served round.

"I must ask you to come to the purpose of your visit," said Mrs. Dunhill.

"Do you know Mr. Towne?" Holmes asked, seemingly oblivious to the lady's urging.

"I do not. I keep to myself mostly. The girl goes into town for my wants."

"That is a pity. To deprive the world of your uncommon beauty. Did your husband enjoy living here?"

"My husband never lived here. I purchased the property after his death. Really, Mr. Holmes, I – "

"I believe Mr. Towne is in love with you. He indicated as much to me in Paris."

I sat up straighter in my chair and, clutching my cup, watched the effect this astonishing revelation had on Mrs. Dunhill. The hard line of her pert mouth softened an instant and her cup rattled on its saucer as she set it down. There was a brief exhalation of breath and a flush rose up from her pearl white neck. Bosom heaving, she placed her cup unsteadily to one side and rose with lithe grace to her feet. Her nostrils suddenly flared angrily.

"Gentlemen, I would ask you to leave."

We retrieved our hats and beat a hasty retreat. Mrs. Dunhill did not show us out. It was fortunate for our driver's continued good health that he and the wagonette were where we had left them. We climbed aboard.

"Where to now, sirs?"

"Towne Manor, if you please," said Holmes.

"What the devil was that all about?" I asked as we made our way down the hill. "Did Mr. Towne really reveal his feelings while in Paris?"

"Not a word of it. I state unequivocally that he has not seen Mrs. Dunhill during his time here."

"And this brings us closer to solving the mystery?"

"I have solved the case," said Holmes simply.

Jakes let us in, moving to lock the door behind him as Towne strode up the hall to join us. Holmes stayed the hand of Jakes.

"That will no longer be necessary," he said.

Towne, witnessing this exchange, exclaimed, "Good God, man! But you said – You've solved it? Is it finally to have an end?"

"Yes, I believe I have. If you would be so kind as to gather everyone upstairs, I shall deliver a full report on my and Dr. Watson's findings."

Towne turned to his servant. "You heard the man, Jakes. Hurry!"

"With your kind indulgence, Mr. Towne," said Holmes. "Would you have everyone proceed to the nursery? This will place yourself and your staff in neutral surroundings."

Towne hesitated as the nursery held unpleasant memories for him. However his desire to have the matter resolved won out in the end and he so instructed Jakes, who ran off to do his master's bidding. Holmes and I followed the master of the house upstairs but we remained in the hallway until Jakes returned with Perkele, Mrs. Grant and young Kelly Duval all of whom bore the exact same looks of shock and curiosity.

"May I have the key to this room?" Holmes asked of Jakes.

Jakes looked to Towne who gave his assent. The key disappeared into Holmes's fist.

"If you all will be so kind as to enter, I shall lock the door behind you. Worry not, for I shall join you presently. There is something I must do beforehand."

The staff made no complaint. Towne held back, reluctant to take orders in his own home but I assured him he could trust Holmes implicitly and to do as he was bade. We entered the close, dark nursery and I heard the door latch click behind me. The solemn atmosphere of the room muted all conversation to the level of church whispers. Towne bore up well though it was obvious it pained him to be there.

Presently there was a low thump at the base of the door, and suddenly Holmes stood among us again. He had so hastily shut and re-locked the door that his presence among us was our first indication of his return. "I thank you for your patience and I assure you it shall not go unrewarded."

"Holmes, please," entreated Towne.

"Yes, let us begin. It pains me to be the one to say it, but it must be said. Towne, your wife was murdered in this house. By the same party committing the thefts. That person is inside this room."

"Murdered! My Evelyn!" Towne gasped.

"I am certain of it."

This revelation set everyone in the house to glancing at one another while Towne battled with his grief.

"For the sake of laying a firm base for my explanation, I should like to establish certain facts as incontrovertible. Towne, your real name is Donald Barker and you made your fortune selling the sideshow concern in which members of your house staff were once exhibited."

Towne was shocked into silence by this but the others offered protestations against it.

"Spare me your denials," Holmes interrupted. "You, Eleanor Grant, your husband was a circus strong man. You were the fat lady of Barker's show. Jakes, your three limbs made you a curiosity and Perkele, whose name means devil in Finnish, performed as a satanic figure with genuine horns upon your head."

Here Holmes shot out an arm and plucked the hat from Perkele's head. Sure enough the man suffered from cortex hyperplasia which took the form of two horn-like protuberances from his scalp. These combined with what remained of his goatee completed his devilish appearance.

"Please understand," Holmes went on. "It is not my intention to bring these secrets to light to humiliate or shame. They are merely necessary to my explanation."

"All right, Holmes!" roared Towne. "We have no more secrets among us."

"You admit to all I have said?"

"Yes, damn you. Yes! It is a shame we sought to lose forever! What of it?"

"A-ha! That desire to bury the past is at the very heart of the matter. You were in love prior to selling your carnival."

"N-No."

"Come now! To Amelia Wood – a strikingly beautiful member of the troupe. You broke off your engagement when you had made your fortune. She was cast aside as was the life you were so desperate to forget."

Towne opened his mouth as if to speak, then hung his head.

"Your greed and hunger for respectability left you blind to the damage you had done to that woman. A woman who lost not only a prospective husband but employment as well. The shame of your actions drove her from the show. A woman who resorted to a loveless arrangement with an older man of wealth. A woman who vowed revenge!"

Towne looked up. "What are you saying?"

"She has taken the name Dunhill, she lives on Telegraph Hill. But you did not only ruin her life and livelihood, but also that of her sister – who is among us this very moment!"

Holmes lunged for a shelf of dolls near the door and flung them aside in an effort to reach the row behind. A high-pitched, keening, blood curdling wail sounded from the shelf.

"Watson, your revolver, quickly!" Holmes hissed.

A shot rang out. Suddenly Holmes raised his hands and backed away from the shelf. My pistol dangled impotently at my side and almost slipped from my grasp when I beheld the target of my friend's search. For perched on the shelf, a derringer in her tiny fists, was the smallest example of womanhood I had ever seen. A human being in miniature, no more than twenty inches in height. Her doll-like features were screwed up into an expression of pure loathing as she menaced us all with the gun.

"I give you the sister of Amelia Wood," said Holmes.

"Very clever, Holmes" said Wood in her childlike voice. "Now stop being clever or I'll put a bullet in you. You, Doctor, drop that revolver or I'll kill your friend, sure."

I had no alternative but to comply and my pistol thudded to the carpet.

"Bullets be damned!" shouted Towne. "Margaret Wood, how dare you trespass in my home! Kill my wife, steal my property!"

"You stole our lives, you snake! Turned your back on us, thought you were too good for us, left us with nothing! Amelia netted that rich old fool and did all right. But what about me? You owed me a living and I collect what I'm owed. So I moved into this house, the house Amelia should have had from you. I had a decent roof over my head for the only time in my life. Food in the kitchen, trees outside. But that was just the beginning. Amelia and I got what we wanted. Everything but revenge. That came after."

"You killed Lady Towne's cat to keep it from sniffing you out," said Holmes. "Then you administered a lethal dose of laudanum to the Lady to deprive Towne of the bliss he stole from Amelia."

"What did I tell you about being clever?" She raised the gun so that the barrel pointed between Holmes's eyes. Then she gracefully dropped to the floor and glared up at us with hate in her eyes.

"I can take no more of this!" shouted Towne. "Put that bullet in me at last and finish it!"

"Oh, no," the tiny Wood shook her head. "I'll not do that. I'll be going now, I think. And you'll never know where we shall strike again. You shall never know peace again, Donald Towne. Mark me!"

Quick as a wink, the tiny figure darted for the pet door and was through it in an instant. Holmes sprang forward to give chase as a gunshot sounded in the hall. He seized the handle and flung the door open. There on the floor, the empty derringer some three feet away, lay Margaret Wood entangled and helpless in Holmes's heavy duster.

Two days later, my reading of the arrest and arraignment of Amelia and Margaret Wood was interrupted by Mrs. Hudson who entered with a deliveryman in tow. The man had a package under his arm addressed to Holmes and I. It was duly signed for and Holmes and I were alone once more. Holmes was eager to have it open, but I wanted certain facts about the case from him first before his questing intellect dismissed them.

"You never did explain how you deduced the presence of Margaret Wood inside the house."

"It was elementary, I dare say," replied Holmes in an off-hand manner, his eyes riveted to the package. He could see, however, that I was not about to abandon the matter until satisfied. "If you must know, here it is. Would you admit that no normal size human being could exit and re-enter Towne Manor undetected and at will?"

"I would. The bars, locks and alarms saw to that."

"Well, there you have it. Now if you'll hand me the letter opener – "

"From this you concluded that the Wood sisters were taking their revenge on Donald Towne?"

"Hardly. It was merely the first piece of the puzzle. I shall lay it out for you. With the nonsense of a haunting disregarded at the start, it was clearly evident upon my arrival that the cat doors were the only means of coming and going from the house undetected. It stood to reason that the thief had to use these passages for want of any alternative means."

"Very well, but how – "

"I am coming to that. If the small doors were the means of passage, then a diminutive human would be the only person able to use them. Such little people are generally found at carnivals."

"Understood. How did this lead you to assume Towne had been formerly associated with such acts?"

"There were numerous indicators along the way. Towne intimated to me that he was in France on business as well as in mourning. His reluctance to reveal anything about his affairs save his urgent need to secure income, stirred my curiosity and I only had to see the mud and sawdust on his boots and the slight odour to his clothes to know that he had been frequenting carnivals in France where such freak shows are still legal. Of course, at the time, I had no way of knowing that his connection to carnivals ran any deeper than this as he mentioned nothing of any pet doors when he recounted to me the tale of the haunting which prompted my telegram to you."

I was most curious to hear how he had made such leaps of logic beyond anything I could ever have imagined based on the same evidence I had been exposed to prior to his arrival and made this clear to him.

"The presence of former sideshow exhibits amongst the staff was immediately evident to me and this led to the supposition that Towne had a deeper association with the carnival trade. The tour of the grounds confirmed what you had imparted to me: that it was an inside job. Add to this the pet doors and the multitude of dolls and my course was set before me. Outlandish though my hypothesis was, however, it could easily be proved one way or the other. I set out to do so."

"What good came from our hanging back upon our arrival from the train station?"

"From what Towne had told me in Paris, there was a distinct possibility that Lady Towne had been murdered. Despite Towne's selfish, self-serving nature, I sensed genuine love for his wife and absolved him of the alleged crime on the spot. I wanted to see if any of the staff displayed guilt upon meeting the man they had wronged. They did not, which led weight to my assumption that someone else entirely was behind the crime. Also, their meek, yet devoted welcome to a man like Towne revealed his prior mastery over them in their previous employment as carnival curiosities.

It was clear they stayed with him because the law banning sideshow attractions left them no other means of earning a living. Such were the castles I had created in the air. I needed proof."

"Then why did you question the staff so superficially?"

"As I mentioned at the time, carnival folk are a close knit bunch. I knew I would get nothing from them directly. Instead I collected what facts about themselves there were willing to impart in order to pass them on to one of their kind who would speak with us."

"Merrick."

"Ah, Watson, you've picked up the thread of it. After feigning bafflement at dinner in case the murderer/thief was listening, we returned to London where Joseph provided the proof I needed. But there was, as yet, no motive. Again, Joseph was instrumental. The woman scorned, sisters injured, thefts and murder as retribution. More suppositions. No facts! A trip to the deeds office might prove illuminating. If the sisters Wood had gone to such trouble to destroy Donald Towne, they would both want to be nearby to gloat in his suffering. With one Wood sister believed to be concealed inside the house, the other would have to take a cottage with a view of Towne Manor as she could not show herself in public lest a chance encounter with Towne ruin the deadly game. Telegraph Hill provides this vantage point. The deed showed that the Hill estate had been purchased around the time the thefts began and was in the name of Rosetta Wood, not Dunhill. No great leap to suppose that she was Amelia Wood, thus I resorted to trickery to prove it."

"How could you be certain she would give herself away?"

"In surprising her with the fabrication that Towne was in love with her, she betrayed herself with an impassioned display of prior ardour. Oh, she recovered herself quickly but the damage had been done. From that moment, I knew I had hit upon the solution. All that remained was to smoke out the sister. After locking you all into the nursery, I hurried to my room for the accursed duster and so blocked Margaret Wood's only means of exit. She was kind enough to put a bullet through the thing in her shock at being smothered and for that I am eternally grateful. Now is that satisfactory to you?"

Listening to Holmes explain his amazing deductive process, the matter seemed simplicity itself. I walked to the table beside my chair and picked up the letter opener.

"Wait a moment," said I, turning with the instrument in my hand. "What about Towne's debts and the shrouded figure which eluded me on my arrival?"

Holmes snorted and sighed. "You simply won't let go of the thing, will you?"

"Well?"

"You'll recall the dug up kitchen garden from which the shapeless vagabond was supposedly stealing vegetables?"

"I do."

"Do you recall any mention of a tiny woman fencing stolen jewels in Higham?"

"No, I dare say."

"That is because Margaret Wood accessed the garden through the cat door after each theft and buried the items amongst the vegetables. That portion of the garden was concealed from the house by hanging branches. Thus the vagabond, under the guise of stealing food, could retrieve the stolen property and be off. I've had a letter from Towne informing me that the black pearl earrings have been recovered from the garden as the hooded figure dared not approach while we resided there."

"Are you saying the sisters had an accomplice? If you'll recall this figure leaped over my head."

"The shrouded figure was Amelia Wood – a former acrobat, remember? A leap as you describe would be as nothing to someone of such skill, strength and experience. The robes were to mask her appearance. As to the finances of the estate, they are precarious thanks to Towne's bungling, which is not a crime so far as I know, and has no bearing on the thefts or the death of his wife. Now are you satisfied?"

I cast my mind back over the affair and could find nothing which Holmes had not explained. I handed him the letter opener and, like a skilled butcher, he made quick work of the wrappings. We both marvelled at what was revealed. Before us was an incredibly detailed model Joseph Merrick had painstakingly built, reproducing 221 B Baker Street. It was precise in every detail.

"Observe, Watson," said Holmes, admiringly. "Here is such work worthy of posterity. Our rattling about the world in search of clues and answers is but gossamer in comparison!"

"There is a card," said I. "It contains sincere thanks to Mr. Singer for many kindnesses. Signed Joseph Merrick."

"By Jove, we have made a detective out of him after all!" declared Holmes.

With that we set about finding a place to display the noble work.

YOU CAN GO HOLMES AGAIN

When I sat down to write my first Holmes/Watson tale for Volume One of this great series from Airship 27 I didn't even know if I'd be able to pull off an adventure Sherlockians would want to read. And it was a tremendous honor to even have the opportunity to try.

So you can imagine my surprise when that first story not only was accepted but made an immediate impact with Holmes fans, culminating with the story being voted the Pulp Factory Award for Best Pulp Short Story of the year! I'm still in shock and find myself glancing over, from time to time, at the beautiful award in its place of honor where I write to make sure it really is my name on the plaque and there hasn't been some terrible mix-up. The creative satisfaction and fun I've experienced writing Holmes/Watson tales is beyond words and this award is just the icing on the cake. I'd like to express my undying gratitude to everyone who read the tale and to the Pulp Factory members who voted for it. The anthology won three awards in total: Mark Maddox also won for Best Pulp Cover and the incomparable Rob Davis took home an award for Best Pulp Interior Illustration. Distinguished company indeed.

Awards aside, it's been a great ride and a privilege working in Arthur Conan Doyle's Holmesian world and I'm still trying to wrap my head around the fact that this is my third go around with the Master Detective and the intrepid Watson.

For "The Adventure of the Towne Manor Haunting" I tried to take a different approach as I've tried to do with my previous Holmes/Watson adventures. My first tale was something of a quest into the abyss during the early days of the duo, the second tale more of an action yarn set towards the end of their illustrious career. So with the story you've just read, and, I hope, enjoyed, I decided to aim at the middle years of their partnership with a bit of a low key approach dealing with perception and interpretation rather than fisticuffs and pistol shots.

The basic set up came from "The Hound of the Baskervilles." In that timeless classic, Doyle has Holmes send Watson to Dartmoor and Baskerville Hall to begin their investigations with promises of joining him at a later date. While reading the novel, it was great fun to see Watson doing the investigating, meeting with the people involved and drawing his own conclusions. However when the dynamic duo reunite later in the story, I was prepared to see Holmes reach quite different and masterful conclusions from the goings on at, and around, Baskerville manor based on the same evidence Watson had interpreted. This did not happen. And, so, the framework for Towne Manor Haunting was born. What follows contains spoilers so I trust you will have read the tale before continuing with this essay.

As to the plot of my tale, I decided early on that Holmes's interpretation of events needed to be so radically different from Watson's conclusions in order for the framework of their separate investigations to hold up. Given the setting of a quiet, rural country manor, what could be farther afield than the crooked, degrading arena of the carnival freak so popular in Victorian times? That contrast, plus the year the tale was set (1887), the year these freak shows were banned, set the stage for the tale to unfold.

The diminutive villain in the piece was based on another real historical figure. Pauline Musters was her name and, before her death in 1895, she stood a mere 23.2 inches in height and made her living as an acrobat and dancer. And what Victorian tale dealing with sideshow freaks could not deal with the Elephant Man? Joseph (not John as depicted in the moving film) Merrick has become a legendary figure and it was with great respect and sensitivity that I included him in the tale. I hope I did so differently than you, dear reader, might expect.

The setting of Higham is also very real and I would like to publicly thank the Higham Village History Group who responded to my queries about the area and helped me get some of the details right. Gad's Hill Place, the last home of Charles Dickens, is indeed on that road Watson takes and through Google maps I invite you to "tread" that road as I did before sending Watson and Jakes along there in a wagonette. Any errors as to the layout of Upper Higham back then are mine and not the fault of the historical society.

This tale also allowed me to continue what has become a personal tradition with these stories: the inclusion of people I know as characters. The first featured my good friend and lifelong Sherlockian Doug Gavin. The second contained a character named Cornelius Rogers, my sister-in-law's father who had passed away while I was writing the tale. The culprit in this tale is the maid, Kelly Duval. Kelly is my niece and she has just discovered the Holmes tales through the first two volumes of this series. It's my hope she'll continue reading these new adventures while seeking out Doyle's original tales. She's got some catching up to do.

I am not finished with Holmes and Watson. Not by a long shot. It's my hope to have a full-length novel completed in the very near future. It's a plot

I've been toying with for awhile now and if I can pull it off, I think Holmes fans will not be disappointed. I would also like to keep contributing to this series of anthologies just as long as Cornerstone Book Publishers and Airship 27 want to do them. Doyle has left us a tremendous literary legacy, one that is just too much fun to be even a small part of.

Until next time, there's a hansom waiting outside at the curb. Let's away! The game is afoot!

❀ ❀ ❀

Andrew Salmon won a Pulp Factory Award for his first Sherlock Holmes story, "The Adventure of the Locked Room" (*Sherlock Holmes Consulting Detective: Volume One*), and has been nominated for an Arthur Ellis Award (the equivalent of the Edgar) in his native Canada. His work has appeared in numerous magazines, including *Masked Gun Mystery, Planetary Stories, Parsec, Storyteller, TBT* and *Thirteen Stories*. He also writes reviews for *The Comicshopper*.

He is creating a Brand/X superhero serial novel currently running in A Thousand Faces Magazine (to read the saga to date, see issues #0, 2, 3, 5, 7, and 12 which are all still available).

He has published or appeared in twelve books: *The Forty Club* (which Midwest Book Reviews calls "a good solid little tale you will definitely carry with you for the rest of your life"), *The Dark Land*, the first of a series ("a straight out science-fiction thriller that fires on all cylinders" – Pulp Fiction Reviews), *The Light Of Men*, which has been called "a book of such immense significance that it is not only meant to be read, but also to be experienced... a work of grim power" – C. Saunders. *Secret Agent X: Volume One* and *Three, Ghost Squad: Rise of the Black Legion* (with Ron Fortier), *Jim Anthony Super Detective: Volume One, Sherlock Holmes Consulting Detective: Volumes One, Two and Three, Dan Fowler G-Man: Volume One* and *Black Bat Mystery: Volume One*.

Andrew's work will also appears in *Mars McCoy Space Ranger* and the upcoming *Mystery Men: Volume Two* (with Mark Halegua) anthologies as well as a revised edition of *The Dark Land* – all from Airship 27.

To learn more about his work check out the following links:
http://www.amazon.com/Andrew-Salmon/e/B002NS5KR0/ref=ntt_athr_dp_pel_pop_2.
http://stores.lulu.com/airship27
www.lulu.com/AndrewSalmon
www.lulu.com/thousand-faces

AFTERWORD - GO SHERLOCK!

It is hard for me to sit here and recall what actually prompted us to do a Sherlock Holmes collection other than the fact that all of us involved with Airship 27 Productions were avid fans of the Great Detective. It just seemed like a good idea at the time. Little did we realize when putting that first volume together we were, in fact, beginning what would become our most popular (& profitable) series since launching our pulp venture.

Volume One not only rose quickly on the sales charts at Amazon.com, becoming one of its premier mystery titles, but it also garnered three of the first annual Pulp Factory Awards for works published in 2009 as handed out at the Windy City Paper & Pulp Convention in April of 2010. Mark Maddox won for Best Pulp Cover Artist and our own Rob Davis took the prize for Best Pulp Interior Illustrations, both for *SHERLOCK HOLMES CONSULTING DETECTIVE Vol. One.* To add icing to the cake, one of the entries in that book, Andrew Salmon's *The Adventure of the Locked Room*, won the PFA for Best Pulp Short Story. Not a bad haul for our first time out of the gate. All this due to the characters of Sherlock Holmes and John H. Watson and their continued appeal to readers all over the globe.

We ended 2009 with the release of our first-ever solo Dr. Watson book, *SEASON OF MADNESS,* by Aaron Smith. Then when Jan. 2010 rolled around, we brought out our second volume of Consulting Detective. This was all on the heels of the successful debut of the new Sherlock Holmes film starring Robert Downey Jr. and Jude Law. Once again we saw our anthology quickly climb the sales charts and it become as big a seller as its predecessor has continued to be. We are very proud of this second volume and fully expect it to garner PFA nominations when Jan. 2011 rolls around. So, we now had two terrific Sherlock Holmes anthologies and the Airship 27 mailbox was quickly being filled with inquiries about when number three would be arriving.

Look no further, Holmes fan, for you now hold that very book in your hands. It was honestly another labor of pure love for all of us here at Airship 27. Honestly, we never grow tired of bringing you these new, classically styled adventures of Holmes and Watson. The five in this volume are as good as any ever written. We'd like to think Sir Arthur Conan Doyle would have a smile on his face upon reading them. Holmes' future seems brighter than ever now, what with a sequel to the Downey movie in the works and with the BBC also launching a fun, new television series starring a modern day version of the irascible, genius sleuth.

What next? Have no worries, dear readers. As long as the books remain successful, Airship 27 Productions hopes to begin every new year with a new Holmes collection and then end that same year with a Watson adventure. We think it's a good idea and so far you've agreed with us. Thanks for that overwhelming support, we truly appreciated more than mere words can say. Note- if this is the first *SHERLOCK HOLMES – CONSULTING DETECTIVE* you've found, do visit our online store immediately where you'll find links to the first two volumes available as well as lots of other great pulp novels and anthologies.

Airship27Hangar.com

Take care and thanks again from all of us at, *Airship 27 Productions – Pulp Fiction for a New Generation!*

Ron Fortier
Ft. Collins, Co.
(Airship27@comcast.net)
(www.Airship27.com)

PULSE-POUNDING PULP EXCITEMENT from AIRSHIP 27:

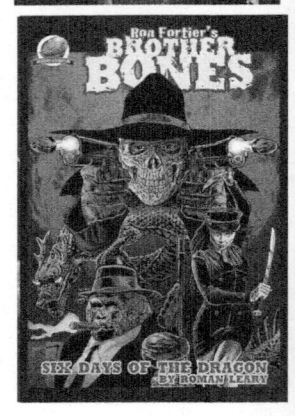

This is just a small sampling of the thrilling tales available from Airship 27 and its award-winning bullpen of the best New Pulp writers and artists. Set in the era in which they were created and in the same non-stop-action style, here are the characters that thrilled a generation in all-new stories alongside new creations cast in the same mold!

"Airship 27...should be remembered for finally closing the gap between pulps and slicks and giving pulp heroes and archetypes the polish they always deserved."
–William Maynard ("The Terror of Fu Manchu.")

PULP FICTION FOR A NEW GENERATION!
AT AMAZON.COM & WWW.AIRSHIP27HANGAR.COM

FROM AIRSHIP 27 PRODUCTIONS- THE GREAT DETECTIVE:

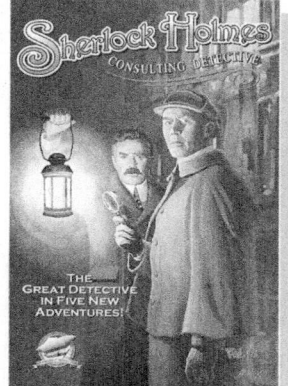

PULP FICTION FOR A NEW GENERATION

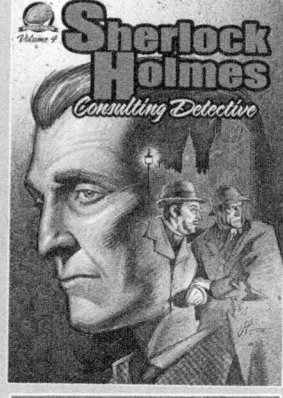

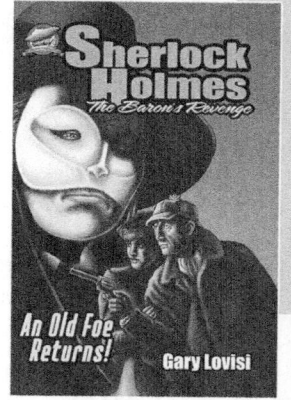

AN AIRSHIP 27 PRODUCTION

NEW PULP

FOR AVAILABILITY OF THESE AND OTHER FINE PUBLICATIONS CHECK THE WEBSITE: AIRSHIP27HANGAR.COM

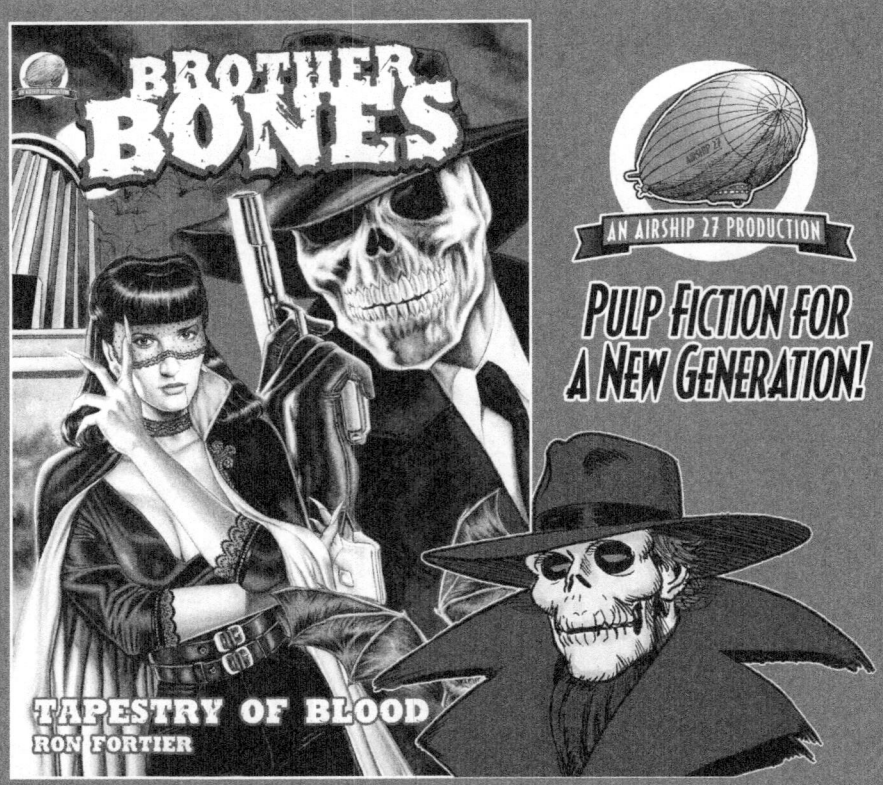

BROTHER BONES

AN AIRSHIP 27 PRODUCTION

PULP FICTION FOR A NEW GENERATION!

TAPESTRY OF BLOOD
RON FORTIER

WELCOME TO CAPE NOIRE

Located on the Northwest Coast, Cape Noire is a booming economic giant whose inner core has been corrupted by all manner of evil. From the sadistic mob bosses who ruthlessly control vast criminal empires to the fiendish creatures that haunt its maze of back alleys, Cape Noire is a modern Babylon of sin and depravity.

Amidst this den of iniquity strides a macabre warrior committed to avenging the innocent and holding back the tide of villainy. He is *Brother Bones, the Undead Avenger* and there is no other like him. A one-time heartless killer, he is now the spirit of vengeance trapped in an undying body. He is the unrelenting sword of justice as meted out by his twin .45. automatics

His face, hidden forever behind an ivory white skull mask, is the entrance to madness for those unfortunate enough to behold it. This new collection features five suspenseful, fast-paced, action-packed stories featuring pulp fiction's most original hero, Bother Bones. Time to draw the shades, light the candles and enter into a Tapestry of Blood

FOR AVAILABILITY OF THIS AND OTHER FINE PUBLICATIONS CHECK THE WEBSITE: AIRSHIP27HANGAR.COM

Printed in Great Britain
by Amazon